'Loads of assurance, buckets of colour, packed with beauti-fully etched observation and piles of raw honesty – this is a debut novel that keeps you wide-eyed with admiration . . . a compact gem'   Tom Adair, *Scotsman*

'A promising debut . . . a strange, funny and capricious book'
                                                    Belfast Telegraph

'There is a witch's heart beating at the bottom of Nick Brooks's debut novel'   *Big Issue*

'Compelling . . . full of quirky characters'
                                            Glasgow Evening Times

'Nick Brooks's entertaining first novel explores the experience of being an outsider looking in, the sense of never quite getting the hang of life. Stylishly written, it has some hilariously quirky moments'   *Sunday Herald*

Nick Brooks was born in 1968 and lives in Glasgow. He has had a number of occupations from cartoonist, musician and stained-glass window maker, to pouring chemicals down toilets for a graphics reproduction company. Most recently, he has graduated from Glasgow University Creative Writing Course. *My Name is Denise Forrester* is his first novel.

My Name is Denise Forrester

NICK BROOKS

PHOENIX

A PHOENIX PAPERBACK

First published in Great Britain in 2005
by Weidenfeld & Nicolson
A Phoenix House Book
This paperback edition published in 2006
by Phoenix,
an imprint of Orion Books Ltd,
Orion House, 5 Upper St Martin's Lane,
London WC2H 9EA

1 3 5 7 9 10 8 6 4 2

A CIP catalogue record for this book
is available from the British Library.

ISBN-13 978-0-7538-1901-2
ISBN-10 0-7538-1901-5

www.orionbooks.co.uk

For my mum and dad,
and for Anna Ehrlemark.

The author wishes to acknowledge the support of the Scottish Arts Council for the purpose of writing this book.

The butcher man was big and brown like a cartoon, drawn in with crayon colours, all darks and blacks, fat cheeks and hair combed over the top of his head that kept flapping down and hanging there, the bald bit underneath like a knee sticking through the torn hole in a pair of old jeans. There was an extra cushion of chin under his face and he wore this white apron splattered with red and dried-in bits of stuff. You didn't like to think where it had come from, except you had to: it was all around. Trays of body parts tilted towards you, offered up with wee pins and flags stuck in them like a parade, saying, Pick me! Pick me! And there was a big picture up on the wall, a mapped outline that divided into duff cuts, good cuts, and best ends.

Denise's granny said the duffer bits were often the tastiest. Pies and bridies and sausage rolls. Grease and gravy that ran down your arm. A pie was better than a sirloin, especially these days – her with no teeth left to chew. The butcher kept up a rhythmic chop-chop at his three-inch-thick wooden board, needing only to glance occasionally down at the dead bird in his hand, the cleaver coming down where it wanted.

'You wanting the feet, Missus?' he asked.

'Will we keep the feet, Denise, what d'ye think?'

Yellow toes stretched out, delicate grey nails curled at the end of each.

'Keep them.'

The butcher brought the cleaver down, tapping it first on

the wooden board – keeping time – then again so that the foot separated from the leg, the blunt nub of bone beginning to seep red from the marrow.

Denise's mouth opened.

The butcher man spun the bird around and did the same with the other foot. It didn't come away the first time, and he had to batter it with the cleaver a couple of times till it parted company with the leg.

Denise put her hands up over her eyes.

'Blunt cleavers,' he said. 'In Scotland – the cleavers are blunt. In Pakistan, the cleavers stay sharp!' He picked up one of the feet and lobbed it over the counter. 'Catch!'

Denise squealed and let it fall onto the sawdust on the floor, taking a step back.

'Denise!' her granny said.

'I said to keep the feet—'

'You're getting to keep them. Mr Ali is giving them to ye.'

'I meant to keep them *on*.'

Mr Ali was laughing. 'Don't you worry, young lady,' he was saying. 'We can wrap them up for you. You can take them home. They can be lucky . . .'

'That's rabbits' feet,' Denise said.

'Rabbits' feet, hens' feet. Pigs' eyelashes. What's the difference? In Pakistan, they don't eat the pig or the cow. Why? Both are ignorant beasts.'

He was bent a bit, looking right down at Denise, the knee of his crown poking through the trouser leg of his hair . . .

'Because one is a filthy animal and the other is holy. I'm a businessman! That not right, Mrs Douglas?'

'Quite right, Mr Ali. Ye've got to make a living, haven't ye?'

'I could have been somebody if I'd stayed in Pakistan. No bother at all. I could have been one of the best, pound-for-pound. A contender.'

'But Mr Ali had to come here,' Denise's granny said. The

words came out but they went off in different directions where you couldn't follow. The only way was to trap them in your headlights, hold them there, white and stunned.

'One of the best. Ha. Could have been. Pound-for-pound, the best Halal butcher in Karachi. But . . .' He made an expansive gesture with his hands. Finally he said, 'Supply and demand, my friends. Supply and demand.'

Denise held onto her granny's hand. She tried to mind if it was a Tuesday that the mountaineer came in. This was a Tuesday. Denise liked the mountaineer.

Her granny and the butcher always talked away but you never knew what they were saying. Words were coming out. Denise watched them dissolve into the air in front of her. They both had these black holes in their faces. Food went in and words came out. The butcher was a cartoon character and her granny was an old yellow photograph, all liney and worn. Denise stared down at the pigs' willies in the tray behind the glass counter, then out the window at the street with the wee bit of spare ground in the middle of the road with the tree on it that the alkies gathered at in the mornings.

There were two of them there already, but they weren't drinking yet. Cars went by so that they looked like they were in a speeded-up film, with only the two tramps not moving. Every time you came to the shops they were there. Once one of them had spoken to Denise while she played outside with her yo-yo. Denise wasn't supposed to talk to him, she knew that. You weren't to talk to strangers. But she saw him all the time so it wasn't really the same. What was in the bottle, she asked him. What was he drinking? He laughed and held it over for her to sniff, and her head jerked back. 'Hair-lacquer,' he said. 'For the night.' He reached into his inside coat pocket and took out a square can with a nozzle. 'Lighter fuel. For the morra.'

'Bitter this morning, intit?' the butcher man was saying, not to Denise. He had a different voice for talking to Denise.

'Oh, terrible!' her granny screeched in her old-lady voice. She could hardly bear to get herself out of bed this morning it was that bad. 'You could see your breath in the air, so ye could!'

'Aye right enough, terrible cold it is.'

Denise's granny had said to herself, 'Elsa, much more of this and you'll be at your end, so ye will. Kill ye this will, sure as anything.'

Denise tugged her granny's hand.

'Och away, Mrs Douglas – you can't be a day over twenty-one.'

Denise's granny cackled, and the butcher man winked a cartoon wink, wiping his hands on his apron and reaching down to one of the trays for a handful of mince. Denise tugged at her granny's hand again.

'A minute, Denise—'

'You wanting anything else, Mrs Douglas? Just the hen and the mince, is it?'

'Eh, pound and a half of your pork links please. Ye any ham houghs?'

'Granny!' Denise was staring out the window, hypnotised. A middle-aged man with a bunnet on, weaving a bit, stepped out from the doorway of the post office across the road and up to the lights. He looked distrustfully out at the road in front of him. He leaned against the railing, pressed the button for the green man then took a step rearward, then another step until his back was against the glass of the shop front. He spread out both palms against it.

'Granny!'

'What *is* it?'

'The mountaineer!'

The three of them stood watching through the glass of the shop front, all of them quiet, wondering how it would go this time. The green man came on.

'Here we go,' the butcher man said.

The mountaineer pushed himself up off the post-office glass and launched himself into the middle of the road, momentum and determination hurling him straight across while engines sat idling on either side of him, the parting of the seas, him weaving from side to side and not seeing anything but the path in front of him, dragged along like a bobbin on an invisible thread.

At the other side the mountaineer careered off to the right of Mr Ali's shop window and disappeared from view. Mr Ali came out from behind his counter and tried to get a better look. Denise tugged her granny's hand, trying to get the words out, all of them trapped inside her, wanting to get them out so badly she was ready to scream.

'What? God's sake, Denise, just take your time—'

'Is he coming back? Is he?'

It was terrible. Denise loved the mountaineer. She loved his red nose and his straw hair. She loved his squashed-up face that ought to have a clay pipe sticking out of it. He was even more of a cartoon than the butcher man. He had tattoos on the knuckles of his fingers, LEFT and RIGHT. Except they were on the wrong hands.

Then she heard the hands slap and saw them press up against the glass of the butcher's shop window moving from right to left. First the right hand, up past the mountaineer's head, stuck palm flat against the glass, then the left pulled free and jerked over to sit parallel to the other as it in turn pulled free and suckered down again a foot further to the right. Then the process was repeated. In this fashion, he made his way across the window to the door of the shop. The mountaineer fumbled for the door handle, and the chimes tinkled as he lurched in the door.

He launched himself again and came up square against the glass counter.

'What can I get you?' the butcher man said. The way he was holding the meat cleaver made Denise panic, a panic like words: it wouldn't come out. Instead she stamped her feet and wrung her hands.

'Calm down, madam,' her granny said.

'Anything particular I can get for you?' the butcher said, his voice quiet and confidential, like a waiter in a restaurant.

The mountaineer stared dully at the meat behind the counter, face raw from the cold, his nose so purple and bulbous it was like a clown's, hair like old straw flapping over the back of his neck and Popeye's girn set on his face. He girned down at Denise and she squealed in to herself. He looked magic.

'Sir?'

The mountaineer reached into his trouser pocket and dug around, then pulled out a crumpled five-pound note. He placed it gingerly on the glass counter, then stepped back to survey the counter once more.

'I says is there anything I can—?'

'Two tinz Superlager. Two.'

The mountaineer's gaze lurched about as if his eyes wanted to escape from his head. Denise stared at him. He was like this beautiful exhibit in a museum. She pictured him stuffed and mounted, standing inside a glass case, a card pinned at his feet.

'We've not got any lager here.'

'Two tinza Superlager, pal!'

'We've no drink. We're a dry store. Haddows is next door . . .'

'Whatveyese goat, thin? Heh?'

'Sausages, pies, mince, steak . . . pork, beef, lamb.'

'Sausages? Whit sausages?'

'Square slice, pork or beef links, turkey . . . what d'you want?'

'How?'

'You came in here . . . you must want something . . .'

'Superlager . . .'

'I've told you. No drink. Of any kind. We are practising Muslims.'

The mountaineer looked at the butcher and at the pork sausages in the tray.

'Muslims, ye say?'

'That's what I says . . .'

'Aw. How . . . ghashtly . . . *stupit* . . . of me . . .'

Denise squealed to herself again as the mountaineer knelt down beside her, grinning a big red grin at her. He thumbed in the direction of the butcher. 'Muslims he says . . .'

'Look, d'you want anything or not?'

'Gie's two pork links well!'

'Two? Anything else?'

'Naw.'

The butcher man sighed, 'That'll be sixty pence please,' picking the five-pound note up off the counter.

'There . . . four pounds forty change.'

The mountaineer picked up the two pork links and fumbled with the coins on the glass counter, his fingers not able to get a grip of them flat on the surface, and shouting, 'Bastars!' he skited the lot off into the palm of his other hand and launched himself at the door again.

'Practising Muslims?' he said. 'Keep it up then. Maybe ye'll get it right one day.' He stood in the doorway, wrestled with the greaseproof paper, held up one of the sausages and looked at it as if it was an unknown lifeform, an alien creature. He took a bite out of it, before disappearing in the direction of Haddows next door.

'Terrible state to be in this time of the morning, so it is,' Denise's granny said.

That was the trouble with this country, the butcher man said, scratching his head. 'Only this morning got his giro, him, and those two there are nearly every day sprawled out on that bit of spare ground over there . . .'

He jabbed a meaty finger at the window. One of the men –

maybe the one Denise had spoken to – was lying flat out on his back on the hard ground, eyes screwed shut and a big dirty quilt thing pulled over him. He looked like he was willing himself to be warm. The other was sitting upright smoking a palmed roll-up and talking to himself. He seemed to be arguing about something.

'They'll be in here wanting a loan of a knife or something later,' the butcher man said, 'once they've had a drink to themselves. They've asked before. Said they'd clean it when they brought it back and everything – but of course, no. They didn't. It was still manky when they brought it back. Nothing like that in Pakistan, heh, Mrs Douglas?'

Denise's granny looked sceptical.

'Aaah, Mrs Douglas! In Glasgow, the streets are covered in dog-muck . . . in Karachi, quite often they're paved with gold!'

Denise's granny laughed. The butcher's cleaver was going again.

'You wanting to keep the head, Mrs Douglas?'

'Denise?'

Denise shrank behind her granny's skirts.

The butcher laughed. 'Don't you forget your lucky hens' feet young madam. There's none of us can afford to turn away luck. Rabbit luck or hen luck.'

Denise took the wrapper of greaseproof paper and put it in the pocket of her duffel coat. She took her granny's hand again. Two swift thumps on the chopping board and the head was flicked quickly over the side into a metal dustbin, by the flat side of the blade. A fleck of wine red landed on the butcher man's apron.

'Blunt cleavers,' he said. 'In Karachi, the cleavers stay sharp!'

Denise's granny would go about the house switching every-thing off, closing doors, making sure they stayed shut to keep Denise's granda and his pals out from under her feet. It was heat they were wanting. Her house was like a furnace, the gas on year in and year out. At night Denise could hear them rattling at the windows trying to get in out of the weather.

It was a good house, a third-floor tenement flat, with peeling plaster outside at the close entrance, coming off in the places where Denise and her sister had picked at it like you picked a scab on your knee. Nobody knew it was them that picked at it. If their granny asked if they'd seen who did it, they just said it was Andy McCabe. If Denise Forrester had known that Andy McCabe wasn't going to make it to his seventeenth birthday she would have maybe felt bad about it. But she would likely still have done it. She would feel bad, but not sorry. At the time though, she had hated him. John Burke and Andy McCabe. Denise hated the pair of them.

Their granda was terrible for not shutting the doors behind him. He'd been brought up in a barn. When Granny had been growing up, they'd never had enough heat. Never enough heat and never enough coal. In those days houses ran on coal. So everybody went about cold. That was how ye were aye making soup the whole time. It heated ye right up. She didn't want Denise and her sister to grow up like that, always cold and needing their dinner like she had been. Her face, gathered in like the skin on your elbow, was slowly disappearing in its own fissures and ravines.

'Look, girls,' she said, pinching the skin on the back of her hand: 'Look at this.'

The skin would stay up there once she'd let go, like the dead skin on a thawing chicken.

'You two try it now.'

Straight away, their skin pinged back into place like it was elasticated.

If you asked her how old she was, she always said, 'Twenty-one. Try imagining being as old as that!'

It was no good – it was buried too deep in the future. Denise's granny said once you were near enough to it, you had to try it on for size. Your own death. See if it fitted. It was like a pair of shoes: it had to be just right, they couldn't pinch too much or you had to take them back to the shop and get another pair. They had to be snug-fitting. Granda's still pinched: that was how he would chap at the windows some nights, wanting in for a heat and to get his old comfy slippers on. Granny felt the draught and knew.

'One size fits all,' she said.

One death to a pair.

Singular.

Plural.

Denise and her sister were scared when they found out about dying. They didn't want to. They liked the sandshoes they had. Their granny calmed them down a bit, sat them up against her huge chest and stroked their hair. Everybody had to get shoes sometime. Right now they only wore their shoes to school – when they got home, they could change into their old comfy, used sannies until the next day. They should really wear proper shoes to go to chapel, if anybody had a mind to send them, but in the meantime . . . The older you got, the more used to wearing shoes you had to get, until you really didn't mind wearing them every day. It was part of being grown up. That wasn't so bad. They both wanted to grow up someday, didn't they?

Denise nodded. She did. Definitely. Her sister wasn't so sure. She looked down at her granny's feet. Slippers.

'Turn the gas up a wee bit will ye, Denise – there's a good girl.'

She turned the fire up again and sat down crosslegged at the other side of the room, as far away from the blast of the fire as possible. It was absolutely roasting in there as usual.

Granny had lived a long time in this heat now, but Denise didn't reckon she could. Her granny looked in travel brochures at holidays in hot places, the Caribbean, Hawaii, places she'd never get to now, she knew, but she looked just the same, just to broaden her horizons. Denise wasn't interested in them. Her sister liked to look at the hot places as well. But heat didn't appeal to Denise.

'You like Egypt, Denise,' her granny said. 'D'ye not want to go there, visit the pyramids, see the Sphinx?'

Denise said nothing. She already had a sphinx she'd made herself. It had been eroded by rainfall. It was a temperate Sphinx. Hers were temperate pyramids.

Denise used to leave the door open in the back room to let in her granda. She would go out and her granny would tell her, 'Shut the door behind ye!' Even after he'd been dead and buried these last thirty years, she was still shutting doors after him.

It was their dad that usually came by to pick them up in the car. Their mum didn't keep well. When they got in she would be lying by the fire in the living room, her head resting on a cushion, with no lights on. It would be getting dark. She had hair that was orange to begin with but went white after an inch or so, because it was dead hair really, only alive at the roots. You could be unafraid of dying if your number had always been up. Denise tried to mind what it had been like, before she had been born, and got this odd feeling. It was a sort of loss. That she hadn't been alive for all the years up until she was born. It was a sort of grief. By shutting her eyes and holding her breath as long as she could, Denise tried to make herself mind before she'd been born, until her lungs were about exploding.

It was no use. She always did breathe in the end. She'd not sorted out a way round that yet. When she was grown up maybe.

When Denise's granny didn't want to talk or be bothered with anything, she pretended she was deaf, and she was – sort of – in one of her ears. She changed which ear it was when it suited her, and she had a hearing aid like a pink snail's shell for it and everything. When she was kidding on to be deaf, you had to say everything twice, shout sometimes or catch her eye. But then you could make her angry by saying swear-words in front of her and she had to keep pretending that she couldn't hear, she couldn't stop the game or you would know, so she just had to sit there getting madder and madder, shifting about in her seat and trying to catch them out—

'*Bums bums bums bums . . .*'

'What's that ye're saying? Heh?'

'*Willy willy willy willy . . .*'

And if you put the telly on as well, she really wasn't able to hear you, she was confused by the noise of it in the back-ground, and would fiddle with the volume control on the hearing aid, sometimes just taking the whole thing out, exasperated. That was when she was at her most dangerous. She would rage about and tell them to get away on out to the other room, away on out of her sight.

She went mad like that 'cause she knew she couldn't let them off and she couldn't be deaf and dumb at the same time. She was just acting like a spoilt wee girl, was what it was. So Denise's sister said, anyway. And everyone said Denise's sister was a lot more grown up than she looked. An old head on young shoulders, the palms of her hands all liney like her granny's. Denise's granny said that probably meant she'd live a long time. She went looking for her lifeline, but wasn't sure which one it was any more, Alison's hands were so scored and wizened-looking, like the cracked plaster on the close wall. That was maybe a good thing, not to know. It was best not to know at her age.

Denise was always a worry. Her granny never had any idea what to do about her at all. All the weans in her class called her names. They never laid a hand on her, though. Not once. They were afraid of her.

'Witch,' they called her. Her with the long dark brown hair and that pale skin, grey almost – ashen. She'd no pals, no friends to play with at all really. Just the dolls and things, the toys she was interested in; the papier-mâché stuff and the animals. Sitting in her room for hours at a time making these papier-mâché landscapes and toy animals, maps and things.

'What ye making, Denise?' her granny was always asking her.

'A country,' she always said. 'A new country.'

She needed the whole thing the way she wanted it, as well. It never got finished, just got bigger and bigger till you had to go in there and tell her to drag the lot outside or take it to bits and start again.

'Is it not nearly finished?' you would always be asking her, Denise probably having been at it for days.

'There's still some more to do,' she was always saying.

And it had a name this country, some name or other, foreign-sounding:

Eulalia.

Even the folk she had living in it had names, all the farmers and townsfolk, the woodsmen and the post-office lady, all the Pugh, Pugh, Barney McGrews right down to the man that delivered the milk and the boy that cycled round with the papers in the mornings. She would be at it every time she got the chance. She would be in and have the papers away, after school, this patchwork of headlines and stories, some of them enough to make your hair curl, like the surface of the moon, dotted with craters and holes, torn bits and the like. She would be in and have them away before you'd a chance to look at the things at all, acting a right madam, so that you had to get two sets of papers in the end just so's you could get a read in peace, and didn't want to have to read the news off the moonscape in her bedroom. That didn't work either. She would be away with that lot as well if you didn't keep a firm grip of them. She had a terrible temper on her, nobody could get her to do anything she didn't want to. Nobody.

She would only eat certain things, and absolutely nothing else. The things she'd eat were:

bread

butter

Nutella

potato derivatives, i.e. mash, chips, crisps, etc. (not potatoes boiled)

vinegar

salt

brown sauce (HP, not Daddy's)

soft drinks of any kind except Dr Pepper

and she would drink water too, but never from the tap. It had to be out of a glass. She would never eat at regular times, but would be up in the middle of the night to get something. You would hear her going down to the kitchen to the fridge, padding about in her bare feet, mawkit from the kitchen floor. You had to go down and tell her to get back to bed or she'd be too tired for the school in the morning, that she needed her sleep like everybody else, and she'd be there with her toast and Nutella. She'd be up in a minute when she'd eaten her piece, she'd say, and continue staring at the TV.

You would put it off of course, but she'd not budge before she was good and ready. You knew fine well she'd have it back on the minute you were out the door. It was a worry what she was seeing at that time of night, what sorts of stuff she was filling her mind with. But after a while, you just left her to it, since you'd be wanting sleep yourself. No reason why everyone had to be dead beat in the morning, up till all hours of the day and night.

Witch, it was, they called her:

'*Witch! Witch! Witch! Witch!*'

A nightmare. Wouldn't let her by in the street or anything. Her sister was fine. No bother for her at all, loads of pals. But folk would throw stones at Denise, if she was out and about on her bike at all, having a hurl or something, but they were rotten shots the lot of them. More likely she would be in her room with her papier-mâché and her animals. No one really knew what was going on in her mind at all. Something was.

That time she ended up in the hospital on the drip she was so thin. Malnourished, the doctor says. Malnourished! She was that grey and thin and pale you could believe it. Malnutrition was what kids in Africa got. No. What they were was starving. So she wasn't quite that far gone yet. The palaver she caused up there, the nurses trying to get her to take things, forcing this stuff into her, things she'd never eaten. Beans, for God's sake. Soft-boiled eggs and soldiers. They didn't have a clue.

It was a terrible worry.

They had to let her go again in the end. They told her she was going to be there till she gained a stone in weight, that they'd stand and wait over her and watch while she ate. She was going nowhere till she put that stone back on again. So she might as well get used to it.

The first time in her life she ever listened to anyone.

Put the stone back on no bother, just so's she could get to

16

go home. She could do that: do whatever was necessary to get peace, get back to her papier-mâché and her animals, her fences and railways and wee towns all painted different colours, rivers and lochs and hillsides, miracle blues and greens, farms and woods and valleys, silvers and greys, sheep and cows and cars and lorries and the like, yellow, brown, black, even though these weren't made of the papier-mâché – she bought them in the toyshops. Sometimes she would go daft saving, wanting one particular kind of sheep or cow, pig or hen, one particular dash of cobalt or silver, signal box or horse and carriage; one very particular kind of steamer for her loch, paint for her trees.

Did she not want some different kinds of animals? her granny would ask, maybe some crocodiles or some elephants or something, 'cause it was always a right pain to go shopping for these things with her, her wanting it just the way she wanted it. And she would not waver. 'What about a llama or two, or an ostrich?' 'Would that not be nice?' She could start up an emu farm or something.

She wanted it the way she wanted it. Fair enough.

She could be a terrible gabbler as well, never saying much in the house, but if she did, the words all coming out in a torrent, no air between them, one word splintering another before anyone got a chance to take it in, like a dam had burst, out it all came. 'Breathe! Denise,' you'd be saying to her. 'Take a breath!' And she'd stop and you could see her trying really hard to slow down, trying to catch her breath, her lips pursing up with the effort of trying to just speak. Then the dam would burst again. It was always these shopping trips that would send her off, all the excitement of it.

Then there was the time she was with her granny and she asked Denise to hail a taxi, she was too puffed to carry the messages all the way back up the road to the house, and Denise tried to flag down a hearse instead and her granny just about had a seizure.

'He'll be by for ye soon enough,' she said. 'Away an' no be in such a hurry.'

Mortified, she was. Tried to baptise Denise at the dinner table, save her soul or something, though her sister hadn't been done either. Chased her round the table trying to fling whisky and ginger over her. Except she wouldn't have it, Denise, she yelped as if scalded when the liquid came near her.

Strange, some dark thing inside her that wasn't like the rest of them at the school, something they could sense a mile off. They didn't like it, they were afraid of it whatever it was.

'*Witch! Witch! Witch! Witch!*'

– chasing her down the street.

'*Witch! Witch! Witch! Witch!*'

– throwing stones after her bike.

Never giving her any peace when that was all she was after. And she'd never get these maps of her finished. There was always more needing done till she had to take it to bits and start again, rebuild the whole thing from scratch, remap all the borders and boundaries and resow the fields, replant the forests, fill the lochs up all over again. If she was allowed, she would maybe just keep on going, till she'd a map the size of the mainland, from Hadrian's Wall to Shetland, she would just keep on going as long as she could. You never knew what was going on in her head, she was just totally away in this world of her own, this land she'd made up and was living her real life in.

She was always getting sick too. She'd take weeks to recover from a cold or a throat infection. She once caught gastro-enteritis and it was coming out both ends. Hello! Cheerio! Destroyed the west coast of her country with spewing on it. That and some book she'd been reading, about Egypt. She was very keen on Egypt: pharaohs and pyramids and sphinxes and what have you. Ancient gods they used to worship, all that sort of thing.

Another thing she collected: porcelain cats, stuffed cats, toy cats, all shapes and sizes, all colours and breeds. She liked cats a lot. Except for the hairless kind. She was sort of prejudiced against them. No wonder. Horrible tickets, those. She used to talk away to them, blether on to them the whole time. She was coming up the path when this black one with white socks jumped out the hedge and went off to one side of her, just staring, and she goes down on one knee, gentle like, and does that shsh-shsh-shshing noise and it comes up to her, sniffing round her hand and letting her clap it. It was mewing away. 'What's the matter with you, you in a huff?' she says to it, and it went swanking about round her legs, rubbing itself against her, its wee bell tinkling. Uh-huh, it says. The toms are bothering me. It was a girl-cat, Denise knew straight off. 'You want your tummy rubbed?' she says to it. Do you? Uh-huh, it says back, rolling down on its side and stretching out its forepaws, the tail lashing away. So Denise was just kneeling there, rubbing its tummy for it but had to be careful, 'cause it was a sensitive thing. A bit shy. 'That's better,' she was saying to it. 'That's better, isn't it?' The best of friends they were after that, it used to come by to see her and they used to give each other presents. Denise would give it milk or some leftovers, whatever was lying about, but the cat, it used to be really thoughtful. It would bring mice, or songbirds or shrews, and lay them out on the doorstep for her to find in the morning. It was really touching, the way it did it. Denise collected them and used to keep them in a shoebox in her room, she was such a hoarder even then. Her mum would have to sneak in when she was out at school or something, so's she could clear up a bit, chuck out some of the junk 'cause she wouldn't do it herself. She didn't want anything thrown out. Not ever.

Two more things: she never ever said sorry. Never. It was just something she just could not bring herself to say.

She could never say sorry, and she could never say no.

Her granny wished Denise would stop encouraging all the cats in the area to congregate in her back yard. They were a damned nuisance, so they were, worse pests than old Polywka next door, with their comings and goings, leaving the back court in a state with their dirt. And they didn't even discourage the mice! The mice were no sooner gone than back again, immune to whatever you flung at them. Traps, poison – it was all the same. You could never have enough traps and you could never poison enough of them. They had too fast a life cycle. They bred like rabbits, so they did. Even old Polywka's plots and plans and schemes couldn't really put a dent in them for long, they always came back again as bad as before, ruining your loaves and leaving dirt in the butter dish. And all the cats leaving dead birds and things for Denise on her doorstep! Terrible.

Some of the things these creatures dragged in.

That time when the old tom from down the back court with the one eye took a liking to her. And he was a loner as well, a battler and a loner, scarred over the snout and wouldn't tolerate any of the other cats to go near him, less they wanted a stripe or two themselves. And he takes a liking to her, starts prowling about the close, waiting to have a word with her on the doormat. An old soldier like him too. Should have known better. Beauty and the beast. It was undignified, the way he started carrying on, leaving these anonymous gifts and hanging about the close, always just wanting to see her or be near her. He knew fine he was far too old for her, that she wasn't interested, but would he learn . . . ?

Hanging about and putting the wind up the younger crowd – if he caught any of them anywhere near her – it wouldn't be long before folk would stop seeing that one about. He would just disappear. Never to be seen again. And there this old tom would be, sat like the Sphinx up on the dyke in the back, keeping his one eye on his patch, master of all he surveyed. Denise liked him well enough, but not that way. He was an ugly old thing, ugly and smelly, and her granny couldn't stand the sight of him, thought he wasn't good enough. All those dead and dying birds on the doormat, squealing still, some of them. He was only good to keep the younger crowd from out the close, 'cause none of them would come near if they knew he was about. Her granny pestered Denise to get rid of it for her, but she should have known Denise wouldn't touch him – or any of them. If there was so much as a fly in her bedroom, she had to sleep through with her sister.

Her granny didn't get it though. It was a mystery to her. Denise never ate meat. She never ate vegetables either. What was the matter with her? She couldn't fathom it. Her mother ate meat – and vegetables. Her father ate meat – not vegetables. And her sister would eat the vegetables at least. So it wasn't hereditary. It wasn't genetic. Nobody could lay the blame at her granny's feet. No.

What was it then? She had no idea. Even the old tom hadn't figured it out. He could see she wasn't taking to the sparrows and chaffinches, so he came up with something else, and when her granny found it on the doormat, she went screaming through to Denise, going, 'Get that thing out of here! Get it out! I am sick to the back teeth with these things getting delivered to my doorstep! Denise—'

It looked like it had wings. In the darkness of the landing it looked like it was fluttering. It was as big as a fist, some kind of black and yellowy-green insect. It made Denise shudder to go near it.

'What is it?' Denise asked.

'Is it alive?' Alison asked.

'Oh shut the door just now, go on, shut it!' their granny said, shivering.

So the door was shut on whatever it was, Denise and her sister spying on it through the letterbox, waiting for their dad to come round and sort it, get rid of it.

'What's the matter with you lot?' he said, the thing resting on the shovel in his hand, him grinning at them. 'Here Denise! Catch!'

He faked a toss of the shovel, but she was away squealing behind her sister, her granny at the back of her as well.

'It's an old rotted bit of cabbage for you, Denise. Look—'

So it was, right enough. An old rotted bit of cabbage stump, probably raked out the bins at the back, the old tom maybe having dug it up or something, totally fed up at not having any luck with the sparrows and chaffinches and that. Who could blame him either? The poor soul had tried everything.

Besides, Denise's dad was always saying that about cabbage, even though he never touched it:

'Food of the gods, cabbage. So it is, Denise, food of the gods . . .'

But Denise didn't care for cabbage either. It was the texture of stuff that was horrible, the way it felt in her mouth made her grue. But in the case of cabbage, she refused to try anything that smelled like it tasted of farts. And could kid you on into thinking it was a giant mutant moth.

But it was a gift. You couldn't throw away a gift. What if the old tom found out she'd slung it out, found it back down in the midden again? She just had to think of something else to do with it.

If you looked round quick enough, he might get trapped in your stare just for a second before he was away. He might be hovering about behind the living-room door, feeling the heat seep out, wanting a warm at the fire. He'd want to take the weight off his feet. Denise thought she heard him chapping sometimes but she wasn't fast enough. She thought she heard him scratching about behind the fireplace and crouched next to it, just her and her sister, no one else in the living room, listening. One scratch for Yes, two for No.

She needed Alison to work out the code. Denise had tried whispering but he never replied, just made these scratching noises. She didn't want her sister to be there – she wanted it to be *her* secret. But it *was* a secret, and only Alison could work it out. Alison tapped up to thirty words a minute in Morse Code. Denise could only manage about three. Alison scrabbled down dots and dashes on her jotter before she staccato-fired back with the underside of a teaspoon against the tiles of the fireplace.

'It must be cold in there,' Alison said.

'Ask him then,' Denise said, her bottom lip sticking out and her arms folded. She was stopping herself going in a huff so's she didn't miss anything. If she went in a huff she would have to kid on she didn't care. Alison tapped out the message onto the tiles:

A-R-E-Y-O-U-C-O-L-D-G-R-A-N-D-A

Nothing.

'Maybe he missed a bit,' Denise said. 'Maybe he didn't hear.'

Alison frowned her old face.

' 'Course he heard me . . . he's not deaf is he?'

'No, just Granny.'

Alison tapped again, with more air in between the taps.

ARE YOU COLD GRANDA

'Are you doing the right Morses?' Denise asked. She was getting impatient.

'Yes.'

'Are you sure?'

'I'm sure. But maybe he's not using Morses. Maybe there's another code. All I can hear is scratching.'

Denise saw Granda hunched up inside his tunnel, scratching away at the dirt, trying to get nearer the fire. He had always suffered from the cold, Granny said. Did she mean the Common Cold? Or Cold*ness*? What had he actually died of? Granny always said he'd had a tragic life. She had heard people on the news and sometimes read them in papers talking about Tragically Short Lives. They would never even get the chance to Fight Bravely against the tiny organisms that were what usually made people die, the ones that moved about through your body unseen, carried along in the plasma current like miniature bombs waiting to go off, latching onto healthy cells like limpet mines, spreading the word, infecting different cuts of meat with their clandestine guerrilla tactics. They would capture a part and make it their own, then convert another part, another slice. They took over the whole map. The word would be spread and the word was Disease.

'Your granda was killed by his lungs,' Granny told them. 'They stopped loving him because they thought he was trying to kill *them*. He wasn't trying to do anything of the sort, of course. But he couldn't persuade them. It was kill or be killed. Expect to go the same way myself.'

She relit her pipe and puffed away on it with an obvious relish.

'Kill or be killed?' Alison thought they might cancel each other out. It was that sort of an equation.

'That's what I says, is it not? It was a very patriotic thing to take upon himself. Really, he was a martyr. A terrible shame it was. Up till the day he died, your granda was never sick a day in his life. Terrible shame, so it was.'

'Was he never ill before that?' Alison asked.

'Naw. He was tough as old boots.'

Denise held her breath at the mention of footwear, and let it stick in there a while. These boots were everywhere. She looked down at her granny's feet, then at Alison. Her sister's wizened face was set and stiff, like a plate of stale porridge. Her granny was wearing her outdoor shoes.

'He didn't get the cold even?'

'Oh aye, he got all sorts. But what I'm saying is he was never ill with them. He just soldiered on. He didn't give them a chance to get a good hold of him. Being brought up in a barn makes you strong that way. He knew they were trying to kill him when he started getting these aches in his side. And later on, he got these headaches as well. He would get terrible out of breath, so he would. He could hardly bend to tie his shoelaces. His hands were affected. His feet as well.'

'How did Granda die then?' Alison asked.

'He fought bravely against it, but it was no use in the end. He was done for.'

'But how was it that he *died*?'

'With his boots on, like a man, of course! How else would he die?'

There might be a lot of answers to that. You could be hit by a car, for one thing. Or a bus, if it made any difference. You could fall down a hole. You could get burnt at the stake. It had happened before. Who was to say that wouldn't happen? There seemed any number of ways. The organs of your own

25

body might take against you in silent mutiny like with Granda . . . that seemed worst of all. *Slow* death. You would most likely be condemned to fight bravely against the ungrateful organs of your own body, which all had the upper hand since they were in possession of inside information. Their spies were everywhere.

It turned out that Granda didn't die of a disease like other diseases. It was asbestosis. All those years that Denise wastes being terrified of slow death as a result of internal disputes between her own organs! There was practically nothing she couldn't worry was going to be the beginning of it for her. The beginning of the end. Denise wanted to face her fear and stare it down. She would be terrified of lung cancer, so take up smoking. She would worry about the brittleness of her bones and so avoid dairy products like the plague. If she ate a bit of fruit she would worry about the preservatives in it. Though she would never eat fruit at all if she could help it, just the occasional apple. Chips and apples were as far as she ever got with fruit.

The night before Andy McCabe's seventeenth birthday, Denise goes into Burger King with her sister and orders two portions of large fries and a portion of onion rings. She also has a large Coke and smokes six cigarettes, three before the meal, and three after.

Her sister has a Spicy Beanburger, which she'll have to take back because there is a dead insect in it. She won't bother to have anything after that. Although there's nothing wrong with the dead insect, except of course that it is dead. Likely, it is nutritious enough.

AREYOUHUNGRYGRANDA

Alison forgot to let more air into the spaces between the words, but didn't say anything to Denise. If they were using the right code it would be good enough. There was a scrabbling noise. Two of them, in succession. A Yes?

'He says he's hungry,' Alison decided. 'We better get him something to eat.'

'Like what?'

Denise pictured the floor of Granda's tunnel, a moving litter of white pink-eyed rodents he squatted on while they crawled wriggling over his boots, the steel toecaps showing through cracking brown leather. Denise shuddered.

Their granny could never work it out. Every day there were new mice droppings and wee bodies to throw out. The back court was full of stray cats but the house was practically over-run with vermin. She found crumbs and bits of bread crust all around the fireplace, sometimes even a tray of milk. It was a mystery where they came from.

'Do you girls still believe in Santa Claus?' she asked Denise and Alison.

'They believe in presents,' their dad said, his light-bulb head sparking on. 'Getting them.'

It was true as well. Denise did believe in getting presents. So did Alison. They believed in that more than anything else. Christmas was a time of wonder for them.

'Why is it you two keep putting down these biscuits and milk by the chimney?' their granny asked, the clack of her false teeth easing the words out.

Neither of them said anything. Denise looked at Alison and Alison looked at Denise.

'No reason,' Alison said.

'Who're they for then, heh?'

'Nobody,' Denise said.

'Mr Nobody? You know Santa doesn't visit bad wee girls, don't yous?'

'Uh-huh . . .'

'You know Christmas is still a whole month away, don't yous . . . ?'

'Uh-huh . . .'

'So no more of this business, then. Christmas Eve ye can put something down for Santa – and that's your whack.'

'Or it'll be whacks all round!' their dad said. He cuffed Denise lightly over the back of her head for emphasis. 'Away and play outside for a while till I see about these vermin for your granny. Go on – get!'

The stanks and drains in the back courts were stopped up
with something that oozed and bubbled every time someone
flushed the lavvy. They burbled to themselves in throaty
voices and wheezed clots of matter out onto the pitted
concrete where the lawns used to be. Denise and Alison were
always getting told to away and play in the back court anyway,
or in the close if it was raining. Away and play hopscotch or
hide and seek. A game of something. Away and play up someone else's close for a change. Sometimes they got ten pence.
Not always, though. The Soods' house smelled good, and Mrs
Sood sometimes tried to give Denise and Alison some of the
stuff they made. The stuff that made the smell. You could
never tell if it was bought or not. These good names the
things had too:
Samosa.
Bombay mix.
Gulab jamin.
Denise played with this boy called Jeedy who had hair like
an Arran sweater, except not so scratchy. Soft. Denise minded
her mum laughing when she found out that Jeedy was brown-
coloured because up until then neither Denise or her sister
had said.
'Black, you say?'
But it was her mum who had said.
Their granny would be in the kitchen, spooning the juice
over a roasting chicken, basting it. Denise hated the smell: fat

and bursting. For a while she wouldn't even eat bread 'cause the smell of roasting chicken was like the smell of new bread baking. Their differences were not so many as their similarities. Their granny pushed at the opaque blob of onion sticking out of the hole where the giblets had been with a spoon, lifting up the tied-together legs like changing a nappy. Denise never wanted to have children either after that.

'Away now and play in the close if it's raining.'

They played on these cold, indented steps worn by the shuffle of the feet of everyone who had lived there before. They went skewering straight up to the top landing where there was a skylight with wire on the inside. It was big, but even so the close was dark. The close lights themselves felt their vocation only dimly. You would be coming back down the stairs with the messages from the Paki's around the corner, doing fine, then – nothing. Pitch black. Your eyes swam about amongst green and red stutters for a few seconds till you could focus them again. They were fine when you went out, but they were invariably on the blink again when you got back with the loaf or the toilet roll. Stained-glass doorpanels blotched the walls ultramarine and burnt sienna. Years later, when she is seventeen, Denise will actually get a job making stained-glass windows for a while, but she will get sacked for being too slow. They have a league table in the wee place where they go to take their breaks and it shows the production rate of each individual that works for the company. There's only about eight people working there, and Denise will always be bottom of the production pile. The company operates a last-in-first-out policy, and Denise will only work there about three months before she gets the shove.

It'll be ten in the morning when they call her into the office and give her her cards, actual cardboard templates for designs Denise has been allowed to make up while business stays slow. But business stays slow the whole time Denise works there. Denise will put them into her portfolio case and take her just-that-minute-finished self-portrait-with-eye-of-Horus shoulder-tattoo from her light box and then she will walk out the door without saying cheerio to anyone. They turn out to be a bunch of cunts, the lot of them. As she walks down the road away from Unit 5, Fastgo Designs, Denise will break into a jog, then a run, down toward the train station.

Granny's nameplate said Douglas but she had told them her maiden name was Lamont. Denise loved the sound of that: *maiden name*. It was mad to think their granny had a name like a normal person, a *maiden name* and that *only girls had them*.

Elsa. Elsa Lamont.

Descended from the French. She had a weird way of pronouncing it as well, totally mad. Everybody else said *La*mont. She said La*mont*. But being from France was something, even if they did eat raw horse and snails. They were both acquired tastes, apparently. Denise was sorry for the horses but not so much for the snails. It was hard to feel sorry for snails.

On the top landing there was someone who shuffled back and forth. They were stick-thin, bare legs and bare arms, leaning over the banister:

'Madden . . . ? Ye there, Madden?'

Sometimes Denise and Alison saw a shadow move in the blink of the lights up above, but could never make out what it was, whether it was a man or a woman:

'*L'homme ou la femme?*

Masculine.

Feminine.

But it was always wanting Madden. That was what happened to you if you asked too many nosy questions, if you didn't know when to keep your trap shut. The lights blinked and you got stuck like that for ever. You ended up looking for Madden, but Madden wouldn't answer.

*

31

Old Mr Polywka lived across the landing from Granny Douglas née *La*mont/La*mont*. He was from somewhere near Russia, somewhere called the Ukraine. He had come here decades before, at the beginning of the War when he was still a young man, leaving everything behind him, except his wife. Mr Polywka used to say his name was actually more Polish than Ukrainian, but if there were any surviving members of the Polywka family then they were still out there in the Ukraine. Or maybe Poland. He did odd jobs for Granny Douglas if their dad wasn't about to help – wee things like wire a plug or change a light bulb. Him and Denise's granny did in all the mice, exterminated the lot of them. Polywka chapped once, twice, three times on Granny's door, and she would open the door a crack and look out, the chain still on.

'Who goes there?' she would say. 'Friend or foe?'

Polywka would look up from under thick brows. '*Hammer-man*,' he would say. 'Perkun division.' And a snapped salute.

Granny would open the door. They always did this. Zegota had been Polywka's codename when he'd fought for the Poles. He'd had a nickname, as well. A codename and a nickname. The Hammer-man. He had waited on the other side of an escape hole, knocked between the walls of two houses. There were many such holes. The Nazi had followed him through, and when he got to the last hole, Zegota brought the hammer down on the back of his neck. He left him there, blocking the hole. The others would have to drag him out before they could follow.

Polywka. *The Hammer-man.*

The mice squeezed into the cupboards and the wardrobe. They got into the bread bin and the butter dish. They chewed the corners of Mother's Pride and shat on the digestive biscuits. Denise's granny got up in the morning and the kitchen floor was a minefield of tiny pellet turds like chocolate hundreds-and-thousands. They were so like chocolate hundreds-and-thousands that when she was very small Alison

Forrester tried to eat them and her granny shook her until she spat them, making her drink cod liver oil, which made her far sicker than the mouseshite had done.

The mice were a big problem. After they killed them, Mr Polywka and Granny Douglas took away all the tiny corpses and all the poison dishes and waited for the next wave.

Old Mr Polywka was sad and serious with heavy movements, spacious Slavic features and kind black eyes. He had been all sorts of things at one time or another. No sight was to be had of Mrs Polywka – only the foot of her bed in the living-room recess. She didn't keep well. Mr Polywka looked after her. He'd maybe give you ten pence to yourself if you ran down to the shops for him and saved him having to go down the stairs. He liked a pie. A pie or a bridie. You had to go down to Gregg's the baker, but Denise wouldn't go because of the smell of the bread, so he would get Alison to go instead. He never asked himself. He whispered it in Granny's ear, and she would put on this face like he'd asked her to clean out his toilet, though she often offered to do just that in return for his mouse-clearing and bulb-changing services, but he aye said naw. So Alison it was that got sent.

Polywka and Granny Douglas sat drinking tea, the front door left open. Polywka left his door open too.

Mr Polywka was only ever after the one pie. Did Mrs Polywka not want something as well? He would just look at you.

'No. Just the one pie. Thank you.' Polywka's right hand came up into a casual salute, the way other folk crossed themselves. He smiled.

By the time Denise Forrester was ten and Alison Forrester was eight, Granny Douglas née *La*mont/La*mont* had got far too old for the stairs, so she moved up the housing list, wanting a first- or ground-floor place, somewhere quieter away from weans and racket and noise. She just wanted to be nearer folk like herself, her own sort. There weren't many of them left. She'll pack up her things and be away one fine weekend, out to newer, sunnier estates. There's nobody much to say cheerio to, only old Mr Polywka, the Soods. Denise and Alison will see old Polywka that last time, stood on his landing with the mop in his hands, swabbing, his black eyes shining from his squat head.

'Mrs Douglas, she's away?' he says. 'Mrs Douglas, she away the now?'

'Yes. She's flitting.'

'Ahh, I know, I know. She's away and shifting the hoose?'

His front door lies open just a crack but you can't see anything much in there, just the foot of the bed and two milk bottles sat on the window ledge. The silver cap is pulled back on the one of them and the yellowy cream separates at the top. The other one is half-empty. The bedcovers are in a state and again Denise can picture Mrs Polywka's feet in there. Sticking out.

Back down the steps, two at a time.

You could hear a thump-thump coming from down in the back court. They would be in blue strips or green, kicking a bruised leather ball against the dyke, the drainpipe spitting away like a cut throat.

Denise wasn't really called Denise anyway: that was mainly in the house. Her name is Anna – like her mum – so she gets called Denise to tell the difference. Her full name is Anna Denise Forrester. The only people who ever called her Anna were teachers at school. Them and her wee sister. 'Anna' or 'Mz Forrester'.

Like her mother, her granny *La*mont/*Lamont* said. Alike but not alike. Yet, thank God. Not yet anyway. Though Denise being ambidextrous as well wasn't a very encouraging sign, especially since if she was stuck, she'd use her left in preference to her right. But she was still more like her sister. Not an immediate likeness, it was more subterranean than that. Denise, darker, the same narrow nose as her dad, fierce eyes and mouth, look of offence; her sister the fairer one, those skinny arms and legs and look about her that made her seem so much the older of the pair. The worker out the two of them. The one you never had to worry about.

Was that a wise look right enough – or just knowing? What was the difference anyway?

Witch Denise!

She got there slowly, her granny said.

Witch Anna!

'She doesn't get there at all,' said her dad.

Mz Forrester.

Her mum said nothing. She was still lying on the floor by the fire.

Witch! Witch! Witch! Witch!

Sometimes, they'd get mistaken on school registers and sit in each other's classes. They'd even swap homework – though Denise could never get her sister to do her punishment exercises for her. The rest was easy. Her sister did the arithmetic and the maths and that; Denise did the drawing and the painting and the papier-mâché sculptures, except nobody was all that much interested in her papier-mâché sculptures – all these animals and landscapes she was forever taking apart and rebuilding, this weird clutter of bits and pieces, pyramids and flyovers, headline stabbings and sports results. Certainly not her art teachers. As far as they were concerned Art began with an onion. Plus chopping board and wine bottle. It all added up: still life.

They got away with it right through the first few years of the secondary, up till Denise's sister spoilt it all by going and taking it seriously. She liked the numbers and the figures and equations, the lack of complication, the lack of necessity to think about them too much. There was a method for everything. If you knew the method, you didn't even have to get the right answer, you just showed your working. Numbers made everything: there was nothing without them or beyond them. Numbers ruled.

Two plus two equals four.

You got given a sheet of paper that was blank. You had to fill it up. What with?

Numbers.

A maze of numbers, abstracts, concretes, decimal points. Pi. Hieroglyphics. Let Denise do the drawings. Let her fill her own pages her own way. Except Denise never filled pages – she took them to bits. She shredded and dissected them, reduced them to the sum of their constituents, then remoulded and restructured them into tectonic plates and continental shelves held together by the dark matter of headlines and murders and

Page Threes. Beneath their torn surfaces an inky corruption suppurated.

By the second year, Denise Forrester was getting further and further behind with schoolwork. It got serious.

'Any further behind and we'll find ourselves in the remedial group, won't we, Mz Forrester?'

Denise wasn't frightened. She didn't care whether they stuck her in the remedial or not. She'd decided not to learn any more. That was in her second year. They made her sit at the front at a desk on her own, a circle scratched into its surface on the bottom left-hand corner. Inside the circle somebody had written:

PLACE LEFT ELBOW HERE.

Denise put her left elbow there. You got the feeling that something would happen if you didn't. But nothing did. It was very frustrating.

At the end of the first term, the teacher had asked her if she wanted to *rejoin* – that was the word she had used – the remainder of the class. It was a trick question, another equation. Denise didn't know the answer. She didn't know the answer or the method. She could show no working.

'Rejoin the remainder?'

Two plus two equals five.

Old Ewart, one leg swinging over the knee of the other, was leaning back in her chair, tilting it. The way a man would. She was folding the black cloak that she always had on over the sleeves of her blouse and clasping her hands.

Was Mz Forrester capable of behaving herself with the others now?

Ewart was supposed to keep a worn leather strap down the inside sleeve of her cloak, even though Denise'd never seen it. It was supposed to be in case they brought back corporal punishment.

Denise said she was.

Was what? Ewart said, the tight bun at the back of her head pulling her eyebrows into an oriental slant.

Capable of joining the remainder of the class.

'I don't think so, Mz Forrester,' Ewart said. 'I don't think so.'

Someone offered her a Polo at break but she said No. She didn't like mints. She'd once nearly choked to death on a Polo. Her dad had had to turn her upside down and shake her until it came out, but it hadn't. Instead, a gold nugget fell out onto the carpet and sat there winking up at her, like a goldfish. A gold filling.

'Throw that horrible thing away, Denise,' her dad said, stalking round the room, limbs all right angles and isosceles legs.

Her mum looked up from her pillow by the fire, rubbing her eyes. 'Can I not have peace?' she said. Her stomach was ill. She was like a pile of cushions, a mattress bound up with rope.

How was the rest of her? her dad wanted to know. He knew how her stomach was. Every day he heard how her stomach was. Had it spread? Into an arm maybe?

Her mum just let out this long sigh and rubbed her eyes. She had sunburn on her face from lying too near the fire. 'Why did you put the big light on?' she said. 'Can you not go next door?'

Denise put the goldfish into her pocket to show her granny. Her granny wouldn't mind her keeping it.

'Fool's gold anyway,' her dad said. 'Takes a witch to cough up fool's gold. Aye. Mouseshite from the one, and fool's gold from the other.'

Denise kept her mouth clamped tight shut.

Left-handed. Ambidextrous.

It wasn't her fault if she had coughed it up. It wasn't her fault she wrote with her left hand.

Her granny said she was like that too. Seeing how she'd write perfectly well with her left or her right hand, her teachers used to skelp her. Take the chalk out of her left hand and jam it into her right; stand behind her and give her a crack on the skull with a ruler or a book if she tried to switch hands back again. But that was still lucky: you'd get the strap if you were a boy.

There had been a boy, Jeffreys, in the class, she couldn't mind which one now. Jeffreys and Valentino. This was after the first war.

'Valentino sat at the next desk and used to make this boy Jeffreys laugh – all knew fine well that he couldn't help it . . . Valentino was always the one that made him laugh. This one time stuff came out of his nose.'

'S'not my fault, Misseez!' he'd said.

'It is your fault Mr Jeffreys,' the teacher would say. 'Valentino makes the balls, Jeffreys,' the teacher would say, 'but you fire them!'

The whole class was silent – all you could hear was the steady munch-munch-munch of the headlice grazing and poor Jeffreys sniffling in his corner at the back.

Denise passed her pen or pencil back and forth between her hands so that no one noticed her preference for the left and always taking things literally.

'They used to say Old Nick himself was left-handed,' Granny *La*mont/La*mont* had once told Denise. 'They could never just leave you alone. A few hundred year back, maybe they would cut your hand off, or drown you or burn you alive, who knows? They might even put you in the Boots first. Never heard of the Boots? Ho!' So Denise should never mind what those teachers say to her – just mind that maybe her granny's granny's granny didn't get off so lightly as herself. Eh!

What were the Boots? Denise wanted to know.

'The Boots were what they used to clap onto a witch. To get your confession.' Denise's granny leaned over in her chair and suddenly clapped her hands round Denise's ankles, making her jump. They felt cold. Slowly Granny began to squeeze her calves.

'The Boots had a screw at the back,' Granny said. 'A screw you could tighten up. They would ask ye questions you couldn't answer, 'cause every answer would be the wrong answer. Their minds were already made up.'

'Whose minds were already made up?' Denise asked.

'The Witchfinders. They wound the boots up so tight that it didn't matter how much you screamed, it didn't matter how much you told them it wasn't *your* fault that the cows weren't milking or the cocks weren't crowing – they were going to get a confession whether you'd done anything or not. You could scream till the marrow oozed out your bones and it wouldn't make any difference. None at all. Round these parts there was a woman used to live away on up at the top of this street. Except it wasn't a street in they days. It was just a seggie lea. An elm grove. A bit of grass, the hummock of a hill . . . there was nothing of *this*.' Granny waved her arm about the room.

Denise thought she meant the gas fire. That was maybe a good thing. It was absolutely roasting hot in there as usual.

'The elms would sway in the wind and folk would think it meant the devil was abroad in the night. They would slink and cower in their hovels, afraid to look out the window in case they were snatched away by something out there . . . whatever it was. They sat by the glimmering ashes of their hearths, the pigs huddled up beside them waiting for their time to come – as come it surely would. You never knew if you were going to wake in the mornings. Anything could happen. You might only have the one or two beasts between yourself and an empty belly. And if the *beast* took poorly . . . !'

41

'What would happen?'

'Well, if there was no milk to be had, that meant no milk to drink. If there were no eggs laying, that meant nothing to take to market. If the pig upped and died, that meant no ham, no fat, no houghs for soup. So you had to make sure that beast stayed alive. 'Cause if it didn't, it might well mean *you* were dead!'

Denise wasn't much of a one for dairy products or pork, so she reckoned she'd be all right.

'Folk had to find reasons for things. They had to find ways of keeping their beasts and themselves alive. They looked for signs and portents all around. They were suspicious and fearful of each other. And they were always quick off the mark when it came to finding some poor soul to pin it on. That was what happened to the widow woman that lived up beyond the seggie lea. Folk didn't like the way she went abroad on a Sunday. They didn't like the way she talked away cheerfully to folk she bumped into when she was out and about. They said she could predict the weather. She would just look up at the sky and see clouds brewing and say: "Rain the morra." Or she would wet her finger in her mouth and go: "Windy the day." But the fact of it was, folk didn't like it that she was a widow that never grieved. They hated her 'cause she didn't go about all humped over with the burden of grief, her face cracked and stained with constant greeting over her dead man. She could get by fine without him. She could take care of her hens and trade eggs and live all by herself without any need for him. And she was well shot of him, since he'd made her life a misery before he'd went and keeled over one morning . . .'

'What happened to him?'

'What happened? Well he'd just been after giving the missus a clout – just to keep in practice, mind – and went down to the run to check on one of the hens that was sickly, when he'd felt a twinge in his gut. A kind of turmoil. A bad egg, he says to himself and goes back to checking the hen. But the turmoil hits him again a second later, worse than before. It wasn't turmoil. It was molten lead. There and then, he drops his trousers and lets fly, arse to the wind . . . But it wouldn't stop, it just kept coming. More and more and more. Everything inside him. Everything. And when he'd finished . . .'

'When he finished what?' Denise was laughing; Granny was sort of whispering and making faces while she spoke, as if she was expecting someone to come in and tell her off.

'Well, he just picks up the hen and wipes himself with it. Pulls his trousers back up, takes two steps towards the house and . . .'

'What?'

'Keels over, stone dead. Turns out he'd shat out his own heart along with everything else. He was totally heartless. And the wife comes down a few minutes later and finds him.'

'What did she do?'

'Do? She just picks the poor wee fella up by the feet and slings him into the water bucket to clean off his feathers. Mind you, him being poorly and all that, it was no great surprise that he was dead by next morning as well.'

Denise laughed, then felt bad. She felt sorry for the hen.

Granny straightened up her face so's you knew she was going to be serious now:

'So that was how folk hated her. She was free, living on her own at the end of the seggie lea, away from the rest of the hovels. So every time something went wrong, the fingers started pointing, tongues started wagging. Her days were numbered. One summer, it rained for three months solid. What crops there were got ruined. The cows stopped milking. The tatties blighted. Folk were starving and weans were sickening and the old yins were dropping like flies. Or they would have been, except an old yin in they days was someone over forty. Anyway, something had to be responsible. Or someone. Some says the author of all their troubles was none other than Old Nick himself, in the shape of a giant tomcat. Others says, no, it wasn't Old Nick, but a witch. Nobody had caught sight of the devil but there was folk that says they'd seen something – in the bare-buff! – out among the elms, thrashing about in a wild sort of a dance, and that it was a young girl – but with the face of the widow woman!'

Denise's granny sat back in the armchair and paused to relight her pipe. Denise footered with the sole of her shoe, kidding on not to be interested, but it was like kidding on you didn't need to pee. A tingling pressure somewhere below your belly-button.

Granny leaned in again, up close. She looked like an old penny.

'And they blamed her for it,' she said. 'They'd found their witch. The next day, they dragged her screaming by the hair, out over the muck and the grass, taking her down to the soldiers . . . and they threw her in the jail, manacled to the wall, in with the stink of rottenness and death. The poor girl had no chance, and she knew it fine. They could do with her what they liked – all she could do was tell the truth. They could blame her with whatever they wanted, they could beat her black and blue, but she wouldn't confess to anything. Never. But of course she did, in the end. It was all over after they clapped her in the Boots . . .'

Denise's granny made a corkscrew motion with her thumb and forefinger, the twist of it giving Denise a sick feeling where the tingle had been a minute before. There was something about it, the slow clockwise ticking of the fingers, that made her want to get up, walk around, leave the room.

'. . . And as the boots tightened, the widow woman began to scream. Each new twist of the key had the whole village shuddering with the terrible animal noise that came from the dungeons. But still the widow woman wouldn't confess. Again, the key tightened. Again, no confession. But the torturers saw only guilty blood spring from her legs. Then guilty marrow—'

Denise's hand went up to her ears.

'. . . till finally she yelped, "Oh Yes! Yes! It was me! I did everything! Yes!" And once she'd started she couldn't stop, the confession comes tumbling out, everything she's done, the spells she's cast, the curses she's put on folk . . . all of it. And the torture stopped.'

Denise looked up, sure it must nearly be over, *this* torture. After a bit she said: 'Did they let her go then?'

Granny laughed, her mouth a red wound. 'Let her go? Not a chance; they throttled her with an old hemp rope, then chopped her into bits and flung her on the blaze. Burnt her into ashes and the rain washed her all away.'

Denise couldn't move. Finally she asked: 'Was she a witch then?'

'A witch? She confessed, did she not? Found her guilty, didn't they? What more evidence d'you want? Guilty or not, they hanged you. They hanged you then they burnt your body to ash . . .'

There was a lesson there somewhere, Denise knew. What was it? Was it the same lesson that that boy Jeffreys had learned? Or was it the one Valentino knew? It couldn't be the *same* lesson, surely?

AREYOUDEADGRANDA

Alison tapped with the teaspoon. Silence oozed through the wall towards her. Again, with more air between the taps:

ARE YOU DEAD GRANDA

The tile she always tapped against was beginning to show hairlines in it. It was getting old.

Denise was wondering about the pyramids: they had been there a long time, but even they wouldn't last. Even they were getting old. Nothing lasted for ever. The hairlines on the tile were beginning to crack like her granny's face. That was what happened when you got older – except for the Sphinx. The Sphinx looked younger if anything, except for the missing nose.

'What was it Granda died of?' Denise asked her granny again. 'How was it he'd been martyred?' Denise saw him in his straw-filled barn, a boy, like she was a girl, cold, swaddled in rags. She saw inside his body, through veins and arteries into where his heart was, red and pulsing, and then his lungs like a couple of dumplings.

'It was his job,' Granny *La*mont/La*mont* told her. 'He had to work in a place where the air was bad.'

'Was it poisonous?' Alison asked.

'No, not poisonous . . . It wasn't like a disease you could catch just by breathing in air that was full of germs. It was a different kind of disease, a modern one. The place he worked was a death trap. Most of the folk working in the place had been there half their lives; they breathed in thousands of these tiny fibres, sharp as needles. The walls of the place were insulated with the stuff. Fibreglass. You breathed it in and the needles worked their way into your lungs and you couldn't get them out again. Slowly, they pierced through the walls and made them bleed.' Their granda had been terrible out of breath, hardly able to walk at all . . . breathing was *murder*.

Denise saw the two dumplings, remembered them leaking blood, and Denise will mind them again when she's about thirteen, when the school shows a HEALTH INFORMA-TION FILM about smoking and its effects.

Lungs on a table. Plural.

Two clootie dumplings.

Death. Singular.

She will sit in the back row of the science lecture room, next to John Burke, the lights will dim and the biology teacher, Mr Thorburn, will tell them all to shut up in a lilting teuchter accent. Denise thinks about him sitting in the dark-ness at the front of the class. She thinks about John Burke sat next to her. She can smell him. The fag smell off his blazer.

'But the thing was,' their granny went on, 'Granda started to get these other ideas . . . He wanted to try and help all the other folk in the place who had this disease: asbestosis, it was called. All the families of the folk who worked in the place formed a sort of group for the sufferers – they wanted the folk that employed them to be brought before law; they wanted justice; they wanted *compensation*.'

Law:

Denise knew it must be a powerful word.

Justice:

Denise knew it was less powerful than Law, because her granny had said it second.

compensation:

47

It hardly seemed to be there at all, it hadn't even been said in capitals.

'Anyway,' Granny continued, 'near the end—'

'What end?' Denise interrupted.

'*The end*,' Alison answered.

'Death,' their granny added, emptying ash from her pipe into the tray on the tabletop at her elbow. Alison and Granny both looked at Denise in a way she didn't really understand.

Granny still insisted that death was not the end. Even the pharaohs hadn't thought it was the end or they would never have done all that preparing for the afterlife, burying the kings with all their treasures and servants and animals . . .

But Denise had to weigh it up. If they were that sure they were going on to the afterlife, how was it that they had built all these monuments that were meant to last for ever? How was it that they had embalmed Tutankhamun and put him inside a golden sarcophagus if they hadn't thought they could keep a bit of him alive that way?

'Near the end,' their granny said, leaning over and lowering her voice as if she was afraid his ears would be burning behind the fireplace, 'Granda got these *ideas* . . . He had thought he could save others. He reckoned he would die just the same, but others might be saved if he took action now. But he hadn't been alone in trying, that was the difference. There had been a lot of them, sufferers and their families. But he had been a martyr, just the same.'

'What's a martyr?' Denise asked, Alison looking at her as if she was thick.

'Someone who gives their own life for something,' Granny told her, settling back in her chair. 'Someone who cares more about other folk than themselves. Your granda was like that, but he was a God-fearing man as well. He knew fine that death was not the end, but the beginning of life everlasting.'

It was the order of things that was confusing. Granny should have said: 'everlasting life'. Most folk would. Except when they were on about God and heaven and all the angels it suddenly turned into 'life everlasting'. It seemed fairer to Denise to have it the other way around:

Life is not the end.

But Denise was always wanting things her own way: she saw pyramids and sphinxes and towns and villages; she saw headlines and black ink and she made them say what she wanted because her own words were always stuck inside her, or came out in a flood with no air between the word in front and the word behind, so that they cancelled each other out. She saw streets she could cycle along on her bike and not have other boys and girls throw stones at her or call her 'Witch'. She saw the shape of her country and knew that its cracks and fissures were just there because she had put them there, and that she had the power to destroy the country whenever she wanted. In this country, Denise was God. If the place got too big for its boots you just tore it to pieces and started again. Why not? It was a free country.

Granda still answered in these weakening scratches, the replies to Alison Forrester's question always coming out garbled, as if he couldn't for the life of him understand what was being asked. Often enough, there was no answer at all, not even a Yes or a No: only silence. Denise and Alison listened to the silence, ears pressed against upturned glasses on the tiles of the fireplace, an emptiness that was incomprehensible and went on for ever. Thinking about it was a sort of loss. For all the times you wouldn't be alive after you were dead. It was a sort of grief. Denise would hold her breath when she thought about it, but it still didn't work. She knew then that she would never be able to hold her breath long enough to find out what she wanted to know.

She couldn't wait until she was actually dead to see what was beyond – it'd be too *late* then. What she wanted was to be near enough to get a quick look, and then come back and live a bit longer. If she could have a wish, that was what she would wish for.

The important thing was to prepare well, Denise's granny said. It was a shame they didn't go to chapel . . . That mother of theirs had let them down. And her faith down as well! It was bad enough she'd went and married a Protestant, but bringing the girls up heathen was surely some sort of a crime.

Her granny was a dyed-in-the-wool, if lapsed, Catholic, but even being brought up by Protestants was better than being brought up nothing at all. Course, Denise's mum had been a right witch herself when she'd been growing up, so it wasn't all that surprising she'd found it so easy to turn her back on the church. She'd never been able to say Yes to the nuns in the convent, and then again there was that time she'd been caught after drinking the Communion wine with one of her pals and nearly got herself expelled there and then. It would maybe not have been so bad, but they'd eaten nothing except the Body of the Host all day and were rolling around the chapel floor between the pews, hooting with laughter.

They tried to give the Sacrament to a dog.

They'd brought it in off the street. Anna Forrester née Douglas cut her thumb with a pocket knife and got the dog to lick the blood:

'Drink of this,' Anna Forrester née Douglas giggled. 'Drink of this the blood of our Lord . . .'

The next morning Denise's mum hadn't been feeling all that well. They were halfway through 'Will Your Anchor Hold' when she'd leaned over and let go into the schoolbag of the girl sitting next to her, totally ruining her arithmetic homework with boaking on it. She got up and ran for the door, one hand clasped over her mouth so that spew jetted out between her fingers in a red floral spray, indiscriminately splattering all who happened to be within an eight-foot radius.

Sister Regina followed the trail of vomit to the lavatory, where she found Denise's mum in one of the cubicles, the door half-open. Sister Regina was holding Denise's mum's schoolbag in her hand, her look a mixture of pity and contempt.

'Anna Douglas,' she said. 'Are you not well, Anna Douglas?'

The answer to that was obvious enough. The working out was all over the floor.

Denise's mum looked up through hooded and teary eyes. She hadn't managed to get any of it in the bowl at all. A crimson pool sat on the floor between her legs, shoes speckled with it. Anna Douglas didn't reply to Sister Regina. Her head slumped forward again and she retched, but only yellow slabber came out.

'What caused this – *malady* of yours, Miss Douglas?' Sister Regina wrinkled her nose in distaste.

'Don't know, Sister,' Denise's mum said, between coughs.

'Come on, Anna, you must have some idea. It's not every day that you turn human fountain, is it?'

'I think it was the . . . porridge, Sister.' Denise's mum kept her head down, facing the contents of her stomach. The girls had porridge for breakfast every single day at the boarding school, sometimes twice, reheated and even more appealing once the thick skin had been peeled off and pushed to the side of the plate with a spoon.

'Porridge? Since when did porridge come in that particular *hue*, Anna? I don't believe I have *ever* consumed porridge of that particular colour and scent!'

It was true. The cubicle smelled more of wine than vomit.

'Congragulations, Anna,' Sister Regina piped out. 'I assume you are also responsible for this?' She opened Denise's mum's schoolbag and produced the empty bottle of communion wine, holding it by the neck and swinging it gently to and fro between her fingers.

Denise's mum groaned. It was the beginning of the end, surely.

'Well done, Miss Douglas,' Sister Regina said. 'You've succeeded where even our Lord and Saviour Jesus Christ could not. *He* was able only to turn water into wine' – she stared hard at Denise's mum – 'Whereas *you*—'

Denise's mum squinted up at Sister Regina.

'*You* have succeeded in turning porridge into wine!' Sister Regina stared at the pool of red alcohol and partially digested oats between the legs of Anna Douglas. 'You're a wicked girl, Anna Douglas, of that there can be little doubt. You'll pay for this, so you will.'

Sister Regina always spoke in this fashion. Years of biblical study, overexposure to other nuns and, with the exception of children, a limited interaction with members of the laity, ensured that her thoughts became terminally atrophied. She grabbed a handful of Anna Douglas's hair and began dragging her out of the cubicle, shouting: 'I'm going to make an example of you, Anna Douglas!'

But it was difficult to see what they could do to you: Denise's mum hadn't cared if she got expelled. She loathed the place already. What could they do, short of having her hanged, drawn and quartered? She would be old enough to leave school in the summer, and that would be the end of nuns for her.

Something did happen to her, though. Sister Regina's curse happened. The curse was the price you paid for growing up in ways you weren't supposed to. The curse would last for years and years and only be lifted by the time her own daughter Denise Forrester is sixteen years old, and her sister Alison fourteen.

Denise's granny often told that story when she'd had a few to drink and a captive audience. It was terrible really, having to listen to the same story over and over again, the details changing but the gist remaining the same. It was a shame for their mum having to listen to it over and over as well. It was like that was all you ever really amounted to with some people. Just these things they decided to remember about you – and they played around with it however they liked and eventually, you *were* that person. You *became* them, whether you liked it or not. Denise knew that was already what folk would be doing to her, trying to trap her like that. It wasn't fair. Her granny tried to make her be things that her mum hadn't been when she was her age. It was like some mad contest. Denise's granny would tell you one thing; her mum another. Denise never bothered what either of them said, just carried on her own way. She still got up all times of the day and night and ate what she liked. She still made her papier-mâché landscapes and talked to cats. She still got called 'Witch' and had no friends, really. It was a shame. Alison, of course, was fine.

Granny *La*mont/*La*mont swayed about the dinner table, shaking pipe ash all over it. She wanted to sing! She wanted to dance! Every now and again she would start up in a cracking voice:

'Rule Brittania . . .
marmalade and jam
co-operative sausidges
and bile't beef-ham . . .'

then she would switch to:

'– a terrible girl your mother was, Denise, a terrible, terrible girl . . . d'ye mind the Communion wine, Anna? D'ye mind that . . . ? Rule Britannia! Marmalade and . . . Here, Denise, see when your mother was a girl, not much older than yourself . . .'

And so it went on.

'God's sake, Mum, give it a rest will you?' Denise's mother said. Her dad said nothing. It wasn't any of his business. He continued to spoon mouthfuls of ice-cream under his moustache, the living-room light reflected on the shiny dome that keeked through his hair.

'But does it not bother ye? The way these two are growing up?' their granny went on. 'I mean, never going to chapel or anything. It'd be better they went to the mosque with Mr Ali than nothing at all.'

'They get religious education at school,' Denise's mum sighed. 'Besides, Mr Ali doesn't go to the mosque any more. Not since he started selling pork, anyway. Muslims and Catholics. I mean, now that Mr Ali's bringing home the bacon . . .' Denise's mum tailed off without finishing her sentence. She puffed at a cigarette, toying with the ice-cream on her plate. She had a sore stomach and ice-cream was about all she could stand to eat.

'It's not the same,' Granny said, waving her whisky and ginger across the table. 'I mean, they should have a baptism, a christening . . .'

'They don't need christening. If they believe they believe, if they don't they don't.' Denise's mum was getting exasperated. She sipped quickly at her vodka, lighting another cigarette off the one she'd just finished.

'But they should get a baptism . . . Here, I'll do it for ye now.'

Denise looked at Alison and Alison looked at Denise. Neither of them wanted baptising.

Their granny dipped her fingers into her whisky and ginger. 'I'll baptise you,' she said, standing up quickly and flicking liquid in Denise's direction:

'You! Denise! In the name of Christ will you stand still and be baptised?'

Denise jerked her chair backward and squealed, setting off round the other side of the table, her granny swinging wildly over the plates and glasses; a big splash landed right on top of Alison's forehead. Baptised at point-blank range.

'Stand still, Denise. It won't hurt. Your sins'll be cleansed and the path to Eternity unbarred . . .'

'Stop it, Mum. Leave the girl alone, can't you?' Denise's

mum was laughing, though, trying to get her mother to sit back down, but laughing just the same. Denise, flying from one chair to another, dodging behind her dad, then her mum, then back again. Finally, she dived underneath the table, into a comfortingly dark place where her granny would never be able to bend down and get her. Her mum handed her down her ice-cream and some juice, and Denise sneaked a cushion from one of the unsat-in chairs. She stayed down there the rest of the evening, listening to them talking. It got to be so she wondered if anyone remembered she was down there. It was nice. Denise would have liked to stay under that table for ever and ever.

She reached into her pocket and looked at the goldfish her dad had shaken out of her. She had wanted to show it to her granny, but not now. She wrapped it in a paper hankie and put it back into her pocket, next to her lucky hen's foot that Mr Ali had given her, even though Denise only used to like going into the butcher's shop 'cause of the mountaineer. When he stopped coming, she began to go off it. The smell was one reason, the ripeness of it. It wasn't so bad as a roasting chicken or new bread baking, but it was rotten just the same. And your shoes would get all covered in this sawdust and stuff, bits of meat. Denise looked round when the chimes went, but the mountaineer had just disappeared. She tried to mind what kind of shoes he'd had on the last time she'd seen him, but it was no use. She kept seeing boots that were beginning to split between the sole and the upper. When you were dead your soul must come floating out of your boots and disappear off into heaven to live with the rest of the souls that had got out alive.

'What's the matter with the young lady?' the butcher man had said, and Denise concentrated on the trays of pigs' willies and the flags sticking out the meat.

'I couldn't tell you, Mr Ali, she's not herself these days.'

Her granny mouthed some words at the butcher, and they both looked at Denise and nodded, then looked at each other and were quiet. Denise stared at the sawdust on the floor. There was no point in coming if the mountaineer didn't come too. The butcher began to whistle and wink at Denise, trying to cheer her up.

'She's missing what's-his-name's Tuesday performances, is what it is,' her granny said. 'Any tongue?'

The butcher frowned and patted the black flap of hair over the top of his head again, smoothing it into place.

'Tongue you wanting, hen? Hold on a minute.' He reached down under the glass of the counter and peeled the grease-proof paper off a great slab of something. It had a glutinous look, like some kind of big eel dragged up from the bottom of the sea, pink and with a whitish skein on its surface. The butcher reached down and tried to grab it up but it slipped away from his hand. It looked like it was half-asleep and not wanting to be disturbed, the purplish tear at the back of it leaking blood into the white tray it sat in.

Denise's hand went up to her mouth.

'C'mere, you,' the butcher man said. He grunted and heaved at it, his hair coming free of his crown again, but the tongue was as slippery as anything, wriggling and squirting out of his hand back into the tray. None of the other meat did anything. It all sat silent.

'Now, just relax there,' Mr Ali said. 'No one's going to hurt you.'

'Heh!' Denise's granny snorted, both hands clasped together under her giant chest, a carrier bag hanging from her wrist. 'That's right, Mr Ali . . . you tell it who's boss.'

He grunted again as it slipped out his hand once more and into the tray. 'Acht!' he said, standing up and wiping fresh smears onto his white coat.

'The tongue is a hard thing to pin down, that not right, Mrs Douglas? Talk its way out of most situations, heh?'

'Absolutely, Mr Ali, but I've been looking forward to some tongue for quite a while now, so ye'll just have to try and persuade it.'

Both Denise's granny and the butcher man started to cackle away, but Denise couldn't see what was so funny. People were always laughing at things that weren't funny. The mountaineer had been funny, but he wasn't here any more. He'd abandoned her.

'Granny . . .' Denise said.

'If you just want to give me a minute here,' the butcher said. He disappeared out through the ribbony curtain into the back shop.

'Granny,' Denise said, again. Her granny was staring at the blue element of the insectocuter.

'Granny,' Denise said again, tugging at Granny Douglas's coat.

'What is it, Denise?' she said, not looking down.

'Where's the mountaineer?'

'Eh, this isn't the day he comes, love . . .'

'Yes he does. It's Tuesday – he always comes on Tuesdays.'

'Are you sure of that, Denise? We don't always come on a Tuesday – how d'ye know he might not have come in on a different day?'

Denise tried to work it out. Maybe he might have come in on a different day. She wasn't 100% sure that the mountaineer didn't come in on other days as well, just to fool people. Denise had never really figured him as existing except to come into this butcher's shop, then disappear off the face of the earth until next time. Maybe that was what had happened to him. Maybe he'd just disappeared off the face of the earth, never to be seen again. Now, Denise couldn't be sure he existed at all. 'Tuesday,' she said. 'This is a Tuesday . . .'

The butcher stepped out from the back shop. 'No, no, he won't come in today . . .' He must have been listening to them through in the back shop. 'It's every second Tuesday he comes.' He looked over at Denise's granny, and their eyes met. They had said something else to each other without making noises with their mouths. Denise knew.

The butcher looked up, out through the window at the sunlight on the road, shining without warmth. He shivered.

'Here we go,' he said. He tightened his lips into a straight line, nodding in the direction of the street. The two alkies were shouting and grabbing each other by the coat lapels, tumbling about in a kind of dance. One of them was swinging away at the other, and every now and again they would both go birling over onto the ground. Eventually, one of them – the smaller one in a herringbone coat with leather patches on the elbows – managed to disengage himself from the other man and ran off a few steps, out of the view of the window. Mr Ali shook his head.

'A terrible lot, so they are,' Denise's granny said.

Denise looked out at the tree with the remaining tramp sat under it, a few desperate-looking shoots beginning to appear on its bare branches. It was getting into spring.

The man sat looking blankly across the road and patting the head of this big dirty-looking mongrel tied to the trunk of the tree. When he went to clap it, the dog shivered and cowered down, presenting its belly to him. The man belted it one across the snout.

Mr Ali shook his head again. 'That one'll be over here in a minute, wanting a bone for the dog. Never buys anything, maybe the odd sausage. But he'll take old bones for the dog.'

'Maybe they're not for the dog,' Denise's granny said. 'Maybe he eats them himself!'

'Chance would be a fine thing, Missus.'

'No chance, you mean.'

'Aye, that's what I mean. No chance would be a fine thing! Comes in here wanting a loan: no chance!'

Both Denise's granny and the butcher started to laugh again.

'About that tongue, Mr Ali . . .'

'Gaunnae gies a lenna wan yir knives—'

A figure, pale skin like plastic and a mouth like an open fly, was standing in the doorway, as though he was using it as a shield. He had the same expression as the dog had when the man clapped it. He swayed a bit as he stood there staring at everyone and no one at the same time.

'. . . a lenna wan yir knives – I'll clean it up, honest I will, gies a lenna wan, eh—'

Mr Ali stared at the man. Denise's granny stared away at a tray of kidneys behind the counter. She had a hand clamped over her mouth and nose. Denise stared right at him, still holding her granny's hand. The man was quivering and shaking like the dog across the road.

'No,' Mr Ali said. 'I've told you before . . .'

'Ten minutes, man, jist a couple minutes fuck, 'sno like I'll no bring it back, man . . . meantaesay ayeways brung it back afore man,' the guy in the doorway was mumbling, his voice a sort of low whine.

'No,' Mr Ali said, slapping his hand on the glass counter. 'Last time I lend you lot one of these knives it comes back all blunted and dirty—'

'MON, YA CUNT! 'Sno as if'll no bring it back – always brung the thing back afore, know what I mean. Gaun man, jist gies it for ten minutes, ya cunt—'

'And I'm telling you NO, and get the hell out of my shop if you're not going to buy anything,' Mr Ali was saying, waving the cleaver in his hand at the man, his head shaking from side to side. The man slunk away out the door and weaved off down the street.

Mr Ali put his cleaver down on the glass counter. He had something looped over the ties of his apron. It was a hook, with a wooden handle. Mr Ali grinned at Denise's granny, the hook held upright. He was like Bluto out of Popeye.

'Those men!' the butcher said. 'Such filthy mouths they have!'

He brought the hook slamming down behind the counter.

'Speaking to me like that!' Mr Ali had the blob of quivering pinkness up in the air in front of him, then landed it down on the chopping board, turning his back to Denise and her granny. The chimes by the door went again. Denise, her granny, and the butcher all looked around. It was the tramp with the mongrel. He stared at the three faces watching him, dog quivering at his feet.

'EMDI COME IN WANTIN A LENNY ANYFIN?'

'Who wants to know?' Mr Ali said. He folded his hands across his chest, the silver hook in plain view. The tramp looked a bit sick at the sight of it. His dog whimpered.

'EH JIST WONDERIN—'

'What did you just wonder?' the butcher said.

'Nothing . . .' the tramp said. 'Well, maybe if yous had any old bones ye didn't want for the dug?'

Mr Ali walked back through the ribbony curtain, then reappeared. He threw a big bone flecked with scraps of meat and cream-coloured fat over the counter onto the sawdust on the floor. The dog began to whimper, and the tramp bent over to pick the object up, keeping his eyes on the butcher all the time. He nodded his thanks and retreated back out the door. He stood in the doorway for a minute, holding the bone out of the reach of the dog, staring at it like it was some kind of ancient artefact, though it was only an old knuckle. The dog tried jumping and snapping at it, but the tramp cracked it over the skull with it, sending it whimpering onto its belly again. Then he began to gnaw at the bone himself.

It was a bit of a hike back to Granny's, especially with having to carry full shopping bags. Denise couldn't really carry all that much but at least she had proper footwear, unlike her granny who'd come out the house with these slippers on. She didn't even seem to know she was wearing them, her face set, concentrating on the road ahead. When she walked, she made these huffing noises. After a bit, they had to sit down on a bench and let her have a breather. Denise let her legs dangle over the side, kicking her heels up until her granny told her to sit at peace. Denise didn't want to sit at peace. Granny was sitting at peace and she didn't look all that much the better for it.

'Just a minute till I get my breath back,' she told Denise, reaching into her coat for her pipe. Her feet were killing her, she was saying. She couldn't believe she'd come out without her shoes. It was that habit of hers, just to keep the slippers on, climb inside her old comfy PVC ankle-boots and go out just like that. Denise said nothing. Dirty-looking pigeons pecked about on the ground by the bench, some of them missing toes, even whole feet.

'Here,' Granny said, did Denise want to feed them? She could take a slice or two of loaf out the message bag and use that if she wanted?

Denise didn't want to feed the birds. They were dirty and diseased-looking. They made her skin feel all itchy.

'Here, like this,' Granny said, scattering crumbs about the

bench so that the pigeons came whirling down and round about them, flapping the air with their greasy wings, jostling and pecking the crumbs from each other's beaks. Denise shuddered at the sight of them, grabbing and tearing, the strong against the weak, clambering and flapping over each other's backs, the smaller ones to the outside pattering around, necks going like clockwork puppets. A horrible sight.

'That one, Granny,' Denise said, pointing to one of the smaller ones, still trying without luck to keep a hold of any crumbs it could get its beak into. It was paler in colour, greyish, and had a brown-speckled back and both its own feet.

'Here, Freckles!' her granny said, sending a bit of crust over with a flick of the wrist. 'Catch!'

But one of the bigger manky-looking ones careened down onto the back of it, snapping the crust out of its beak and then, oddly, sort of balancing on top of it and doing this strange-flapping routine, sawing the air with its wings and nodding back and forth.

Denise's granny was black-affronted; right in the middle of the street they were, in front of everyone!

'You filthy brute, leave her alone!' she said, standing up suddenly, grabbing Denise by the hand and waving a shopping bag at the birds. 'Come on, Denise,' she said. 'Time we got you up the road.'

Denise's granny set off at a hell of a pace, far faster than she normally walked, moving with a rolling sort of gait that was probably the fault of her wearing slippers instead of shoes. Denise could hardly keep up. 'Slow down,' she said, but her granny ignored her, huffing away on up the road. Denise couldn't understand what was going on. The pigeons had only been playing a game, hadn't they? What was wrong with games? Denise didn't like playing games herself, but she knew other people did.

When they got to the corner of the street, Denise's granny had to slow down, wheezing heavily and looking dead pale. Denise had never seen her look that way before. It was scary.

'Granny,' she said, tugging her hand: 'Granny, what's wrong?'

Her granny leaned against the railings, puffing. 'Here, love,' she said, handing one of the shopping bags to Denise. 'Take this a minute, will ye?'

Denise took the shopping bag and stood uneasily by her granny's side. She looked not well at all. She handed Denise her purse.

'Stop a taxi, will ye, Denise? We'll take a ride home the day.'

She kept on wheezing, the sound coming from somewhere away deep down inside her and rattling all the way up. Denise nodded. She looked up and down the street. There was a black car in the distance, coming towards them. Denise stepped down off the pavement and waved and jumped up and down.

'Not that one,' her granny said, tutting between wheezes, yanking Denise off the road by the collar. 'In the name of Christ, Denise, what d'ye think you're playing at?'

'You said to stop a black cab,' Denise said.

'Aye. A black cab I says . . .'

Denise looked at the vehicle as it passed.

'That was a hearse,' her granny said, pressing the button for the green man to come on. 'What's your hurry?' she said, a grim look setting on her face. 'They'll be by for ye soon enough. I wouldn't be in so much of a rush if I was you.'

The green man came on and Granny set off into the middle of the road, trailing Denise by the hand.

'Are we not getting a taxi any more?' Denise asked.

'No. We'll walk. Wasted enough money as it is . . . sides, it'll do us good.'

Denise didn't think it was really all her fault. It had looked like a taxi from where she'd been standing.

*

Elsa *La*mont/La*mont* got a terrible scare that day outside the
butcher's. She was sure she was dead meat. But the hearse had
sailed by leaving no trace of a wake. All the same, it was a
portent. Time was no longer there just to be wasted, and she
began to round up the rest of her affairs, stopped entertaining
Mr Polywka and made a final effort to rid the premises of
mice and cats. The poison had only a short-lived effect on the
vermin, but cats didn't breed with the same intensity. They
couldn't recover their numbers so quickly. Denise and Alison
began to notice a smell among the stink of drains and
midden, a smell that was familiar but new at the same time.
The brittleness of the spring air couldn't subdue it entirely;
the days were beginning to warm, shoots of green springing
up through the cracks in the concrete where the lawn had
been, and the smell of rank meat ripened. That was what the
end would smell like: the bloated body of an old, scarred tomcat lying among the cabbage stumps and empty tins of beans
of a back-midden in a crumbling tenement.

First one body turned up, then another. Denise wanted to
know what had happened to them, but Alison had no answers
this time, and Granny said less and less. More and more, she
kept her hearing aid turned down or off: you practically had
to shout to be heard. She was shutting down.

Denise was helpless, Alison indifferent. Neither their mum
nor their dad seemed to have any solutions either. Denise lost
count of the number of times she asked her granny for help,
but she would just snort, relight her pipe and go: 'Witchcraft!'
then refuse to say anything else.

Alison tapped a message to Granda through the wall:

WHY ARE THE CATS ALL DYING

but the only thing that could be heard was the usual
scratching. Denise was beginning to doubt he was there at
all. What with the warm weather on the way, maybe he'd
not needed a heat so much. She looked quickly over at the

window to see if he was looking in, but there was nobody there again. She'd thought she could hear sick, laboured breathing; she had thought she would see a man with hands curled inwards, shuffling forward painfully, lungs on fire. Granda had been a martyr, he had died for the other folk in the factory he'd worked in, but his wounds had never been visible. Only when Denise had watched a thousand TV documentaries, heard a thousand news stories on TV, seen the power of a visible injury, had she any inkling how much of a handicap an invisible injury must be to a martyr. There was no bleeding from Granda's hands or feet. The wounds were imaginary; the wounds of a man who knew he would die and that, no matter what anybody said, there could never be any compensation for that. Not for him, at any rate. The day after the earthly remains of Andy McCabe are scattered on the eighteenth green at Gleneagles, and the crowds have already begun to forget who he'd been, Denise Forrester will remember this about her grandfather, a man she never met, and experience a sudden stab of grief for him, and for Andy McCabe too. Though not so much.

'What is it called if you bleed like Jesus?' Denise will ask Alison, as the next day turns out to be no different from the one before, despite everything.

'Stigmata,' Alison will reply, frowning so that her face becomes just like her mum's and her granny's and her dad's all at once – three generations simultaneously flitting across her brow.

They walk on for a bit in silence, then Alison asks: 'Why?'

Denise Forrester, biting a fingernail and grinning, just looks at Alison and then says: '*Psychostigmatic.*' And refuses to say anything else, and Alison will storm off in a mood, sick of her sister.

Jeedy picked the dead cat up by the tail and swung it over his head, stepping closer to Denise. Jeedy was angry about something. Jeedy was always angry about something.

'Get away!' she shouted.

Andy McCabe and John Burke sat on the steps of the back court, laughing, Jeedy shouting, '*Jee-day! Jee-day!*' the cat arcing around his head. He did a sort of dance and made faces as well, like he was a mad Zulu or something. Then he let go and the cat sailed over the dyke into the next court, panelling through a pair of underpants on the washing-line and disappearing from view. One of the women looking out the window, three-up on the other side, leaned out and started yelling. Jeedy turned round and stared at her.

'Wasn't us, Missez!' he yelled, then made a dash for the mouth of the close. Denise didn't bother running. If there was any justice in the world, she'd get off scot-free.

Jeedy and Andy McCabe were getting folk to pay them to dispose of the bodies. They had a black bin-liner and slung them in that, then took them off and flung them in the river with a couple of bricks inside to weight the bag. A pound a corpse they were charging, and doing not bad out of it. John Burke wasn't involved. He couldn't stand to be near dead things. When Denise got back to the close, Jeedy and Andy had a hold of another one – twisting and screeching and spitting.

'Bastard!' Jeedy said, letting go suddenly. 'Scratched me!'

Andy McCabe was laughing. 'Shouldn't try to grab it by the back first – you need to pin its forelegs . . .'

Andy had it held down by the back, practically crushing it against the floor with his full weight. The cat was terrified.

'Let it go!' Denise screamed at him. 'Leave it alone!' She went for Andy, clawing him with her nails, him jumping back out of reach, the cat tearing off down the back steps of the close and out into the back court and away. Andy stood, dabbing at his cheek, Jeedy laughing now and Denise panting hard, shaken.

'What were you doing that for?' she yelled.

Jeedy looked at her. 'We get a pound for every cat we get rid of,' he said. 'It makes sense,' he went on. 'Besides, they have nine lives. We were only going to kill them once.'

Andy McCabe jumped in with: 'You should have seen it, Denise – we get all these kittens and put them in a bin and fill it with water out a hose and then we stick the lid on it and just wait and wait and when we get the lid off again they just all float about. Mental, so it is. Mental.'

Denise stood, her hands tightened into walnut fists. She looked over at the bin-liner. She looked at Andy McCabe. She looked at the words coming out of the hole in his face. They were ugly words, but carried no more weight than any other kind, dissolving away into nothingness, becoming air in front of your eyes.

'You're talking shite, Andy man,' Jeedy said. 'We never touched any kittens. We never killed any cats, Denise . . .' Jeedy shook his head at Andy and went to pick up the bin-liner in the corner. He held it up in one hand and shook it. Something heavy inside swung about. 'This is all we do, Denise,' he said. 'We get rid of the dead ones. We've found about five so far, but we never killed any.'

'Cross my heart and hope to die, we never,' Andy said.

'Shut up,' Denise told him. 'I don't want to hear any more.'

She went running out past Jeedy, down the front steps and into the street, nearly knocking Mr Polywka over on the way.

'Where you going in such a big hurry, young lady?' he said, bending to pick up a bag of onions that'd fallen from the top of the brown paper bag he was carrying. But Denise kept on going, down the hill to the bottom and away around the corner as far as the traffic lights before stopping. She stood, looking out across the road at the world beyond. She wasn't to cross on her own. She pressed for the green man, waiting for something to happen. The button didn't seem to do anything.

The intervals between the changes from green man to red man carried on regardless.

The green man came on and Denise stood, watching the traffic, wondering whether or not to cross the road. One of the drivers was looking at her: she was the only person there. They were waiting for *her*. Denise clenched her fists and tried to think what to do. She had never crossed the road by herself before – she would get into trouble if she got caught. That was definite. The green man stared back at her from mid-stride. Denise put one foot out onto the road, then another. Then she crossed over to the other side, a feeling like bubbles fizzing trapped up in her chest, trying to get out through her throat and mouth, and even when she got to the other side it didn't go away. It was a mad feeling, like when you went to the carnival and had just come off a ride on the dodgems or something. Denise loved the carnival, but this was better somehow. By doing nothing but pressing a button you could change everything, make things STOP or GO for yourself, even if it was just kid-on and it happened without you anyway.

It was only when Denise looked down she saw that she'd forgotten to change out of her school shoes, the ones she was meant to take off when she got out of classes. Denise felt them loose about her feet, broken in a bit, comfortable. She was used to them now. She walked along the pavement, in the direction of the shops, seeing the bodies of cats piling up on pyres; smell of burning meat and hair, black figures reeling in a black night silhouetted against an orange blaze; the Curse hanging before her, Denise taking one step and then another, creeping towards whatever it was, on the brink of something that turned into a mirage as soon as it was within reach. The feeling of being the only one who didn't understand was almost enough to crush you; she could feel that weight on her chest. It was relentless. It followed her everywhere. You could try and control it, but your working had to change all the time, there was no right answer, only the method mattered, it was all you had. It was an impossible situation.

She was at the crossroads again, waiting on STOP to change into GO, red man to green, not knowing whether to go or to turn back. She could see the butcher's shop. She could see the two men with the dog outside it, someone else between them, grabbed by either arm. His head was down, but she knew it was the mountaineer. The two men holding his arms took turns to punch and kick him. He was half doubled over. One of them flung him back into the partially closed iron shutter of the shop. A clattering.

She was powerless, the lights unchanging.

The men kept hitting him, punching and kicking. The dog barking and dragging at the mountaineer's trouser leg, him dropping a handful of notes onto the ground and them beginning to curl away in the breeze. One of the men let go and bent to scramble about after them. The butcher man was coming out the shop, meat hook in his hand. He pushed the shutter up so he could get out. The other man punched the mountaineer in the face, a wet clack, nose splitting open and blood spattering in droplets onto the ground. Denise saw the man turn from the mountaineer to the butcher – saw him take something shiny out from inside his coat. The thing lashed through the air. The mountaineer raised his hand to fend off the blow. Denise begged with the traffic lights to change. The mountaineer was sitting on the ground, hand up to his throat. Blood blurted uselessly out between his fingers. Denise forced words into her mouth and spat them across the street at the butcher.

'You should have put him in the hospital!' she yelled across the road at the butcher. The mountaineer's eyes stared.

'That's how the police catch them! You should have put him in the hospital!'

Denise's dad came and picked her up from Mr Ali's shop. Denise sat staring out the window at the stain on the pavement. Her dad came in and went over to Mr Ali. They spoke quietly; Denise couldn't hear what they were saying. She knew it was her they were talking about, but it wasn't Denise that had got her throat slit on a busy street while it was still daylight out. It wasn't Denise who'd robbed an old tramp while folk walked by on the other side of the street and paid no attention. No. She was innocent.

Denise's dad fingered the peak of his cap, then smoothed the epaulettes on his police jacket. He liked to look spick and span. He worried about dandruff.

'The old boy had lost a lot of blood. He was gone by the time the ambulance came,' he was saying to Mr Ali. 'And for what? Just the giro? No great loss, mind.'

'Animals, so they were,' Mr Ali said. 'Malevolent animals, the lot of them.'

They wouldn't get far, though. They weren't what you could call 'career criminals'.

Mr Forrester didn't like to catch the butcher's eye. He kept his gaze over his shoulder, staring at the picture on the wall, the one of the bull with all the different cuts on it. He was wondering what the trade name for a cut throat would be. A Halal cut, likely. They were a wild lot, so they were.

It was a bit of luck Mr Ali had been around to look after

70

the girl, he said. Christ knew what state she'd have been in if he'd not been there.

'Just to be looking at her now, you would think nothing had happened,' Mr Ali said. He himself had a tired look about him. His eyes carried big bags under them.

Denise's dad thanked Mr Ali again and went over to Denise. She was dangling her feet over the side of the window ledge, head twisted round to stare out at the street. The blood was different from the blood inside the shop. It was redder. Not so dark. Denise shut her eyes and tried not to see the mountaineer's face behind her lids. It didn't work. His mouth opened and closed silently. His eyes stared up at nothing, helpless and not understanding. Denise tried to think of something else.

'You ready to come home now, Denise?' her dad said, quietly patting the top of her head. 'You hungry?'

Denise nodded. Her dad looked over at Mr Ali and winked. Mr Ali leaned over the glass counter and scratched the bald bit on the top of his head. He was thinking about going home too. It was getting on now.

'Okay, then,' her dad went on. 'We'll get you off home and get you into bed, heh? An early night'll do you good after all this *excitement*.'

That was the word he used: *excitement*. She didn't know what it was that she needed to go to bed early for. But it wasn't because of *excitement*. She bit her lip and stood up, though. The chimes tinkled on her way out the door.

It was a prison sentence. Unable to sleep, she lay staring at the darkened walls, watching columns of light sweep around the room, only knowing that time was passing because her heart was still beating inside her chest, regular as the minute hand of a watch, b-dum, b-dum, b-dum, waiting until the house was silent and she could creep downstairs, switch the telly on and let brightness and colour and daylight in again. And the house would settle into its own night rhythm; the clank of pipes and the creak of ageing floorboards, relaxing, breathing after the tautness of the day. Then Denise would feel like she belonged.

The punishment was sleep. Denise was awake. But this was *her* time. She'd often thought about running away one night, but didn't know anywhere to go. She could go to her granny's, but it wouldn't take anybody very long to find her there. There was nowhere else, and she didn't fancy the idea of living in a garden shed or underneath a flyover. She'd seen the sorts of folk that lived in those places. Sometimes, Denise left her room, through the window, out over rooftops and trees, the shapes and shadows that clung between their boughs. The soles of her feet sprang lightly from smokestack to telegraph pole out over the poisoned world where everything was already dead, moving through walls and rooms and lives, over fences and railways and towns all painted now in night colours, rivers and lochs and hillsides of shadow and pitch, farms and woods and valleys; silvers and greys, sheep and cows and cars and lorries and the like, lamplit orange and steel grey, everything carved in black ink, places without limit. There were always imperfections and adjustments needed; more needing done till it had to be taken to bits and started again, rebuilt from scratch, all the borders and boundaries remapped, fields resown, forests replanted. Let Denise fill the pages her own way; shredding and dissecting, reducing them to the sum of their parts; remoulding and reshaping them from dark matter and torn surfaces. Below, figures crawled like malevolent insects, carrying clubs and broom handles, going after every cat they could find, starting with the old tom, smashing its spine with iron bars, driving the others across rooftops, bludgeoning every one within reach, trapping those that tried to escape in the corners of lanes and alleys, forcing them into bin-liners and dustbins. They dumped sackloads of half-dead cats in the back court. Then they gathered round and staged a trial: there were guards, a confessor, and a public executioner. After pronouncing the animals guilty and administering last rites, they strung them up on an improvised gallows, laughing. A scarred snout dangled from a noose. Seven lives to go.

The faces turned. They came toward her.

Hands reaching out to grab her, sticks poised to break her back, flaming torches raised to set her alight. She saw herself hoisted up on the gallows, saw them loop a noose around her neck, felt the choke of it and wondered vaguely as her breath began to putter out how many times they'd kill her, how often would be enough for them . . .

Denise was standing behind the kitchen door. Her mum nearly didn't see her and had to catch the door in time before it bashed her in the face.

'Denise,' she said. She shook her by the shoulder, but Denise kept staring, a look of fixed terror in her eyes . . . she seemed absorbed, lost. Denise's mum felt the hairs on the back of her neck stand on end. She shook Denise again and again and tried to get her to move. 'Denise,' she said, quietly, 'come on now, love, wake up.' Her mum tried again to get her to move. Nothing. The muscles in her body were rigid and stiff and couldn't be coerced, a muscular premonition of something worse that was to come. Something real.

Denise's mum was about to shout to her dad for help when she snapped out of it. She mumbled something about being choked, about wanting to breathe but not being able to. Her mum cupped her cheeks in her hands and looked into her eyes. They were normal again. Wherever she had been, she was back.

'Denise,' her mum said, suddenly cold. 'You've been sleepwalking . . .'

'Sleepwalking . . . ?'

'Yes. I came down for a glass of water and you were here. What were you dreaming, pet?'

Denise stared at her mum.

'What was it?' Her mum stroked her hair, and with the back of her hand, her cheek.

'It was a . . . map.'

'A map?'

'A map . . . then a map of the map. I don't remember any more.'

Denise's mum stared at her.

'I'm tired now,' Denise said.

'Yes. Go on up to bed. You've had a long day.'

Denise climbed the steps like someone already asleep; the exhausted tread of a wean up too late at night who'll remember nothing of the previous night when she wakes in the morning.

It was odd to think of Denise like that. A child. There was nothing childlike about her. There never was.

And when she becomes a teenager, there is nothing teenage about her either. There never is.

Mz Ewart wanted answers, but Denise only had questions; one question led to another and another, they multiplied and went scuttling out of reach. She tapped at the chalked scratchings on the board with a ruler. Denise continued to stare out of the window, letting the question fall to the floor unanswered. Mz Ewart scattered drifts of dandruff around the room. Rajan Sood had his hand up.

'I'm talking to you, Anna Forrester,' Mz Ewart said. 'Do me the courtesy of answering my question.' She tapped the blackboard again with her ruler. The chalky marks read:

$3.14 = ?$

Denise stared out of the window, not answering. She had been tricked. Lied to. Here she was, after a year, still sitting at the front of the class at a desk on her own. Once upon a time, Denise would have liked to rejoin the remainder of the class. Not now. She would answer no more questions like the one on the board.

'It's Denise . . .' she said. 'My name is Denise Forrester.'

Had she said something? Mz Ewart asked her, head bent slightly, quizzical expression on her face. Denise stared out at the playing fields. When she'd been small, there were no playing fields. There were no houses. There were only back courts and tenements. But that was before. Here, there were only playing fields and cul-de-sacs; anonymous two-storey buildings and detached homes; bungalows, a couple of Italian cafés.

Denise looked at Mz Ewart and realised she wasn't there at all, that no one in the class was there at all, that she didn't have to follow their method, their working. She looked at Mz Ewart and all she could see was meat.

'Would Anna Forrester care to repeat what she just said?' Mz Ewart said.

Denise said: 'My name is Denise Forrester. My name is Denise Forrester, and I am fourteen and a half years old.'

'That's not what I asked you, is it, Mz Forrester? What did I ask you? Tell me,' Mz Ewart said, the ruler pointing straight at Denise like a knife. 'What was it that you were asked, Anna?'

Denise said again: 'My name is Denise Forrester and I am fourteen and a half years old.'

'Mz Forrester – I asked you a question.'

'Mz Ewart – I gave you an answer.'

For a minute, Denise wondered if Mz Ewart really did have a belt up the inside of her sleeve and if she might really hit her with it. Denise had never spoken to anyone like this before and wondered what was causing it. It felt good.

'*Denise* Forrester,' Mz Ewart said, lips thin and slitted, the colour draining from her face, 'you have, for the best part of a year, narrowly avoided a stint in the remedial group. You have dozed through the year . . . the simplest questions have been met with blank stares. What would you propose I do with you? Would you *like* to spend some time with the remedial group?' Mz Ewart turned, folding her arms under her chest. She looked at the class.

A cold feeling spread its fingers over Denise's back and shoulders, a sweat beginning to prickle the edges of her cheeks.

'Perhaps,' Mz Ewart said, a slight smirk appearing on her face, 'we should ask the class what should be done with you, Mz Forrester? Let us be democratic . . . Turn and face your classmates, Denise.'

Denise turned and looked at the faces. For a minute, the

only one she could put a name to was Rajan Sood. The rest were just lumps of meat. She hated them. Andy McCabe was sat at the back, mouthing something:

'*Witch!*'

Denise couldn't hear the words, but that didn't mean they weren't there. She looked at the other boys and girls and she could see them all doing it, mouthing the words silently, and she could hear Mz Ewart asking them, what should be done with this *girl*? What sentence should be carried out, on this . . . this . . . left-hander!

Denise Forrester wouldn't stand for it. Not any more. She looks at Mz Ewart and fixes her to the spot with her stare, cold and sharp as a dagger, then she picks up the books on her desk, folds them across her chest and walks towards the door. When she gets there, Denise will turn and say the only words she can think of at the time, and even they'll be difficult to get out, so difficult does Denise find it to speak in front of people:

'Fuck off.'

And Mz Ewart stands still, speechless, frozen.

So there was power in words after all.

Denise's granny moved about the place in a sort of crouch these days: she seemed to be getting smaller. Denise and Alison could both mind when she had been huge, like a giant, indestructible. Now she had become this shrinking, wizened thing that never seemed to leave the house and always kept its hearing aid turned down. If you asked her something, she ignored you or said: 'What?'

She was a ghost of her former self all right, and it was a shame. Always up in the middle of the night these days, off to the lavatory every ten minutes and no great sleeper now either. She would be up half the night, reading travel brochures over and over. She had this idea that she was away off to Egypt – though the furthest she'd ever been was Cornwall. Excepting of course that, away back in history, she had come from France, she was Clan Lamont French, so that was always something. But this business about Egypt was a right nuisance.

'Where's she going to get the money to go to Egypt?' her son-in-law asked.

'She's got her pension,' her daughter said.

Alison and Denise said nothing.

It was warmth she was wanting. She was always complaining about the cold, never warm enough even with the gas fire on all the time and the heating bill through the roof, the slates and tiles loose and in disarray; the insulation an ancient, primeval wool of some kind that hadn't been replaced for years. The stairs were getting a bit much for the old biddy. It looked for certain the only place she was likely to be going would be a ground-floor place out in one of the newer schemes, somewhere tucked out of sight, away from main arteries and busy roads; away from gangs of roving youths who threw bottles at each other and vandalised bush shelters; somewhere with fewer stairs and *weans* and *racket* and *noise*. She wondered if such a place might really exist, or if it was just a figment of some town-planner's imagination; a place of cul-de-sacs and pathways and underpasses, of whitened buildings like a set of bleached false teeth against the slate skies. The sort of place you went to die: the old folks' graveyard. And she would go there willingly as well, this was the thing. She could aye picture it: her version ringed with cast-iron fences, nightwatchmen permanently on duty, concièrge at the front hall so's that you never had to answer the door personally. Heaven.

'I reckon it'll be a below-ground-floor place before then,' her son-in-law said, though not to her face. He said it to her ears. He knew fine well she was deaf as a post.

She mentioned nothing to Mr Polywka. He came, said his codename, flashed a salute and cleared away the drifts of dead mice behind the cupboards, flinging them into a steel bucket by their tails, their tiny pink hands curled in towards their chests, mouths set in miniature frowns. For a minute or so, Polywka would stand uneasily with the pail in one hand, looking at the piles of dishes wrapped in newspaper that sat on the table, or pick a book up and stare at it, before putting it back into one of the cardboard boxes that sat by the front door, then quietly excusing himself and going next door again.

'Mrs Polywka keeping all right?' Denise and Alison's granny used to say, once or twice upon a time, but she wasn't really asking anything. It was just something she said to Polywka. They were very limited conversationalists, the pair of them, so they were.

When Denise Forrester meets Mr Polywka on the close landing for the last time, before her granny flits, she notices something about him that she has never noticed before: how completely alone he is. She knows, then, that there is no Mrs Polywka; that there hasn't been any Mrs Polywka for a long time. She can feel it in the way auld Polywka stands there, looking at her, like the light has been turned out on him for ever. Denise knows this, and never wants to have it happen to her. For a minute, she will feel a terrible sort of pity for Mr Polywka, but it will be overtaken, dragged away in the under-tow of another moment, forgotten. Denise Forrester stands a few steps down from Mr Polywka, in the blinking close lights, his look the look of a man who barely exists, stuck in an ageing picture-reel thrown by a faulty projector. Her granny would become an old yellow photograph, Mr Polywka a crackling black and white film; Mrs Polywka nothing at all, a non-presence, like her granda, or them up the stairs:

'*Madden . . . ? Ye there, Madden . . . ?*'

Singular.

Plural.

Denise moved into the single bed in her sister's room but it was too small for the both of them. Her sister twisted about during the night, kicking out in her sleep the way dogs do. After dinner, they sat in the room together but separate. They didn't like the same games and never played together anyway. Her wee sister liked a kind of game of tennis that didn't need a ball or any more than one player. She played it on paper, with lists and crosses and dice. She had jotters and jotters full of these games, leagues and tables all played this way.

Lists and crosses and dice.

Denise would be reading, or maybe drawing with an HB pencil, filling in the margins and covers of jotters with swirling hieroglyphs and encrypted swearwords. You started at the back of your jotter and worked in reverse. You stopped when you got to the end of your homework.

There was a war going on between them; equations and long division tried to restrain insurgent marginals, and the other way about too. But the marginals would lose, they always did, and Denise's Indian ink and brush were in the other room. Her room. She wanted them but she wouldn't go in there, not now it was under occupation.

They were ignoring each other again. There was no point in bothering to leave the room once they were allowed the three-bar electric fire on. They rubbed the soles of their woolly socks against the rungs, watching the spark of fluff and dust as it dropped into the orange of the element. Denise could keep this up until she felt the burning of her feet. The window sucked inwards in its frame and the rain lashed it. Denise sat with her homework on her lap, opened at the day's page, smothering under those inky monsters: long division and fractions. She could hear the telly on downstairs, but that room was no use any more either. All the rooms except this one and the lavvy were no use any more. Not even the hallway or the landing. Her sister didn't understand. If they had a fight she still said, 'It's my room. I can do what I like in my room.'

She had to learn. It was better for her if she learnt now.

Denise in there with Alison was no use though. School was getting worse. Her eyes filmed over, spreading space into a blur every time; it was an agony to keep them open. An agony. Her dad couldn't understand. What was the matter with her? She wasn't thick was she? He knew she wasn't thick.

Her lip was split and swollen up, purple like a bit of overripe fruit – her sister's tooth was cracked. Denise lifted – was *flung* out onto the landing, just with the backswipe of the hand. It was only a tap, really. Then she was in a heap, not knowing which way round she was, everything thundering, her dad's shovel hand hovering before her.

'What have I told ye?'

There *was* something. What had it been?

'Leave your sister alone!'

They moved Denise down the stairs, into the living room. She could sleep on the couch in a sleeping bag. She was right under her old room. It creaked at night, as if the bones of the house were stiff, needing to settle themselves for the evening. Cracking and splitting. It let her think the house still liked her, that it was maybe still her friend. This was just a matter to be waited out.

Now, there was a rasping noise at night like when air loosened from a stabbed spacehopper. Except now the blade sawed down through the ceiling. A throaty sound.

Denise was going into the lavatory when her granny stood there in front of her, in nightie and slippers, all shrunken. Denise had to step aside for her quickly, looking away, a feeling boiling inside her and the hairs up on the back of her neck. It was like her face had caved in, collapsed on itself during the night. Denise had never seen her look so old. The eyes didn't even see her. Granny *La*mont/La*mont* stepped forward into the light of the bathroom, the door clamping behind. Denise made her way downstairs, the blood in her head gagging the sound of Granny's thin trickle. She tried not to picture it in her head, but *it* insisted, kept appearing there, even while you were back and lying in bed. The floorboards resettled themselves and the ancient bed mattress wheezed. Denise was nearly away to sleep, just nodding off, when a clogged cracking brought her back again. Her granny coughing. If it hadn't been for that, it might not have seemed real.

Granny arrived on the doorstep on the Sunday afternoon. She was wearing her see-through plastic headscarf knotted under the chin and carrying her customary polyethylene bag. She had slippers on inside her brown zip-up boots. The old walking stick with the wood darkened at the handle where she'd been holding it. 'Your poor auld granny walked the whole way,' she said to Denise and Alison. It was five miles from where her new place was. She had been walking half the day.

Denise could hear the sticky rattle of her breath at the end of her sentences, the strain in her voice. There was a smell of something off her. Decay.

She'd come for her tea, she said. It was a Sunday. Brought these for the weans . . . Granny *La*mont/La*mont* took a crumpled poke out of her pocket and clapped it into Denise's mum's hand, unbuttoning her coat and hanging her walking stick over the bannister.

'Have you a drink of water for your poor old granny, then?' she said. Denise's mum handed her the bag.

Boiled sweeties

black-strippet balls

cinnamon balls and humbugs.

They had all clotted together in the bag, so that when you went to get one they were warmed and glued and you had to pull it apart from another and then spend ages picking the paper off of it. It was best just to eat the paper as well.

'Not until after they've had their tea, right?'

There was soup. Her mum made soup all year round, still hoping Denise would take some one day. Denise didn't like the texture of soup, 'cause of the floaty bits in it. In the summer her mum might give them salad of tomatoes and lettuce, after the soup and before the meat. Denise didn't like the texture of tomatoes and lettuce. There was lentil soup from ham ribs or a hough and broth from a bit of flank mutton or boiling beef. *This* was chicken soup with rice in it. Steak pie, potatoes, Brussels sprouts. Custard and rhubarb. Denise didn't like any of it. The custard had lumps and the rhubarb was too sweet. Too sour too. She sat mute, in front of the telly till everyone came in and stopped her watching it.

Denise and Alison sat on the floor 'cause of there not being enough seats for everyone. Denise hated sitting in chairs anyway, but Alison liked it 'cause it felt grown-up. The news was put on, covering the sound of Granny's lungs. They all sat quiet, watching. Something was keeping talk out the room.

Granny farted. She did it twice and both times she never said anything. She acted like it hadn't happened. 'Cause she couldn't hear it, it was like she reckoned nobody else could hear it either. Their dad acted like it was normal. If Denise had farted he would have said something. He would have said, 'Lavatory is the place for that sort of thing.' Her mum did it sometimes as well; lying in the floor, head on a cushion by the fire, she would let off and act like nothing had happened.

The room was silent apart from these submerged noises that sounded like they had come from underwater. Trapped farts. From when you didn't lift your bum up to let them get out.

'*Woof-woof!*' Denise's dad said. They all started laughing, everyone except Granny *La*mont/La*mont*, who had to keep kidding on she couldn't hear.

Her dad shifted in his seat and rustled the paper a bit. He got up and leaned over to turn the telly up. There was a war on somewhere, Africa maybe, and a big cloud of fart was hanging in the air above the room. But nobody said anything about it.

Denise was to take her granny up the stairs and show her where she would be sleeping. She was to get fresh linen and pillow slips out the hall cupboard; she was to dress the bed in them. She was to bring all the dirty sheets down the stairs and leave them in the laundry pile. Show her granny where she could hang her things up and not take all day about it, her mum said, 'cause Granny was tired, Denise could see that she was tired, could she not? Her mum took Denise to one side in the kitchen, yanked her by the shoulder and told her to get that look off her face. Her granny was old and not well. Surely Denise didn't mind giving a sick old lady her room for a while? She needed that bed more than Denise did.

'And I expect you to behave yourself around her, d'you hear? None of this' – she stuck her bottom lip out in imitation – 'None of that. She's put up with you and your sister often enough. All right?'

Denise nodded yes.

'Good. Now get off up there and make sure she's everything she needs. Off you go now.'

There was this feeling that hung in each room like bad air. Denise might have to suddenly close the door again behind her and give up something, a room, a space, not wanting to share it with anyone, whatever it was. It was no use if it was shared. It had to be her space and that was all. Sometimes she could feel it when a presence came into the room behind her. If she was watching the cartoons before the news, she could feel something come in. It would sit down in the armchair, while she stared, crosslegged in front of the screen. Denise wanted to turn round suddenly and have the presence absent. But no. She was always there.

This time, she thrust a crumpled note into Denise's hand.

'Not a word to your mother. Agreed?'

It was a fifty-pound note.

'Not a word now, all right?'

Denise knew what it was for from her quick look away and back to her paper.

It was for the room. It was for lodgings.

Then, the old lady took an HB pencil and began scratching herself across the top of her head, through her thinning hair, then behind her ears and down the back of her neck. Next, she directed it to her false teeth, working the point in between the gap, into the corners. She sat with the pencil sticking out, wedged in tight between the two front ones.

Denise stood up. She went up the stairs to the small room and sat down on the edge of the bed. Alison was playing again: lines and crosses and dice.

Her sister looked up. 'See what Granny gave me,' she said, holding out her hand. The note lay flat and smooth, like it had been ironed that way. It was another impossible sum. You had to say the words out loud and then look at the paper and even then it was impossible that those two things could add up to this other thing. Of course, you couldn't keep such a lot of money. But you could pretend for a bit.

Alison was going to get sweets with it. Lots of them.

Denise went up to her mum in the kitchen. She was washing dishes with the radio on. Denise stood there waiting. Her mum was humming a tune.

'Mum?' she asked.

Silence.

'Mum?' she said again.

'What is it? I'm busy.'

'Look what Granny gave me.'

'Oh, well, you can get yourself some sweeties.'

'But—'

'Did you say thank you to your granny? Mind and share it with your sister.'

'She got money too,' Denise said. She held out her fist, the note inside crumpled into a ball. Her mum let her put it in her palm; it began slowly unfolding, opening up like an origami flower. She looked at it.

'Right,' she said. 'Just you wait till your daddy comes in. Just you wait!'

'But Granny gave it to me!'

'Fifty pounds? Come off it . . .'

'She did! She gave us both fifty pounds each!'

'Each? What have you been putting your sister up to, eh? Fifty pounds each!' Denise's mum slapped the straightened-out note onto the worktop. Then she went over to her.

'Off your granny, eh?' She shook her shoulder. 'And what was that in aid of?'

She went through into the living room and nudged her mother awake. She had been sitting half-asleep in the arm-chair by the fire and when she opened them, her eyes went around not knowing anything, lost, and she said: '*I've still got all my own hair, ye know!*'

Denise's mum said something low and quiet and Granny began to stand up, pushing slowly up from the chair until upright, even though upright was slightly crouched. There was a click from both knees.

'Let them keep it, Anna, it's for them.'

But Denise's mum pushed the crumpled ball into her hand. 'It's not on,' she said. She could stay as long as she liked, she was welcome, more than welcome, she knew that. This was not on, though. Bribing the weans . . .

Then she went out the room, closing the door behind very quietly.

Granny *La*mont/*Lamont* sat back down and looked at the TV. She scratched her scalp. She looked bewildered. Denise looked at her and bit her lip. She could feel her ears burning.

She had taken her rain cap and coat and gone out the door. There was a taxi waiting, a minicab, the engine running, and Denise was back in the room. *Her* room. The smell of oldness and decay would go in a while. The sense of it not being hers would dissolve. She sat on the edge of the bed, then went over to the windows and opened them full. She went into the bathroom and sat down on the seat. There was no one to say cheerio downstairs. They were all out. Even her mum. Alison was out playing somewhere. There was no one to say: 'Come back next week.' There was just Denise, then the sound of the motor on the tarmac outside.

She sat and stared at the glass sitting on the unit beside the bath and it snarled back. The washed-out pink of gums; grinning, hard, sharp incisors in the corners, the flats of the front two like spade heads. A silvery line of tiny bubbles ticked up from the glass bottom, regular as the minute hand on a watch.

Denise went down and opened the front door before her granny got a chance to ring the bell again. Her face was sucked in, jutting, like an accusation.

'Fogot um!' she was saying. The taxi driver was looking over at them, the engine running.

'Fogot um! Upshtairsh. Ma teef. Falshersh!'

Denise held the glass out and away from herself, a bit of water slipping over between her thumb and the side. Granny took it and fished out the pink insides. They slipped into place with a click, and her face was human again. She handed the glass back to Denise, tapping at the ground with her stick. Her head had a kind of wobble. Her jaw too. Denise had never seen her do that before, but she knew that her granny would have that wobble from now on. The wind had changed and it had stuck.

Granny looked up at the sky and then back down again. She stared at Denise, her forehead all shiny and reddened.

'I had a brother fought at Gallipoli, ye know,' she said. She mopped her brow and swatted at the air with the hankie. 'Never heard of it, have ye?' she said.

'It's in Turkey,' Denise said. 'There was a battle there.'

'In Turkey. Aye. In it, right enough. Beautiful, so he told me. On the seaside. He learned to swim there, George did. Mastered it, ye might say.'

'Did he not go swimming at school?' Denise asked.

'At school? Ho. You swim yourself, don't ye?'

Denise nodded.

'At the school, is it?'

Denise looked at the ground.

Her granny swatted the air in front of her again.

'That's not swimming, though. Is it? Is that swimming?' She stared at Denise. 'Is that swimming?' she said again. 'Well?'

'No,' Denise said.

'No what?'

'No it isn't . . . swimming?'

Her granny took the glass back out of Denise's hand and looked at her. 'No,' she said, 'not indeed. Not by a long chalk.'

She tilted the glass and drained the water in one gulp, put it back in Denise's hand and clasped her own tight over it, staring. Then she took a fiver out of her purse and handed it to her.

'Mind and not mention it to your mother,' she said. 'Or

it'll likely be the last ye see of me round here. You hear me? The last!' She turned and walked stiffly down the front path.

It must have been a couple of days or so before anybody noticed Granny *La*mont/La*mont* was dead. She'd moved into the new flat – it couldn't really be called a tenement – only two days before. Everything would still be sat in cardboard boxes around her; a newspaper she must have been reading flapped against her chest; half-drunk mug of tea tilted slightly between the thumb and forefinger of her left hand. Her eyes were open staring at some hairline crack in the ceiling plaster. Her mouth, too, had been open. The gas fire blazed away on a full heat, ignorant of the death of the host. The first thing Denise's dad had noticed when he opened the door with the spare key was the fug of hot air that came to meet him in the hallway, though he'd made nothing of it; it was just uncomfortable. It was only once inside he noticed the pile of leaflets and fliers that had collected on the carpet by the door.

'Elsa?' he says, quietly, not wanting to give her a fright if she was just dozing.

The hall is in semi-light, the living room door closed. 'Elsa?' he says again, slightly louder this time. He puts down his carrier bag with the shopping his mother-in-law had asked him to bring her: bleach, Jif, Brillo pads, a half-bottle of whisky – 'for cooking with' she'd told him. He smiles to himself thinking about it. She's probably pretty well-done at the moment, in this heat. He closes the front door behind him and bends to pick up the leaflets and fliers, before going into the front room. He chaps lightly on the door before pushing it open, caution thrown to the wind. She's expecting him, after all.

And there she is, fast asleep on her armchair, the one she's had since before he and Denise's mum got married. He walks slowly about the room, taking off his jacket and slinging it over the back of the couch before sitting down. The heat is unbearable. 'Jesus Christ,' he says under his breath, before remembering she can't hear a word anybody says – unless she's a mind to. Maybe he ought to give her a tap on the shoulder or something. Wake her from her beauty sleep. He can't be sittin' here all day!

Denise's dad crosses and uncrosses his legs, before picking up a week-old copy of the *Sunday Post* from the couch beside him. He flicks through the pages, turns to The Broons and Oor Wullie, then puts it back down beside him again. He coughs: 'Ahem!'

But she can't hear him. Next he gives the old biddy a wee nudge, and the newspaper on her chest slides to the ground. He better get that teacup out of her hand. She'll likely spill the bastarding thing. He crouches over her hand, facing away from her, and eases the cup from her fingers and puts it back down on the occasional table at her elbow, next to the dish with the cherry Bakewell slice on it. There's hardly a bite taken out it, so he picks it up and crams it into his mouth, wiping the crumbs off his moustache with the sleeve of his shirt. It tastes a bit stale, if anything.

He walks through the living room and into the kitchen, in a recess at the back, where he runs a glass under the tap and takes a drink of water. The old biddy is obviously totally out for the count, so he goes back through and picks up the carrier bag and brings it into the kitchen, begins putting the shopping into the cupboards – the cleaning stuff under the sink, the foodstuffs in the one above and left. And the whisky? He tests the weight of the bottle in his hand, bouncing it off his palm. Then, he untwists the cap and takes a quick gulp, replaces it and sticks the bottle in the cupboard next to the rest of the grub.

Denise Forrester's dad wanders back through into the living room and turns the fire down and opens one of the windows above the main window. Then he goes over to the sideboard and writes a message on the notepad there before placing it on the table at his mother-in-law's elbow, next to the mug of cold tea. Then, he walks out the front door, closes it securely behind him, gets into his car and drives home. He is wondering what there is for dinner when he gets in.

Nothing stirs in the living room of the house he has just left, nothing except a bluebottle which buzzes in erratic circles around the room, before alighting on the face of Granny *La*mont/La*mont*. It wanders over her cheek, before disappearing momentarily into her open mouth.

The note on the pad reads:

MESSAGES IN THE KITCHEN. NO CHANGE. BYE FOR NOW.
PS: CAN YOU TAKE GIRLS SATURDAY?

and is unsigned.

It will be another day before anybody discovers the body. The smell will alert the folk living next door.

Denise watched the food come and go, the dishes proffered up to her as if to a sullen deity in need of appeasement, and she refused them. She turned the other cheek, the skin drawn in close to the bones, and stared sideways out of windows, through doors left ajar, at spaces with nothing on the other side of them. Everything was just this moment; the here and now, and the thoughts in her head slowed to make sense of the here and now; the *her* and the here and the now. Her mum would come chapping quietly on her door, but she didn't answer. It made no difference what she said, whatever was outside would come in anyway, whether it was invited or not. There was no justice in it; it was just the law of things. The cheek of it, her granny might have said.

'Denise? D'you not want some bread and Nutella?' her mum asked, looking round the door. Denise sat on the carpet, doing nothing. She couldn't get interested in anything. She looked up at her mum, saw the worry on her face, the whiteness of the hair she kept wiping out of her eyes with her free hand. In the other, she held a plastic tray with two slices of toast on it, spread with Nutella, and a glass of juice. Her mum had never bothered to bring her food before. Not ever. It was weird. Ever since Denise could remember, her mum, her dad – even her granny – had refused to give her food she wanted. It was left up to her to feed herself, which she'd done, never taking any notice of mealtimes or anything like that. They were just times of the day: there didn't seem to be any reason for eating then. Denise ate when she was hungry.

She wasn't hungry at the moment. She was tired. Dead beat. There was nothing in her belly, but there was no empty feeling there, no absence to send her into the kitchen. Nothing.

Instead she would go to sleep at teatime and get up in the middle of the night, somehow the darkness horrible to her in a way that hinted at something primeval, something barely recalled. She would go downstairs and eat a slice of toast or drink some juice when no one was about, no one that could pester her. But it would sit uncomfortably inside her, the taste of it would contain no pleasure, and she would push the plate aside and switch the telly on and stare at it until someone came downstairs and told her to put it off and go back to bed.

'D'ye know what time it is, Denise?' whoever it was would say.

She didn't care what time it was. It wasn't important. Only appetites had to be paid attention to, and she didn't seem to have many of them. She still had to go to the toilet and pee or shit – though less and less – and she still needed to sleep – more and more – but timetables were bottom of her list of things that needed paying attention to, and nobody had ever had any success at making Denise do anything she didn't want.

After a while, rubbing their eyes and seeing it was no use, whoever it was, mother or father, would sigh and go back upstairs and leave her alone. Denise would wait a few minutes, then turn the telly back on with the sound down low and stare at it until it got light, flicking absently between the channels until she could hear the first of the birds outside. Then, picking up the last of her slice of toast, she would retreat back through to her room and wait until she could hear movements in the others, signs of life, stirrings in the hallways and the clearing of throats; first a male one in the bathroom, a snort and then a sound like retching followed by running tapwater; grunting and heaving as her dad forced his body to respond. Then, a more discreet one muffled by a hankie in the bedroom, a feminine slurp of catarrh loosening in the lungs, shaking itself awake and into the first light of day. Noises. Portents. It seemed these noises were what living was all about. Unspeakable, immutable.

She wondered what noises she was made of. Maybe they were as disgusting to other people as the sounds of other people to her. Noises that were part of the workings, the machinery; systems and constellations of organs inside the body, the slow glug of the blood around the veins, the ooze of matter converting into flesh that would eventually convert back into matter. It went round in circles, the secret life of matter that had converted into other matter: that was all there was to it. If Granda still existed – if *Granny* still existed – it was only as a spatter of particles that had joined up with other particles in new arrangements or none.

There was no one behind the skirting-board. There was no code that contained any answers; only ceaseless workings. Systems, methods, wrong answers.

Denise wondered if she had been a wrong answer. Certainly her mum had said she had been a mistake.

An accident.

Denise knew that if she didn't eat, then she would be eaten. The law of the body. Already she was being eaten. She didn't care.

The food was placed in front of her, then taken away, untouched. Denise decided to put her affairs in order.

Her mum sat with her in the back of the ambulance after she went blind.

Denise had minded feeling weak, but there was nothing weird about that: she always felt weak. She got up out of her chair in front of the telly, and at first it was as if she'd stood up too quickly, the room swimming, darkening. Denise held her hands up and looked at them, a feeling like blood slowing inside her limbs, the awareness of the blood moving inside the veins, the feeling of the veins inside the muscle, the feeling of muscle contracting. She couldn't feel her fingers. Then there was no sensation in her hands and forearms; they seemed to be turning inwards, freezing, her vision clotting, and then the terror of her breath refusing to come, the air refusing to enter her lungs.

'*Mum* . . .' she tried to say. But she was alone. She tried to lean back on the arm of the chair. She could see nothing. Her legs would not obey her; she staggered back. There was a sunburst of blotches, orange and green in front of her. Her head felt like metal inside. She tried to speak. It wouldn't come; words never came easy. No sensation. Then, a sharpness on the back of her skull.

In bed in the hospital, Denise tried to remember what else had been there. She wished it had been a glorious white light. She wished she had floated above her body. But there was nothing. Only the orange and green bursts and the blackness. Now there was the whiteness of the plastic curtain around her bed, the whiteness of the nightdress they had put her in, the whiteness of the bed linen. There was a white cast on her other arm, from wrist to elbow.

Her mum and dad sat at her bedside. They looked grey, ill. Her mum's hair tied back, her dad sitting straight up. Behind them, next to the window, someone else was staring over at them. A man with a coat over his arm, and a bunnet on his head. He fingered the palm of his left hand, then his right. The brightness of the window made it difficult to see his face. But you could tell from the bunnet that he must be older. Only old men wore bunnets.

'Denise,' her mum said quietly. 'That was a terrible fright you gave us . . .' They'd found her lying on the living-room floor, curled up, knees drawn up to her chest and her hands turned inwards. They'd had no idea what was wrong, but she'd not wake up.

Denise was too weak to speak. There was a tube going into her at the wrist, held in place by a piece of clear tape. At the side of the bed was a kind of stand, with a bag of clear fluid hanging from it, into which the tube ran.

Her mum followed her stare and then said: 'That's to make you feel better . . . it'll make you well again. So's you have the strength to eat.' Her mum looked down into her lap after she said that. It was like she'd said something rude. The man by the window fingered the palms of his hands, said nothing.

'Sorry,' Denise's mum said, still not looking. 'I know you don't want to eat just now.'

Food. Eating. If Denise had eaten anything then, it would likely have killed her. But there was something else in her mum's voice as well, something different. It was like an admission of something. It was like she was saying sorry for something that Denise had needed to hear for a long time. It frightened her.

Her dad was breathing heavily through his nose; he looked sorry for something too. Even his breathing was guilty.

'You better start taking care of yourself, young lady,' he said, then shut up again when Denise's mum slapped his shoulder.

'Well she will,' he said, his voice not sorry but indignant. 'Lucky it was only her arm she broke this time, and not her neck.'

Denise's mum skelped him one again, and he shut up.

Denise wished they would both go away and leave her alone now. Let her sleep. She was tired out.

'Are you all right just now?' her mum asked. 'We've brought you some things to nibble if you feel like it – on the table. Just chocolate and stuff. An apple. Just if you feel like it . . .'

Denise nodded, then closed her eyes. She felt a hand stroke her cheek.

'Who's that?' she heard herself say.

'Who, love?' Her mum's voice.

'Over by the window . . . the old man.'

'There's nobody by the window, Denise. You're dreaming. Sleep now. Get rested.'

As a baby, Denise never *ma-ma'd* or *da-da'd*. Nothing like that. Not for her. The first thing she said, a full eighteen months after she fell out of her mother, was *mine*. The thing of it was, though, her mum had known that was how it would be, even as she swelled up like a balloon. This child was going to rule her life from now on, was going to be at the centre of her universe, and it was a burden. Not just to carry Denise about inside her belly. That was bad enough, what with the lack of sleep and the endless visits to the lavatory, seven, eight, nine times a night, what with not being able to bend over and get her shoes off and getting sick in the first mornings. Not just all that. There was a feeling Denise's mum used to get. It was the feeling like this infant didn't really need her at all. Like she was just a carrier-bag, the incubator.

And her mum couldn't give her anything more than she was already giving her: food, nine months of her body, a lifetime of worry . . . there wasn't *room* there for any more than that. There was barely room in the bed for her and Denise's dad either, what with Denise crowding them both out, stealing their nights off them, squeezing in between them like an over-full hot-water bottle. A nightmare. For nine months all that was said in the parental bed was: 'Can you not shift over a bit?'

Denise's mum had the days till conception marked out: she counted them off, the days till she was going to be free.

Nine months. Nine full months of penury. It was a long time, no doubt about it.

*

Denise's granny said that it was the most natural thing in the world; a truly beautiful and miraculous thing. It didn't seem so beautiful to Denise's mum. It was a miracle that it was possible – that went without saying – she was aware that her body was undergoing a miraculous transformation, that a miraculous thing had taken root inside her belly. But they could grow the same miracle in test-tubes these days, could they not? Probably it could be done just as well in a milk-bottle or a jam-jar. There was no way anyone could convince Denise's mum that all *this* would fit easily into a test-tube. It was plainly out of the equation. There wasn't a chance in hell.

And the birth itself was inconceivable. You had to shove it right to the back of your mind, or let it drive you round the bend.

'What about a section?' she used to ask Denise's dad. 'Maybe it would be best to just have a section?'

'Fat chance,' he said. She was perfectly healthy and robust. What did she want to go and cut herself open for? Childbirth was the most natural and beautiful and miraculous thing in all the world, was it not? For thousands of years, women had been shiteing out weans behind bushes, in the dirt and darkness, out of sight of menfolk. Frankly, Denise's dad reckoned it was a lot of fuss about nothing. It was only an inherent genetic inability that prevented him doing it himself.

Denise's mum moaned aloud, feeling a bit of leakage in the bladder area. It was a conspiracy. Her mother, her husband, her GP, the neighbours, all of them. Everyone. They were all conspiring. She couldn't believe she had fallen for it. Hook, line, and sinker. Sister Regina's curse had her floored for the best part of every month; there was no respite from it. As soon as her pains ended, the periods began again, without relief, on and on, so that it seemed a blessing when she'd tested positive, a blue streak of joy held in the palm of her hand.

A miracle.

But the feeling didn't last long; the pains were replaced

with morning sickness, her outfits stopped fitting and she looked at herself in the mirror, her body like a laundry bag full of damp clothes.

The thing growing inside her was at it as well. It kicked and twisted, shifted about and generally made a nuisance of itself, exactly the way Denise would behave when she finally did emerge, a screaming, bloody, mucus-covered scab of pink-pulp the size of a couple of bags of sugar, two months premature.

And the miracle is that when she holds this grotesque bag of skin against herself, before the midwife takes Denise away and puts her in the incubator, Anna Forrester *believes*. She believes it *is* a miracle, a beautiful, extraordinary miraculous miracle.

But this feeling passes, as it must, and other feelings replace it, as they will.

The world was suddenly still. Everyone in the ward froze. Denise's dad stood – still in his blue uniform and cap – one palm shaking the hand of the doctor, over the drained body of Denise's mum, a pair of large shears for cutting the umbilical poised in his other hand.

'Say cheese,' the nurse said, poised with camera, before the room crackled blinding white. Denise's mum saw black shapes swim in front of her eyes. Dirty big black shapes clotting before her, against walls and ceiling, blotting out the daylight. She thought, the words seeping like exhausted neon in the black, half-a-second before losing consciousness:

NEVER . . .

then, a quarter-second before:

AGAIN . . .

Later, she and Denise's dad stare at the foreign body in the incubator. It looks like neither of them, there is nothing recognisable about it at all. It's like a sumo wrestler in miniature. Denise's mum searches hard but can't find any connection with it. It has nothing to do with her. It doesn't even have a name they can agree on. They just call it the 'wean', or 'the wee yin' or something like that. It lies there, totally still, apart from the flutter of its tiny chest, plastic tubes going into it, wrapped in white cotton nappies.

Denise's mum turns away from the incubator and shuffles back through to the ward she's bedded in. Denise's dad stands there a minute longer looking in at her, chapping on the sides of the perspex box she'll be living in for the next wee while. Denise is ignoring him, a policy she will carry on for most of her adult life. Then he puts his cap back on his head and follows her mum through to the other ward.

Denise's mum climbs back into her bed and lies, trying not to think. There had been no beds in the maternity ward, everything was taken. After a bit, they'd stuck her up here in the cancer ward, figuring she'd be out in a day or so. She was staring across at the decaying body in the bed opposite, some poor creature so crumbled and withered that it was only 'cause they were sharing a ward that you could tell she must have been a woman once. Now, a sexless husk was all that remained. Beneath the bedcover was some sort of frame, like a big box. Nobody had yet come to visit her, whoever she was, whoever she had been. Denise's mum stared back up at the cracks in the ceiling.

This wasn't the way she'd expected to feel. Not at all. She couldn't even feel relieved about not having to carry around this ton weight with her everywhere. If anything, she felt the opposite. It was a sort of grief. For the emptiness she was feeling inside her. It was a sort of absence. She kept on staring at the wall, feeling like she was committing some terrible crime. Not wanting her own child. Not caring anything about it. What it was called. Whether it was a boy or a girl.

She was trying not to think about how she would feel if it died.

And in a way that was what she wanted, because then she knew she would feel grief for it. And she would be cured. She wouldn't be a bad person after all, 'cause she would feel a terrible grief that she'd never ever be able to recover from – and it would prove she had cared about her baby after all. This was what she was trying not to think about.

But these feelings pass too, as they must, and other feelings replace them, as they will.

When Denise is finally allowed out of her perspex box, when it is finally decided that she will live after all, she doesn't complain about it. She clings to her mother's breast, eyes prematurely staring, in a way she will not do for the rest of her life. For the rest of her life, Denise will need nobody. That's the way it will be. Denise's mum wants to make her daughter need her, wants to hear her ask something of her, wants to hear her say Yes to her. But it'll never happen. It's as if Denise, two months early into the world, wrinkled like an old lady and raw like a skinned rabbit, has decided that if nobody needs her, then she'll need nobody either.

She'll look up at these people around her, these bickering, lumbering giants, and feel only a vague kind of disgust. She never knows why. It's just a feeling that's always there. She doesn't seem to want any part of them, these creatures. She has the feeling that these people, whoever they are, have nothing to do with her. The older she gets, the more she has the feeling that these people are imposters, chimeras. Somehow, she must have got taken away from the hospital by the wrong family. Her real mum and dad are still out there, somewhere.

It was only half-true, Granny *La*mont/La*mont* reckoned.

She brought Denise in close to her chest, hugging her so she could hardly breathe. Her daddy was no use. Granny *La*mont/La*mont* had never liked him. But Denise's mum had gone behind her back, got herself knocked up by some foreign man who'd gone to sea the next day. It was only when she knew he would never come back that she'd went and married that . . . that . . . *eejit*!

Who was Denise's real daddy?

'Your real daddy . . . ? Your real daddy was a sailor. He came to Scotland on a great big merchant ship – a sailboat, such as they used to make in they days . . .'

Denise's mouth opened; it was more in hunger than in awe. She felt the rumble in her belly and knew, deep down, she'd been weaned too soon, that everything her granny told her was true. Her daddy was a sailor man, like Popeye, a face like a burst orange and muscles like steel cables charged with lightning. Her granny talked on and on about the sea, foreign parts her real dad had visited, told her how he'd carried nothing more than a navy blue duffel-bag over one shoulder. His whistle had carried up dark streets and over slate rooftops, the thin soot-blackened tenements arching their backs toward the sound of his two lips pressed together, the tune an old sea-shanty from the whalers who still fished the South Seas, who froze to the decks in ice-storms off the Newfoundland coast, who grew blond beards that got bleached by the bitter winter suns and stiff with flying fish and herring that got tousled in there, their arms blue with tattoos, coiled serpents and anchors aweigh, skin like old leather . . .

'*Farewell and adieu to you, fair Spanish ladies* . . .'

Her daddy could charm the cats from the rooftops, have them follow him down the road, trailing after the sound of his two rosy lips pressed together. And where the cats led, the girls of the town would follow, away on up after his rolling gait, jackletless in midwinter, shirtsleeves rolled up to the oxters, the bunnet on his napper set at a jaunty angle.

Where was he going, they all wanted to know. He'd been the talk of the town, not a door he passed would stay shut but the women would be out and following the trail he made through these dark streets, the gaslamps running their length like flickering tinsel. Denise's daddy kept strolling on and on, ignoring the laments of the cats and the wails of broken-hearted girls. He knew exactly where he was headed.

Where? Where had he been headed? Denise wanted to know.

To his one true love, of course. He'd no time for those other women who could be charmed by the sound of his siren-whistle. Not at all. He'd been at sea for two years without setting foot on dry land . . . He'd been all around the globe, and not set eyes on your mother in all that time. And now he was heading home to her, the sweetheart he'd left behind.

Denise felt her heart in her throat, a word that fizzed like dissolving bubbles: *sweetheart.*

'That was your mother, Denise,' her granny said. 'He'd come all the way back to her. He lifted his fist to the door of her house. Chapped a first time, and from where your mammy sat by the coal fire in her long silk nightdress and shawl, comb and glass in her hand, the smell of brine and seaweed wrapped around her and carried her to the door . . . She'd waited a long time for this night, waited every night for the sound of whistling to carry up the road toward her, waited for his three-times knock on the door. Now he was here. What she'd wished for all those nights ago when he'd kissed her and told her he'd be back to take care of her and the babe she'd be carrying in her arms, the poor wee babe that'd never set eyes on its daddy.'

Denise held her breath.

'Your mother went to the door as if in a trance. She stood by it as she'd stood many nights in the past, hardly daring to believe it was true, that he was here at last. She heard him chap a second time, and had to lean a bit against the wall, her heart was beating that fast. She yanked at the chain on the door, and there came a third chap . . .'

'What happened?' Denise was asking. She smelt sea-air in her nostrils, saw a man wait, fist raised, navy blue duffel-bag over one shoulder, shirtsleeves rolled up and a tattoo of an anchor on either arm. A clay pipe jutted from his mouth . . .

'Well,' Granny said, 'your mother flung aside the door, oblivious to the cold and the frost, her body wrapped in tentacles of briny air and the smell of seaweed . . . She flung the door open and . . .' Granny's voice trailed away.

'What?'

'There was nobody there at all. There was no one stood on the step with a duffel-bag over their shoulder. There was only the night and the cold and the frost. There was only the sound of a tune being whistled, fading softly back over the roof-tops . . .'

'*Farewell and adieu to you, ladies of Spain . . .*'

'And the sound of a sailor's boots tack-tacking away off down the streets towards the shipyards – never to be seen again . . .'

Through a black haar, Denise saw the dark outline of a figure recede, a trail of seawater following him down the cobbled lanes, his clothes sodden and strung with fronds of kelp.

'Why did he not come back?' she asked. Her eyes were wet. She felt tears there, but they didn't roll down her cheeks like normal. They were frozen tears.

'He couldn't, Denise,' Granny said, relighting her own pipe. 'He had drowned away across on the other side of the world, his ship had foundered in the South China Sea, gone down with all hands lost, save one, the ship's cook, who was found floating in a dinghy with a slow puncture sixty miles from shore, half-mad with thirst and sunstroke . . . It was in the paper three weeks later: *EULALIA* COOK SAFE AFTER SHIP LOST IN SOUTH CHINA SEA.

'A tragedy, it was. A terrible tragedy. What your mother had seen was a portent. It was your real daddy saying his last goodbye to her, his last farewell.'

Later, Denise would see the injustice of it. If her real dad could come and say cheerio to her mum, how could he not know the ship was going to sink in the first place? Why did he have to let himself go down with the ship? How could he not have warned the others? A big question mark seemed to hang over the whole story.

Denise never acknowledged that the man her mum was married to was her father after that. She called him that – but that was only a word. It meant nothing to her. Some words were easy come by:

DAD = the tall skinny man with the blue uniform, the brown moustache and the truncheon that rested by the wall in the room he slept in beside Denise's mum. The tall man that lived in the same house as the rest of them, ate at the same dinner table, watched the same telly. But he had slipped into the empty space her real dad had left. Surely her mum could see that as well?

Neither of them deserved Denise. Her granny would take her away, she said, she would take her away and they could live together in her flat. When it was the right time she would come for Alison as well . . .

'No!' Denise said. She didn't want to share her granny with anyone, especially not her sister. *Mine*, she would say, so that everyone understood.

Her mum was useless, her granny said, not sending her to chapel, not having her baptised. If Denise was to suddenly up and die, she would never get into heaven – she'd be a soul stuck in limbo. A poor lamb, lost from the rest of His flock. If Denise could only stay with her, then everything would sort itself out in the end. They would all get into heaven if they could all stay with Granny *La*mont/La*mont*.

Denise remembered something from when she had been very small, something she could only conjure into existence by sheer force of will, so dim was the picture inside her skull. She had been lying inside the bars of something like a prison. Her cot. She could make it shoogle if she moved about, but she couldn't stand up. The room was dark, except for a vertical light, like a wedge against the wall. The door. Something dark had filled it, something had looked in on her, stood there, a black shape against the light. She began to cry. The shape came toward her and she cried louder. The shape shook the cot, so that it moved about underneath her, she was rolling from side to side.

'Shhsh . . .' a voice said. A hiss like steam escaping. 'Shhsh . . .'

The tongue froze in her head, she stopped screaming, the terror backed off. The figure got up and went out again. Then, the door was completely shut and the terror was locked in the room with her, the shape of it somewhere outside the bars of her cage, pacing around. In the darkness, Denise could see nothing. Nobody. Absolutely nobody at all.

Denise's mum went back to the cushion by the fire, the curtains drawn and the telly flickering black-and-white matinees from years before across her face; Ginger Rogers and Fred Astaire . . . the clack-clack of their heels as deafening as the music that made them move surefooted as they flew across the screen, their world a crystalline and shimmering shield protecting them from the banality and dullness on the other side of the screen. Denise's mum lay motionless, her face mottled like raw mince from lying too close to the fire. Then, Denise was aware of another presence.

In the corner of her room, something squawked and bleated. There was a new smell as well. Alison.

Alison reached for a doll. Denise grabbed it away.

'*Mine!*' she said.

Alison burst into tears. Denise stared at them, these strange shiny trails that crawled across her face like glitter. She dabbed her finger against them. They were wet.

Denise couldn't remember having ever done the same thing. She held her breath and waited, but the tears wouldn't come. It was like words. Words and tears: neither of them would come. Her mum didn't seem to notice she had come in. She was sitting in a chair, light from the screen of the telly flickering across her face, the rest of the room dim and shadowy. Black and white. The colour of the past. Denise stared at her mother's face, looking for signs of herself. Sometimes, just for a second, you could see it in the eyes, but not always. Sometimes it was in the set of her mouth, or the frown on her brow. Sometimes it was in the tilt of her head or the way she clasped her hands. There was no one special place.

Denise's mum stared at the screen. People were shooting at each other. There was screaming and noise. Denise's mum was doing something with her blouse: her hand had sort of disappeared inside the sleeve, was crawling back up inside it. Denise felt uncomfortable. She tried to make herself shrink. She wished she could get up and go, but she couldn't – she was stuck there, frozen. The hand wriggled about inside the blouse and
slowly
it climbed
out
the sleeve
again
something clasped
in the palm –

her bra.

Her mum let the thing fall on to the floor and pushed it to the side of the chair with her foot. She never took her face from the screen.

Denise decided it was maybe an idea to go and play with Alison.

When she got to the room, Denise couldn't get the door opened. Alison had rolled across the floor in front of the door again, playing the draught-excluder and barring entry. Denise wanted to scream. Alison did this all the time, but it was *her* room! It belonged to Denise! She had never asked for this intruder to move in. She had been quite happy on her own until this *thing* had arrived. But Denise could say '*mine*' all she wanted: it was Alison who had the room now. Denise battered on the door with the flat of her hand.

'Alison!' she yelled.

There was only a sort of burble from behind the door.

'Open the door!' Denise shouted.

It was no use. Alison would be there for hours. Denise sat down on the hall floor and made a low, groaning noise to herself. Her mum came to the door of the living room and looked at her.

'What's wrong?' she said. It wasn't really a question. It was just a noise she made, like Denise's groaning. It meant something, but not what the sum of its parts added up to.

Her hair looked very white, and her face as if one side of it had been slept on, the side she had kept her head propped up with her hand. She looked thin and worn out. Denise felt something about that too, but she was unsure what it was, since the sensation never seemed to stay the same. It was a sort of pity.

Denise couldn't recall a time when her mum had worked. Not since before she had been born, she thought. Years and years and years ago. Nearly four and a half. An eternity. It was impossible to imagine her having done anything Before Denise.

As far as Denise was concerned, her mum ceased to exist before her own birth, though, of course, Denise had no idea that she *had* been born – she was way to wee for all that.

Denise asked her mum what she'd done before.

Denise's mum looked at her.

Do? she said. What did Denise mean '*do*'?

Denise had no idea what she meant by that. What did anybody do? Grown-ups did different things from weans, she was sure of that much. Her conclusion was correct.

The man that lived in their house and said he was Denise's dad got up in the mornings and put on a blue uniform. He drove about in a white car with flashing lights on the roof. People called him *pig*.

'Did you have a . . . *job* . . . like Daddy?' Denise would say the word, but it sat on her tongue like thick skin on curdled milk: *Daddy*.

Yes, her mum said. She had a job. A hell of a job, was what it was . . .

'What job?' Denise wanted to know.

'Carrying you about for nine months. And then that sister of yours . . . Hell of a job, so it was . . .'

Carrying Denise about for nine months before she had been born? And then her sister? What did it mean? There was something missing. Definitely. And it was ages till she finally found out, as well. Years and years. When she's about eleven, Denise asks her mum and dad where babies come from. Of course, she's asked that before – hundreds of times. But she never got a straight answer. She just got told she was too young to understand. She didn't feel like she wouldn't understand, though. She felt as if she could understand as well as anybody else, better maybe. It was as if they didn't trust her with the facts.

Denise's mum is laid down by the fire, in front of the telly, and her dad is in the chair behind, reading the sports section of the newspaper. He looks like he's made up of wooden clothes pins, his head so round and smooth, all except for the hair like Friar Tuck around the sides, and the brown moustache above his lip. He looks cheerful and cross at the same time. He always looks cheerful and cross at the same time; Denise wishes he would just be one or the other. Cross would be best, because cheerful is dead annoying.

'Where do babies come from?' Denise asks. Alison looks down at the game she's playing, pretending not to hear. She's decided that if she just stares at the one spot on the board in front of her then somehow no one will notice she's there.

Her dad immediately sighs and crumples his newspaper down so he can look over at her. He looks cross.

Denise's mum looks up from her pillow by the fire. Denise's dad looks at her mum.

'Well?' he says. 'Are you going to tell her or what?'

'Me? Why should I tell her?' Denise's mum turns her head back to the fire.

'You're her mother – it's your job.' Her dad lifted his paper up so you couldn't see his face. 'Do they not teach them in school these days?' he asked, the paper still covering his mouth.

'I don't know,' her mum said. 'They gave her a lesson on—'

Denise interrupted, the words bursting out in a torrent, no breath between the one before and the one after.

'Andy McCabe told us that the lady gets all hot and has to take all her clothes off but the man doesn't need to take off all his 'cause he's got a thing then the lady rubs up and down against him until they have an organism and the organism makes a baby and that you don't get the organism if you've got your clothes on and then you have to carry it around for nine whole months and then put it in a plastic box with tubes and that keeps it warm until it hatches and then you get a baby but then he told us that you can't have the organism if you stand up 'cause of the gravity and if you put a rubber on your pencil then you can't have the baby either and—'

'Enough!'

Denise shut her mouth tight. Alison looks up from her game, catching her dad's gaze as it ricochets between Denise and himself. Too late. He freezes her to the spot with it.

'You! Alison! Away and play in the other room now!'

'But—'

'But nothing. Go on – get!'

Alison bursts into tears and begins to mumble about how it's not fair, she hadn't done anything wrong, then she sort of grinds to a halt. As she walks out of the room, she shoots Denise a vicious look. She hates her. It's all Denise's fault. It's always Denise's fault.

When Alison is out the room, Denise's mum sits up, looks at her, then at her dad. 'All right,' she says, 'there's a few things here that obviously need straightening out.'

She gets up and goes into the cupboard behind Denise's dad's chair. He looks up at her, baffled. Denise sits still, her legs crossed underneath her on the carpet. She hates chairs. One of the things she decides is that she'll never sit in chairs when she's grown up. But she will, even if she doesn't know it yet.

Denise's mum hands her a book from the cupboard. The cover is plain black. Denise holds it in her hands and looks at it.

'Open it up then,' her mum says, arms crossed, looking down at her. 'You wanted to know. You won't know unless you open it up.'

But Denise is afraid of what she'll find inside, afraid that the answer won't add up, the questions she has are so many, it can't surely be the same answer for every one. Denise's hands tremble. She opens up the cover. Inside is a totally blank page.

Denise is glad. The white page makes her feel a bit better. It's comforting, this white page. She lets the back of her hand stroke it, a good, clean feeling, a pure whiteness reaching out from between the covers, pressing against the back of her hand.

Her dad stares over at her, his nose poking over the top of his paper, a paper covered in hideous black squiggles, wriggling like worms. The marks are permanent. Denise shudders and closes the book, turns it face-down, pushes it across the floor.

'What?' her dad says. 'What is it now?'

Her mother stares down at her, a feeling of helplessness settling over Denise again like a shroud.

'How're you not wanting to see, Denise?' she asks. 'Are you frightened?'

'No.' Denise isn't frightened. It's not fear. It's something else, something hard to explain.

'Denise?'

She looks up at her mum. She breathes deeply for a few seconds, wanting the words to come out right, not just spurt across the room like they always do.

'Denise?'

Denise is calm. She can see whiteness before her eyes, a silk screen between her and the rest of the world. Then she says, as slowly as she is able:

'I want to . . . *wait*.'

Denise carried white nothing between her and black nothing. She sort of knew, inside, that they were both the same, somehow, the line between them only standing to highlight their sameness. That didn't matter. You could choose either; colour or the lack of it made no difference. Sometimes Denise chose black; sometimes she chose white. She almost never chose grey, but it seemed to seep out of her body anyway. She hated the grey. She looked in the mirror and saw grey. Grey flesh, ill from never eating anything green; grey nails, grey lips. She walked out onto grey streets in the mornings and sat in a grey classroom, while teachers made her try to think grey thoughts. Even her school uniform was grey. There were places in the world where things weren't grey. Egypt was one. Eulalia was another. There was colour in these places. Denise had been to Egypt, in her head, taken it and made the bits she liked into her own country, painted it with colour. And underneath, seething, there was always the black and white.

Sex was a grey area. Denise knew, and she didn't want grey. So she would wait. She would wait until it was clean, white, pristine, or dirty, black, squalid. But she was determined there was to be no grey.

Of course, that was all right in theory, but the practice was different, and later on Denise reckons there's a good deal to be said for the working out, though in that context *method* turns out to be an entirely different thing. Often as not,

Denise gets herself to arrive at the right answer. God forbid. But He was nowhere to be seen.

Denise studiously avoided learning anything from books, or from pictures or even from the conversations that went on in Smoker's Corner between lessons. The boys seemed to know a lot about it. Andy McCabe knew a lot. He even had pictures of things, totally disgusting things that you had to keep staring at over and over. He'd got them off his dad, he told them.

'Your dad just gave you that magazine?' Denise said, incredulous.

'Naw! I took it out his collection – he'll never notice. He's got loads.'

The cover of the magazine said: ALBINO WIVES

Denise didn't really know what an albino was, but the folk inside were dead weird-looking. Their hair was all white and they had these pink eyes with no lashes. But just the women. The men all just looked like dead big hairy fat blokes.

The normal guys were doing stuff to the albino wives, except there were big black marks covering it up. Some of these big black marks said: CENSORED

You wanted to see what was under the big black marks, but then you were glad you didn't have to. It gave you a weird feeling to look at the pictures, they didn't leave all that much to the imagination. Not really. It was a shame, because Denise was beginning to like imagining all that stuff. She sort of kept a white screen between her and the pictures in her head, smoothed off all the hard edges. Sometimes, she would try and imagine all the details as well, though. That gave her a feeling too.

There was a big circle of folk around Andy McCabe and his magazine. Some of them were trying to get a hold of it, so they could see better.

'Fuck off!' Andy said. 'You'll tear it! Fuck off!'

Denise couldn't imagine wanting a picture of an albino

wife that badly. Or a normal bloke. All the normal blokes were totally weird and disgusting-looking. They were totally hinging. Totally.

Something was happening to Andy McCabe as well. He looked different somehow. His skin was terrible, for one thing. Denise couldn't mind his skin having been so bad before. All these red plooks with yellow heads on them around his chin. Nowhere else, just his chin. Gads.

But there was something else as well. Sometimes something happened to his voice. It went all kind of squeaky, then it went all kind of deep. John Burke was the same. It was like they were speaking in small letters, then the letters went to capitals. Weird as fuck, so it was.

'check oUt the fAnnY on tHAt!'

'eh, nAW! . . . aW bALDY!'

There was a word for these things.

Wankers.

That was it. They were wankers.

There was something about them. Andy was a different shape now, broader across his shoulders. When they'd played in the back courts and middens, he'd been this wee stunted shite, all pale and skinny. A totally different person. He was always hanging about, telling lies and stuff. Denise had hated him then. Now, he had this kind of smell as well. He was still hingin', but sometimes something happened to Denise and she wanted to touch him. Or something. It sent a shiver down her to think of it. Andy McCabe. Gads.

Denise had changed too. She'd been terrified of it. The Curse. She had been spared it this far. Not any more. She'd sneaked about the place, thinking folk could smell it off her, the blood, thinking that everybody knew, thinking there was a great big sign floating over her saying: DENISE FORRESTER IS ON THE RAG

She is fourteen years old before it starts; late by the standards of the rest of her year. But then, Denise is out of kilter

119

with the whole world and besides, all she ever eats is crisps, bread and chips, which doesn't help. She had gone in and out of shops and classrooms and doctor's surgeries and guidance panels. She had bumped into people on the street and stroked cats and clapped dogs and said hello to the next-door neighbours. It felt like they all knew. Her cheeks burned every time she opened her mouth, every time someone spoke to her, every time someone looked in her direction. She could feel herself go bright red, like a blood signal, an admission of guilt. It was as if the organs inside her were trying to betray her. She had no control over them; mutiny could be triggered in her blood vessels by just entering a classroom. A uniform eyes to the right, and she became a rash of blushes, skin on fire.

There was no respite in sleep. Dreams followed her under the duvet; she would be stood in the same classroom doorway, completely naked. Faceless people stared at her body, everyone except Mz Ewart, who was Mz Ewart but not Mz Ewart, who stared at her as if she was some kind of vermin, some sort of bug. Denise felt her nakedness, skin like rice paper, tits just buds. Sparse growth between her legs.

Someone had chalked something on the blackboard:

DENISE FORRESTER IS A TITLESS BOOT

Denise covered her chest with an arm; her other went to cover her fanny. It was cold, there was a sound like old pennies falling onto marble, and she looked down at the redness dripping onto scuffed flooring.

Denise started avoiding people as much as possible, which was only slightly more than she already avoided them. She'd never been a people person. Her mum didn't really understand what was going on: Denise kept on asking if she could get a cat again. For company. She hadn't done that since she'd been a little girl; they'd said no then. They were hardly likely to change their minds now she was the age she was.

'Cats are a nuisance,' her granny used to say. 'Peeing on everything . . .'

'And it'll be us that ends up looking after it when you can't be bothered!' her dad said.

'What about a dog then?'

Her mum hadn't cared either way. She was dead beat, was what she was.

Denise needed the company, though. She avoided practically everyone. She was sure she must smell. Liz Tonner in her class smelled. She smelled of pish and puberty. She picked her nose and ate it too.

Denise spent all her time washing. She practically shone, she was so clean. She smelled like a newborn baby, spent all her money on deodorants and creams and perfumes. She wondered if she had covered her own smell up, and what it was like. It was impossible to smell your own smell. She could smell, in her memory, what her sister smelled like, what her mum and dad smelled like, even what Andy McCabe smelled like. But she couldn't picture her own smell. Now, she had covered it up, but she knew it would always be trying to sneak through her defences, leaking out into the atmosphere like some poxy cloud, or a splash of wine in the public baths. She could never let herself rest.

Swimming was the worst. She was terrified to go swimming, except she wouldn't ask any teachers for a sick note so she could get off. That meant telling someone. So she forgot her stuff. As much as possible she forgot her stuff. Everyone else went in but she stayed in the gallery, reading.

She had never read so much in her life, but the words were confusing; now more than they had ever been. Before, everything was just her on her own. There was no past and no future; everything had been *now*.

Her and here and now.

Books said otherwise. She didn't like it, but there was nothing else to do in the gallery, nothing except listen to the screams and shouts and splashing, listen to the pool attendant blowing his whistle, look for signs of blood in the water. The first thing Denise did when she opened a book was stare at the blank, white comfort of the very first page. Only after contemplating that could she bear to go on.

And it was hard to concentrate. A sentence she read might say something like:

I speak not of the calumny of the moment, which hovers over a character, like one of the dense morning fogs of November over this metropolis

but by halfway through it would have become infected, say something quite different, something sweet and truculent and unbearable, the same words repeating themselves in endless formulations that always said the same things, always the same words, always the same pictures:

pushing stiff   in me hands   wrapped round   back   mouth mouth wet on   mouth hips on my hips   my face no   on my back no mouth   weight on   my   weight   in me   weight squeezing

She couldn't stop. There were parts missing, vital parts, a skein or something covering them, a white sheet between her and them. She crossed her legs hard and tried to concentrate on the books. But there was always an ache there. Always. And she would have to put the book down again. It made the head swim to think about.

She stared at the wet bodies bellyflopping into the pool, the plastered-to-scalp hair framing boy faces with adolescent bodies; the backs and shoulders scarred with plooks and cystic acne, the broadening shoulders and white, white skin that only boys had. The water leapt around them, their presence a pleasure of frothy white-blue foam.

Denise was the only one in the public gallery. Her book was dry as old leaves and the water was cool and wet. It would be great to sink into it. Magic. But she wasn't much of a swimmer; she would end up stuck up the shallow end with the numpties, more than likely. Already, she could see it was her lot to be stuck in classes full of numpties, like in the remedial. Just to look at them was mental, the way they hung on to those polystyrene boards as if they were trays covered with food, trays just out of reach.

Someone tapped her on the shoulder and she jumped. Jeedy. And that guy who never said anything as well.

'Fuck's sake,' Denise said. Her chest was thumping.

'Heh!' Jeedy said. 'Give you a fright, did I?'

Denise nodded, feeling her cheeks redden. Why was Jeedy speaking to her? They used to speak. Before Denise's mum and dad had moved away from the tenement. It was to do with growing up, she knew. That didn't help any. It was to do with him being a boy and her being a girl.

'Look at them,' Jeedy said, pointing. He grinned white teeth over the water. His face was so black. Every time he was up close, Denise had to fight not to stare at him. A velvety blackness. She remembered the feeling of his hair between her fingers. The guy who never said anything was quiet, sat beside Jeedy, his headphones on as usual. He smiled at Denise, then quickly looked away.

'Bunch of divots, so they are,' Jeedy laughed. He had a magic laugh. She could smell the fags off him; he must have just put one out before coming in.

'How come you're not in with them?' Denise asked, her voice taking this tone she never meant it to.

'It's *wet* in there . . .' Jeedy looked at her.

'You could do with the wash,' Denise said, then regretted it straight away. She never meant it to sound like that.

Jeedy shot her a look. 'Could do with one yourself,' he said. 'Pure stinking you are. Why're *you* not in with them?'

Denise looked down at the book. 'Forgot my kit,' she said.

'Aye, right.'

'I did as well.' She could feel her cheeks getting redder. He must know, she was saying to herself. He must be able to tell. Be able to *smell*.

'Yeh . . . so did I.' He smiled at her again, a gentler smile. You couldn't see his teeth this time. 'What you got next?' he asked her.

'Double arithmetic,' she said. She didn't mention the remedial. Jeedy was good at that stuff without even trying. It made you feel dead necked-out sitting with him, though. 'You?' she asked, looking up and then back down at her lap again quickly.

'Fuck knows,' he said, like he was angry about something. Jeedy was always angry about something. 'I ain't fucking going anyway, whatever it is.'

'How not?'

'Can't be fucked. Might go to the caff instead. Might not. See what this cunt wants to do.' He elbowed the guy that never said anything, who looked up at him, surprised, then went back to staring at the pool and nodding to his headphones.

Denise didn't know what to say, so she kept quiet. Jeedy was quiet too. She liked that about him. She began to relax.

'So how come you don't talk to me any more?' he said, after a bit. He was looking at the pool. His face was steady and serious. Denise felt a twinge of something like panic, and her cheeks flared up again.

'I don't know,' she said, very quietly. 'I wanted to . . .' Jeedy was angry. Still. He had lots of anger. You could tell. Denise was angry too, but not like him. There were different sorts of anger.

They were both quiet again for a while, watching the surface of the pool churn over the bodies, the striplights reflected off the torn surface like some luminous jellyfish. Then the end-of-class bell rang. Folk began to climb out of the water and shuffle shivering into the changing rooms. Jeedy stood up.

'I'm going,' he said. 'Want to come?'

'Yes,' Denise said. She got up and followed him out. A couple of seconds later, the guy who never said anything got up as well, trailing after the pair of them.

The morning after her mum walked out, Denise's entire body was painful to move. Her head felt like it had a steel plate behind the forehead, a plate that was conducting an insistent low-frequency current directly into her brain, played between unwilling nueroreceptors and braincells gone into mourning. When she moved herself, a dizziness overcame her that was so strong she leaned over the side of the bed and convulsed: stringy gobs of saliva came out. It felt like her stomach was going to follow them.

Denise tried to think. She tried to think why her mum had gone, but she knew it was 'cause the Curse had been lifted. Denise had inherited it.

She lay back and closed her eyes, panting slowly like a stray cat in the sun, dry rasping huffs that hardly caused her chest more than a flutter.

Her mum had abandoned her years before; had never really been there for her at all. Denise was glad of feeling so terrible; when it passed she knew all she would feel was numbness, and that she would feel guilty for feeling that same numbness. It would almost have been better if her mum had died. And in some ways, that was what Denise wanted. She wished her mum was dead, so that she would feel this terrible irreplaceable loss, this pain that would haunt her for the rest of her life, a pain that would let her know that she really had loved her mother after all. At the same time, she was wishing either her mum was dead, or that she herself had never been born. One or the other.

It was quiet; late afternoon sometime. Definitely after lunchtime. The house kept its silence, refusing to judge, indifferent. A trail of vomit ran from the downstairs kitchen to the upstairs toilet; big orangey-brown pancakes of sludge that reeked of alcohol. In the kitchen were broken dishes and glasses; Denise had to watch she didn't get any glass skelfs in her feet. Bottles and overflowing ashtrays lined the worktop. The back door was open. Denise pushed it wider to let the air in. Denise fanned the door a bit, then clicked it shut behind her, suddenly aware of herself in her nightie, her legs goose-pimpling against the brisk air.

In the living room, she found her dad lying like a fat slug on the carpet in front of the fireplace, his back to her. In the darkness, he looked like he was hugging a pillow or quilt or something. The curtains were drawn. Denise walked over, careful not to step on any ringpulls or ashtrays. The crack of light from the curtain cut the features of the bodies, one with her thumb in her mouth, curled in against the arms of the other. It was Alison. Her hair was plastered over her face, and her dad's breathing sucked in a wisp of it, blew out again then sucked in again. Neither of them stirred.

The sight of them like that, together, stung. Blood was rising in Denise's cheeks. She couldn't mind a time when he had ever held *her* like that; she couldn't mind a time when she had wanted him to. His body lay there on the floor like a side of meat, the flutter of hair against his mouth the only indication he was alive at all. Denise went back through to the kitchen and started to clear up the ashtrays and bottles, slinging everything into black bin-liners. The sound of the bottles crashing against each other sang inside her skull. She put the radio on loud; that hurt too. The sight of them lying there like that was worse. The noise would wake them.

Something came back to Denise then, rose to the surface of her brain like a bubble rising in bathwater, a memory like a bad smell. It was when she was first sure there was no connection between her and her dad. She had been playing on the floor; there were building blocks, yellow, red, green and blue. She could see her pink fingers like sausages grabbing for them, the room lit like an old colour Polaroid, everything saturated in light that wasn't real light, wasn't the light of *now*. She felt someone lifting her, carrying her up in the air, and then she was hanging above that man, the one that wore the funny hat when he went out to work.

'How do yous two not play together for a bit?' a voice was saying. Granny *La*mont/*Lamont*.

She put Denise down on the man's lap. His legs felt bony under her, his voice uncomfortable, strained. Denise looked up at his face; it seemed to slink away down, as if his features were trying to escape from it. Hairs crawled out the edges of his nostrils like spiders' legs.

It was excruciating.

Neither of them had any idea what they were expected to do. Her dad stroked her hair, awkwardness seeping from the touch of his fingers. She'd been able to feel the discomfort, even through her own.

'Maybe another time, eh?' her granny had said, swiping her up again and putting her down on her own lap.

Denise and the man stared at each other. Some sort of understanding had been reached, something had clicked into place.

Denise was saying to the man:

Leave me alone.

The man was saying:

Suit yourself.

An invisible umbilical cord connected her to her mum, but with this man there was nothing. He might as well have been a ghost. Nobody.

Now, here he was, fully present. Asleep on the floor with her sister. With Alison it had been different. She seemed to want all that kind of affection. She was always after all the attention, needing folk to notice her, needing them to tell her, 'That's good, that's great.' And they did too. Denise baffled them. Alison was a relief. If there was a party or something, she was the one in the middle of the room holding court, or singing a song, the one that was getting the compliments from the grown-ups and that. Straight away after she'd come in the door from school she'd be there under your feet, wanting you to pay attention, listen to what she'd done that day, telling you what so and so had said to so and so, what had happened in her arithmetic class, how her spelling test had gone.

Denise floundered in everything, but Alison had a plan. The plan was very straightforward. The plan was to succeed.

And success depended on Denise's failure. That was why they'd stopped sitting in each other's classes. Alison didn't need Denise's pen and ink; but Denise needed Alison's working out. She needed the equations. As far as the school was concerned there was nothing above or beyond them. Numbers ruled. Once Alison had that figured out, there was no more need for empty wine bottles and chopping boards. They were useless: still life. They went nowhere and they took you nowhere except the dole or some useless FE college full of guys like John Burke that couldn't manage in the real world and would be left behind by it. It was sure as anything that folk like him would still be doing their album covers and sculptures and stuff when they were thirty years old. They'd have moved maybe a few streets away, or they'd get a flat up the town or something; a council flat if they were lucky and knocked someone up. Alison could see that far. It wasn't for her. Denise was welcome to fill up that page all by herself.

Where Denise slopped papier-mâché, Alison formulated tables; when Denise was skipping over slated rooftops, Alison slept like a calculator turned to 'off'. The 'how' of things was what she wanted to understand. It was simple. Lines and crosses and dice. The fittings of tiny golden cogs and wheels;

mechanisms in balance, their ticking the slow tick of life itself.

And then there was sex.
   And to understand sex, you had to *do* it.

Anna Forrester had her reasons for leaving; had been living with them for a long time. Years. When Denise and Alison had been just girls, she'd said she had a sore stomach; Denise had felt that she was the cause. Her mum always seemed to be in pain when she was around; it must be something to do with her. Her mum was either angry or ill or both, and it was Denise who was the common factor, the link between them. That was part of the Curse as well. It wasn't limited to her mum.

Anna Forrester had never gone back to work for any length of time after Denise was born. A year later, she was expecting again. And the rest of the time she was off ill anyway.

'Why don't you work like Daddy?' Denise had asked.

Being a mother was work as much as she could cope with, she said.

Their dad just humphed and went back to his paper.

Granny decided it was politic not to express an opinion. She said nothing when her daughter took time off work again and again, before she was on the sick permanently.

Sometimes there were brief spells where the skies would clear and Anna Forrester would have a kind of *lift*. Sometimes real life was a possibility; there would be a way out, another road to take. Your life could go right or it could go left. Somewhere along the line Anna's had gone left, when it should have hung a right. Somewhere along the line pills and treatments and doctors' appointments had taken over, nappies and bottles and interrupted sleep had taken over, exhaustion and permanent pain and never having any energy at all had taken over.

And there was no one to talk to about it. There was no one who would listen. Certainly not her husband. Sometimes she looked at him and she didn't recognise him at all. Now, he was an alien presence. What was he doing in her house, sleeping in her bed, eating the food she cooked, at her table, in her kitchen? In her body. And who was that creature who looked so much like him? The creature that had flopped like a polythene bag full of offal out of her own insides?

Denise's mum, Anna Forrester, would look at these people and wonder who they were. Who she was. Then she would feel ashamed, disgusted.

She looked first at one daughter, then another. She took pills and mopped her brow with her hankie; a hankie she kept down her sleeve like an old woman. Like her mother. Christ. Already she was turning into her own mother. It was a cheat. It was a fix. The man she shared her bed with, her house with, her daughters with, didn't understand. Didn't care. He had been the least part of the process: a teaspoon or a test-tube could have accomplished the same. It wasn't him who had his body possessed; it wasn't him who had spent ten hours being stretched and split and finally lain so exhausted that to do anything other than sleep was too much.

No. It wasn't him. He hadn't anything to do with it.

At night, in the dark, she would be stirred from sleeping, not fully conscious, feeling hands on her, feeling him press up against her, nudging his prick in between her legs . . . Sometimes she would say quietly: *no*. Sometimes it was she who let her hand drape across his chest, let it reach down over his waist and hips, and it would be him who would turn over, grunting.

That was the way it always seemed to happen.

Never in the sunshine, in the afternoon, on clean silk

sheets; never in a hotel in Paris or a Caribbean island; a hay-loft or sun-freckled green field by a river. Never other than in this darkness, on the edge of sleep; sweat mingling with hands, genitals, and taste of this faceless stranger, taste of alcohol on her breath, on his breath, spreading herself out over him in the dark, coiling herself round him like a black smear, his eyes shut, hair tangling about his face and the heat of her, the folds of her grinding against him, slippy with moisture, his fingers gripped tight round his cock, in her, holding himself there because it might go, it might leave him any second, sleep might overtake, lying there, still on his back, only the shudder of her hips and the arch of her back keeping him there, and then feeling it go from him, feeling his firmness slip away, knowing that she was feeling it go from her too so he would start moving in her again, trying, trying to keep it all going, hoping the momentum would last, his hand still there, sticky from her, his other hand holding her between the crouched fat of her thigh and belly, helping her, and himself, feeling himself almost all spent and her not there yet, not there nearly, but still rocking, rocking, not willing to give up yet, there was still time, and then no time left, all done finally, having to stop anyway, finally having to breathe again anyway because there was no use in it now, there was nothing left of him and nothing left of her either.

And then she flopped down too, a greasy feeling of his chest hair against her, wanting to hold him between her legs like that, but he was practically suffocating in the colourless mass spilling from her head, getting in his mouth and up his nose, then finally extricating his hand from under her weight. Feeling her holding him in there, not minding. Feeling her clench him with her molten insides like she would his arm with her fist, saying, 'Keep it in for a while, keep it in,' and then him slipping out anyway with a sound like a wet kiss:

Smack.

Dull light coming in through the slats of the blind. Her still awake, twisted in the heat. Right arm gone dead and her slack jaw patterned by the sheets. Slack and sore. He was awake as well, she knew. He was facing the woodchip, but she could feel the wakefulness in the lie of his body. The sweat on his side had gone cold.

'*Come back*,' she remembered saying once.

He turned and looked at her. Her hair was plastered to her cheek.

'*Where have I been?*'

'*You were away.*'

'*How could you tell?*'

'*You turned your head.*'

He turned onto his back and yawned. The sheets on her side of the bed were riding up a bit, sticking to her arm, ribbing uncomfortably beneath.

'*Well, I'm back now.*'

But he was already nearly asleep. Anna could feel it in the lie of his body.

Then the crying would start in the other room. The sheets still damp, neither of them asleep more than ten minutes after. There was a knot in her gut. She clicked the light on at the bedside table, shutting her eyes again quickly, blinded. He went, 'Put that thing off, will you . . .'

She ignored him. 'You going to go, then?' she said. He turned onto his front and stuck his head under the pillow. She threw the quilt back. There was blood on the sheets. She felt like laughing, she was so fucking – *fertile*. She took a tampon from the box in her dresser drawer.

She put on her dressing gown and followed the heaving, racking noise of Denise into her room. She never bothered to put the light on, just opened the door a crack to let a bit of light in from the hallway. It was a nightmare. She'd been fed only a couple of hours back. There was never enough for her. Sometimes when Denise started her racket, her mum woke with this feeling like there was something sitting on her chest, like in the stories her mum used to tell. She'd believed them as well. All this stuff about changelings and cats that sucked the breath out of your lungs while you slept. Stole your life slowly. Now Anna Forrester knew that all those old stories had been true. Every word. They had been warnings.

It was Denise who was sitting on her chest every night, sucking the life out of her slowly; it was *him* lying on top of her every night too. Even if she went on top, it was still the weight of him that was squeezing the puff out of her. Night after night.

There was no respite. The days and nights would stretch out into infinity.

She was looking into the deep space of the bedroom: she could make out the shadow of the cot, see it shoogle slightly, an arm waving.

'Shhh, Denise,' she said.

The screeching continued. She couldn't go into the room. She could not. Picking this changeling up, touching it, maybe having it clamp onto her sore, leaky tits made her want to spew. Honest to Christ, she got the heaves just thinking about it. The next day, she could have stood it. In the morning she could have stood it. But not tonight. She hovered by the door, not knowing what to do. She went back to the bathroom, ignoring the noise. She opened the cabinet and took out a bottle of paracetamol. There weren't many left. She'd get some more in the morning. She looked at the bottle, the cap. Opened it. It was suddenly a strange thing; she had never examined the bottle before, and she couldn't mind a day she'd not swallowed a couple of the things since she'd been twenty years old. She stood there looking at it; at the cap, the label, the brown glass. The thing in the other room continued to scream. Anna Forrester unscrewed the cap, emptying a few of the tablets into the palm of her hand. White. Hard. Beautiful. She put a couple in her mouth and held them there. She looked at the cap, turned it upside down. There was a circular bit of sponge inside it. She'd never noticed it before. She picked it out of the inside of the cap. The surfaces of the pills in her mouth began to feel pitted, a bitter milkiness beginning to tang. She'd never allowed herself to taste them, not for years anyway. Maybe it was a good thing to taste them, to feel them, to fully taste their bitterness. That way at least you were aware of them. Maybe it was better just to suffer. She looked at her face in the mirror, leaned down to the tap and took a gulp of water, then threw her head back and swallowed the pills. She felt them all the way down.

The bathroom door opened, and *he* came in, hand fumbling at the fly of his pyjama trousers. The bags under his eyes sagged like his wrinkled scrotum. She looked quickly back up at the mirror, the steady sound of his urine hitting the side of the pan like the sound of a marble rolling round an aluminium sink. The sound, the intimacy of the act, repulsed her. It was an intimacy she could live without. Early on, when they'd not been seeing each other long, he had asked her: '*How long is it you wait before you don't mind having a shite in front of each other?*'

He actually seemed to think that this would be a desirable state of affairs. '*Don't worry yourself,*' she told him. '*Till death do us part's not that long to wait,*' she'd said.

'That wean's still greetin',' he said.

'I know, I'll see to her in a minute.' She kept her gaze fixed on the mirror. Her hair was changing its colour, there was a coarsening as well. She was looking old before her time, right enough. Maybe it would get the colour back in the summer, when the leaves on the trees were out. Maybe sunshine would cause it to sparkle and photosynthesise again Come into full bloom or something.

'Can you not see to her now? I've got to work tomorrow . . .'

'So have I.'

'*You* can call it work. Lazing about the house . . .'

'Away back to bed. I told you I'd see to her in a minute.'

'What's that bleeding on the sheets? You never told us it was your bad week.'

'You never asked, Duncan.'

'Aye well. You should have said earlier.'

'Sorry. Forgot. You can stick them in the wash, can you not?'

'Typical. Get muggins here to do it! Who's paying for those sheets anyway? Who pays for everything in here?'

She didn't answer that. They'd been a wedding present, but there was no point reminding him. He stood over the lavatory, hawked, spat into it, then flushed it and went out again. She stood for a minute looking at her face in the mirror, hands clasped on the cold porcelain of the sink. Even her face didn't seem to belong to her. It was the face of someone else. Once it had been her mother's face – she could see how similar they'd become over the years. Sometimes she caught a glimpse of her reflection in a shop window and had to look again to make sure it wasn't her mother.

She went through to the room with the cot in it, still not able to go in. The screeching had calmed to just this regular wheezing gurgle, a sound that kept itself going by momentum alone. The baby wasn't crying; it was more advanced than that. It was as if this crying was some sort of parasite that had attached itself to the baby; was feeding off it in the same way the baby fed off its mother. She pushed open the door of the bedroom and went in.

'Shssh,' she said. 'Shssh . . .'

She closed the door behind her, so that it was dark. It was better in the dark somehow. She didn't want to see the face of the baby. She wanted to feel anonymous. She rocked the cot back and forth. She still couldn't bring herself to pick it up. She said her daughter's name to herself, like an incantation, wanting to break the spell, wanting the power of the word to infect her, overcome the desire she had to push her daughter away.

'Denise,' she said. 'Denise. Denise. Denise.'

It took a long time for the baby to calm down. The wheezing became more and more irregular, until finally it stopped and everything was quiet. It was beginning to get light out, in the world beyond the curtain, the world where life was going on. She could make out the shape of Denise's head and body now. She watched her chest rise and fall, tiny hands held perpendicular at the shoulders, as if she was surrendering, her pillow a white flag framing her head. Anna left the room, closing the door as quietly behind her as possible.

She got herself back in under the covers, and lay back. She knew he was awake. He rolled over to face her, nudging his hard cock up against her thigh again, his arms falling over her breasts. She rolled over onto her side, so that they made spoons.

No, she said, very quietly. *No*.

The next day had been the worst, before Denise had realised what needed to be done. She had lain in bed, hung-over, and stared at the walls and ceiling, followed their cracked ravines like dry riverbeds and brought faces to life, there, grimacing on the plaster. There was Granny *La*mont/La*mont*. And half of Granda, bunnet on his nut. Back from the dead. But of course Granda had never really been *alive* anyway. He'd never been more than a puff of smoke let out of a bottle, curling slowly towards the sky where he would eventually join in with the rainclouds that shunted from one end of the horizon to the other, before coming back to earth with the deluge again. Denise put him back in the bottle again and screwed the cork back on tight.

At sixteen, Denise filled in the gaps between when her dad was there and when he wasn't, a black hole that had sprung open between his words and her silence. She ironed her sister's clothes in the mornings, got her up and ready, sent her off out the door. Denise goes to school less and less herself, until finally she leaves quietly by the back door, before they expel her officially. The reasons are never clear to her.

Suspension for scrawling on a desk with a scalpel; suspension for refusal. It all added up. After a while, anyway.

It doesn't matter what for, the reasons told you. Just because.

Because and because and because.

Denise thought of her granny and wished she was there

with her, wished she could conjure her back into existence, wished she would come back and take care of everything for her, make it all better. There was no magic for this situation, no genie was going to appear and put everything right.

It was up to Denise now. Her dad hardly even noticed, him being away half the time, busy with other things, trying to find other things to fill up the empty space his wife once occupied.

But no. There was only absence in the bed next to his. Palpable, living absence.

Denise was never sure when she was first aware of things not being quite right, things not being the same way they were in other houses. It seemed like everybody knew but her: Alison, her granny, everyone. Why had nobody bothered to tell her? All the time she'd been up in her room making her sculptures, mapping and remapping, *things* had been going on right under her room, right below her in the other rooms in the house, those same other rooms that ceased to exist as soon as Denise walked out of them.

She had noticed her mum put things down in a heavier way. She noticed the level in the vodka bottle. Though they never had a drinks cabinet, just the two bottles: whisky and vodka.

His'n'hers.

Masculine.

Feminine.

It wasn't as if her mum and dad ever fought that much or anything. For years and years it was as if they were just ignoring each other; they lived in the same house, but that was it. They'd got separate beds not long after Alison was born. In the same room, but separate.

Unnatural is what it is, Denise's Granny *La*mont/La*mont* had whispered to her, years before. Denise had never known what she meant. It was the only way Denise was able to remember it being. What was unnatural about that? Denise had never known them to sleep any other way than unnaturally. It's only when Denise herself starts wanting to sleep, naturally, with other people that she realises this isn't the way everybody sleeps when they get married. But of course it'll be a long while before *sleep with* will mean simply that to her.

'A husband and wife ought to share the bed,' Granny *La*mont/*La*mont said. 'That's the way it's meant to be.'

'Why?' Denise asked.

'So they can make a baby,' Alison said, knowing the answer as usual.

Denise frowned.

'You two never mind about all that the now,' Granny said. 'Yous are too young to be thinking about that kind of thing.'

But it was their granny that had started it. In more ways than one.

Maybe Denise's mum was expecting her real dad to come home any minute, Denise wanted to say, but stopped the words coming out and making a mess. Her granny had told her not to mention that. It was their secret. Denise was good at keeping secrets. It was a side effect of never being able to get her words to come out.

It was like their mum would sleep anywhere – anywhere at all – except with their dad. Armchair, living-room floor, couch – anywhere. You never saw them touching or anything, there was no hugging or kissing. You never saw them speak to each other much, it was more like they spoke this mad other language that was all just grunts and groans, muttering and sharp looks. The language of grown-ups. They hardly needed to say anything, but you could tell they understood each other fine. Denise had trouble getting words out, but she could follow what they were saying to each other, no problem.

The conversations were always the same. Her dad would come in from his work, fling down his cap and loosen his jacket, grunt something; where was his tea, why was the place such a tip, what were they two doing still up ... Not *questions*; he never put question marks at the end of a sentence, whether he *looked* it or *said* it. There was never any *why?* And there was never any interest, either. Later, thinking about it, Denise can never remember if her dad ever asked her mum how she was; what she'd been doing; where she'd been that day. Never.

Denise's mum would wear this set expression on her face, the one she used against everything. Her expression said it all:

Leave me alone.

His expression answered back:

No.

In the evening, they both sat there, only the tinkling conspiracy of ice in glasses between them, of those same glasses being put down and picked up off tables, each with one at their elbow. Denise's mum put things down heavier and heavier. Something happened to her voice when she spoke. If she spoke.

Denise's mum moved from kitchen to shops; bathroom to living room, standing to lying in front of a television set that was almost never switched off, though she never seemed to be actually watching it. The programmes were like the level in the bottle or the white pills she kept in the bathroom cabinet; they filled some kind of gap. The telly flickered away in the corner, throwing out its warmth across the room to her, nourishing her on a diet of the *Six O'Clock News*, cartoons, repeats and old black-and-white films. Transmissions from the real world.

Denise couldn't stand it. She would head on up to her room to escape back to her own fascinations. Painting watercolours onto the window panes, transforming the view beyond the window, redrawing it in her own likeness. Sometimes, she would prise the balls from used roll-on deodorants with a teaspoon and hold them up to the light. Her mum found a shoe-box of them under Denise's bed. What did she want those things for? she asked her. Old deodorant balls . . .

She collected unique things: a golden filling that looked like a fish; the mummified bodies of mice and sparrows; roll-on balls too. Inside each one was an air-bubble, different each time. They were like snowflakes that never melted. You could keep them for ever.

'Get rid of them, Denise,' her mum said. Her mum always told her to get rid of the things she collected. Denise remembered how she'd pleaded with her to let her keep the mouse bodies the old tom had given her. She had been going to bury them properly, she said, somewhere that no animals could smell them and dig them up again. Nonsense, her mum said, and threw them on the midden, where the cats would find them and carry them off once more.

Denise took to hiding things, putting them places where nobody could get at them, or just carrying them about with her everywhere with her, like she did with her golden fish, somewhere out of the way of her mum. Denise didn't know *why* she wasn't allowed to keep things; she just knew that she was always having to hide them or they would get thrown out. It was like her mum didn't want her to have anything of her own; it was the same with her landscapes. It was a terrible shame really. She was only pleasing herself.

Her mum didn't want her to collect things; she wanted to remind her that she was still there, that even if Denise didn't want to acknowledge it, she was still her mother and it was her who had final say over what went on under her own roof. Denise needed no one but herself; her mum knew this. And she felt guilty 'cause the reason Denise never needed anyone was because her mum had never needed Denise either, had regarded her with suspicion ever since she had been born. Denise's mum knew that it was her fault, so she couldn't help looking over Denise's shoulder. Denise was her first; she was still making mistakes with her. Alison she was determined to get right, except she only had Denise to go by and she wasn't at all sure she'd got it right with *her*. Nobody told you these things. You never knew what you'd done right. You just had to make it up as you went along.

Denise carried her fish around with her everywhere. She decided never to show it to anyone, not even to her granny. It would be her secret fish. But she does finally show it to someone when she is sixteen: a jeweller. She shows it to him because she wants him to make it into an ornament for a necklace; she wants him to hammer it into the shape of a D.

D for Denise.

Of course, the jeweller says, but he'll have to add to it, there isn't enough of the golden fish there to be going on with.

Fine, Denise will tell him. Do what you have to.

And when it's made Denise pays the jeweller with money she's stolen from her dad's wallet while he lay asleep on the couch in the living room after a shift, one hand edging down the front of his trousers, his moustache catching spittle from his open mouth. She'll put the necklace on and walk out of the jeweller's shop and down Byres Road, school blouse opened at the collar to show off her new cleavage and her new necklace with the golden D made from a goldfish she coughed up when she was just small and which she has never shown to anyone; Denise will walk with this new necklace, this secret, hung around her neck for absolutely anyone and everyone to see. For the whole world to see.

No one notices it for days.

Her mum has been gone months.

Her dad hasn't noticed anything for years.

Inside, Denise knew it was his fault their mum had gone, his fault for not noticing, for never trying, for only half-caring. But he was still there, in the end. At least he was still there for them. The Curse had been passed to Denise and there was no reason for her to stay any longer. It had been the Curse that had kept Anna Forrester née Douglas tied to the house. Not her husband. Not her kids. It was being crippled that had kept her there. And himself? He'd never shown any interest in her after they'd got their separate beds. That was a long time not to be interested. Denise's mum had got up one morning and had some kind of a flush, some kind of wave passed over her and she broke into a sweat, nearly passed out. A new development. It happened again and then again. Other symptoms too. In the plumbing. After a while she made her way to the doctor, this feeling of terror, that some new and even more horrible thing was about to befall her. She had coped with the Curse for most of her days: at least it had been reliable. Now it was taking a new twist. It wasn't fair. There was no justice. Anna Forrester swallowed the word back down, like she'd swallowed all those pills, the ones she'd been swallowing for years.

The doctor looked over his notebook at her, uh-huh-ing a bad coffee-and-cigar smell over her as he sat on the edge of his desk, one knee crossed over the other, shoes black and shiny, neatly pressed pinstripe suit and clean fingernails. His face had a serious look. He was at least sixty, and his face was covered in broken red veins, his nose almost a different colour entirely from the rest of his body.

'And these flushes,' he said, scribbling in his notepad. 'Are they much different from your usual ones? Frequent?'

He tapped his fountain pen on the notepad. A splot of ink jolted out onto the paper; he was reaching behind him for a blotter or something. He didn't seem to be listening. As he half-turned, his face went red with the effort, his nose turning an even deeper purple than it had been. He panted a bit.

'I get them most days now,' Anna said.

The doctor had a hand up to his chest as if he had a bad heartburn. He took a couple of pills out of a bottle on his desk, then went over and filled a crystal glass with water from the tap of the surgery sink jutting from one of the walls.

'Sorry,' he said. 'These flushes, you say? You get them during the day?'

'Ehm . . . yes. They make me feel faint.'

'They make you feel faint. Nothing wrong with that. Fine. Hot flushes make me dizzy as well. Just experienced something similar a moment ago.'

'But what is it that's causing them? Is it serious?'

'Serious? Absolutely it's serious.'

Anna felt herself get cold suddenly. This was it. The big one. Cancer. The Big C. She had known it all along.

'You're getting old, Mrs Forrester. What could be more serious than that? Look at me! Old.'

Anna Forrester looked at him. She opened her mouth to say something, and then shut it again.

'Time is catching up with you, Mrs Forrester,' he said, smiling at her in a not-unkind way, so that his eyebrows formed two crescents on his brow. 'Perfectly normal,' he added. 'In due course. You seem to have succumbed earlier than usual. Nothing to worry about, though.'

Anna Forrester felt limp, like all the tension had been knocked out of her body.

'Now, I can give you a prescription for some of these symptoms—'

'No. No prescriptions.'

'Are you sure, Mrs Forrester? Not for the dryness or—'

'Nothing. No prescriptions.'

Anna Forrester felt herself changing now, felt herself aware of molecular readjustments and recalibrations taking place inside her, felt their constellations shift and begin to pull in different directions from before; cell by cell, nucleus by nucleus, dying egg by dying egg. In only a short time, then, there might be a chance – a last chance – at life. At living. She pushed the thought out of her head. No. Day by day. For now. Moment by moment. Wait and see. Wait and—

No. No more waiting. She'd waited long enough as it was.

At sixteen, Denise tried to end two years of shy flirtation and an ache that seemed to be taking root inside her like a tumour, on top of an old mattress by the railway embankment, in a fumble of hands and underwear and a terrible kind of excitement that was a kind of fear she wanted to go on for ever, but which actually lasted only about twenty-five seconds before Denise was sat upright again, straightening her clothes, looking down, looking away, looking anywhere except at the person sitting beside her. If she did look, she'd only have seen this person fumbling with his own flies, his dick looking dead and ugly and old just before he tucked the thing away; the angry look returning to his face.

Even now he was angry.

pushing stiff   in me hands   wrapped round   back   mouth mouth wet on   mouth hips on my hips   my face no   on my back no mouth   weight on   my   weight   in me   weight squeezing

Denise had wanted to wait, except Jeedy said he couldn't use those things. Condoms. They hurt him, he said. Now Denise wanted the waiting to end but he couldn't get it up!

Why was he afraid of a johnny, she wondered. It's just a bit of rubber, she said. Why would he be afraid of a bit of rubber?

It wasn't fair.

stiff   in me wrapped round   back hands   mouth wet   on hips on my hips   mouth my face yes   inside me yes   mouth yes   weight in me   weight   in me   weight   pushing yes   again   yes

The thoughts, the pictures, would have to stay where they were for the moment.

Alison had her own ideas. She would watch Denise and Jeedy walk up the street together, lagging behind with Andy McCabe and John Burke. Her sister's friends. Not hers. Denise's. Alison wanted to say *mine* but couldn't. It was like Denise was always taking things off her. Even things she didn't want. Things she didn't care about. It wasn't fair. Alison saw the way they both looked at Denise now, Andy and John; quickly, then away at something else; their feet, a lamppost, Alison. She hated them for it. She hated them and she hated Denise. Denise most of all.

Andy McCabe said: 'Can't stand that guy.'

John Burke didn't seem to be listening.

Alison giggled.

It was 'cause of Denise growing up, and Alison stuck with this fourteen-year-old body that nobody wanted, not even herself. Everyone was always saying how much older she looked than her sister, how much more mature and sensible and grown-up she was, but it was something to do with her expression; her eyes; the way she held her mouth, the proportion of her cheekbones and the angle of her neck. It had nothing to do with her *body* at all. More than anything Alison wanted it to have something to do with her body. *Now*.

There was obviously something wrong with her. There were other girls in her class that weren't as developed as she was; she had the tits and the hips and was getting periods and everything. It was like some sort of big conspiracy. Nobody was letting her grow up. They still wanted to see her as the wee girl she so very nearly wasn't. She was trying her hardest too. Denise was always getting to things first, claiming them, grabbing them out of Alison's hands and going: *Mine!* Alison wanted something of her own for a change, not hand-me-downs and cast-offs, not second-hand stuff that her sister had already drained the pleasure from. Alison would watch Denise walk up the road with Jeedy, see Andy and John sneak furtive looks at her sister and know she had to do a lot of growing up and she had to do it quick. She decided the whole process needed speeding along a bit. She looked up at Andy McCabe and John Burke. Andy was getting to be quite nice, though he had pretty bad skin and was kind of a prick.

She decided on Andy. It would be simple: she'd just walk up and suggest it. It was delicious to think how easy it would be. There wasn't much about him that she liked, except that he was a boy, older than her, and he liked her sister. That was reason enough.

He wasn't any great looker.

She tried to come up with a better one.

He could be cruel, nasty, but he was sometimes funny, sometimes he'd given her a laugh. Sometimes. That was something. Yes, Alison reckoned, Andy would do the job. For now anyway. Alison needed someone to *do the business* with. She needed someone to *succeed* with. He would be the least part of it. Then she could move on. It'd be over.

Alison fought Denise every inch of the way; tried as hard as she could to scupper her efforts to take over from their mum. If her mum could go and leave her, then there was no one you could trust any more. It was as if she'd always known this would happen; now that it had, it was almost a relief. So far as Alison was concerned, it was only Denise that never seemed to suspect; she'd never understood what kind of an equation her family was; never understood anything about her mum or her dad or her sister. How could Denise expect Alison to take her seriously? It didn't matter how many school blouses she ironed, or how many slices of toast Denise made for her, she couldn't replace their mum. Their dad had soon settled into letting Denise keep everything under control – she was good at control, always had been – but Alison could not accept this new set of circumstances as anything other than temporary. Now, she was going to come into her own, she was the one who was going to get the attention. She was determined. She was going to have her cake and eat it; she was going to have Denise's share and eat it as well if she could get away with it.

Their dad did nothing, had become even less of a presence in the house than before. Denise hardly noticed him now: she had taken over. She was doing all those things she'd never bothered with before, 'cause if she didn't then no one would. That was the only reason. If she'd been on her own, if the house was hers, then she'd never have bothered: she didn't care what kind of squalor she lived in; it was immaterial to her. But it was the decay around her – in *this* house – that she couldn't stand. She had never known it to be anything other than spotless: her mum and her granny, both of them, had made sure it was always immaculate. And they'd taken it for granted, all of them. That was just the way things were. Now it made her stomach turn to see dirty plates and unhoovered carpets. It nauseated her to see a stained lavatory-bowl or a grimy-looking sink. She would gag and retch as she dragged matted, greasy ropes of hair from the bathroom plughole, purse her lips at overflowing bins. She'd become house-proud by osmosis.

And then there were all the pairs of dirty underpants and knickers, smelly school socks. There was an order that needed to be established. There was a hierarchy that needed to be created. Denise was the one to do it; no one understood better than her how necessary she was becoming, how indispensable she would be in this new arena. It was true it was not an arena of her own creation, it was true she had never asked for it, but she had been in training all her life for this moment. She was a natural.

The pants and the socks could be trained: she'd force them into the washing machine and onto the clothesline. The dishes could be made subordinate to the sink, the dishcloths and mops dance to her tune. It was simple.

'You, Denise, you take these plates and wash them,' her Granny *La*mont/La*mont* had told her plenty of times. She'd always resented it since she never dirtied any herself, at least never more than a plate or two. Toast didn't create that much of a mess.

'You, Denise, take this Hoover and run it around the carpet,' she'd been told by her mum. 'And use the attachments!'

Her dad never told her to do anything, just sat about reading the paper.

But every once in a while, he'd come into her room, step in when she was in the middle of something: painting, looking at her books on Egypt, sculpting. He never knocked. And there had always been a discomfort about it, an embarrassment that clung to skirting boards and electricity outlets, that seemed to charge the air in her room with a vague static, an energy that threatened. But with her mum in the house, it had been kept in check. Now, with her mum gone, it had started again. There were never any knocks. Never any May-I-Come-Ins. The door would just open and he would stand there, staring at her. His face always heavy and slack so's she could tell he'd had a drink; he'd sway in, never asking her permission, his eyes saying what was on his mind:

You think this is your room?

And she would feel herself shrinking into herself, this invasion more than she could bear, the same as her fear of the dark when still a child.

When she was sixteen, Denise Forrester listened to what the other girls said about boys: what they'd done with them, *when*, *who* and *how*. She tried to copy the way they flirted in front of the mirror in her room, put on make-up and dyed her hair even darker. Her skin seems translucent, like rice paper a thumbnail could tear, faint blue lines under the surface.

That was the night her mum walked out on them.

So, at sixteen, Denise got drunk for the first time and went tottering from one room to the next, outsize whisky tumbler in one skinny hand, the liquid sloshing a pungent trail onto the carpet; a trail that disappeared like breadcrumbs picked away by wild animals in a forest so that you wondered if you'd ever find your way back, and if anyone would care if you did.

After her mum left, Denise remembered a dream she'd had the night before. It was like some sort of premonition, as if it contained some immutable truth, some kernel that could be prised from the dream's shell. Spaces were contracted and oblique, events distinct but lopsided. The faces of the people in it had been opaque, their voices cartoon voices, their features cartoon features. It was like the dream of somebody else, except all dreams were like that. That was maybe why folk were always telling you about them afterwards and sounding so surprised. Denise hated dreams because the dreams were always nightmares, and she always remembered them when she woke. There was no respite. There was no rest. Ever. The absences of the day projected in Technicolor onto the backs of your eyelids. They were a sort of grief for the day, a sort of loss.

In this dream, Denise remembered leaving the swimming lesson, and a feeling of defeat, of humiliation. That wasn't so odd. Feelings of defeat and humiliation were familiar to her. So far so good. She'd remembered being forced to take part in the lesson, her usual tactic having failed her at last. Even having the Curse wasn't enough to save you sometimes. Not from dreams, anyway.

'Everyone has to take part in the Lifesavers' Test,' the teacher had said, a man she didn't know from any waking place but she recognised just the same. 'Everyone has to practise for it,' he told her. 'Even a witch like you.'

She stepped out of the baths into air that cut, air that burned like menthol throat lozenges. There were nondescript buildings looming on a horizon that was like a painted stage backdrop. Denise's plastic carrier-bag handle cut into the skin of her wrist, leaving a reddened ring mark around it, the wet hang of cloth and the chlorine smell leaking into her nostrils from the bag. The skin on her hands was shrunken white and wrinkled like a baby's and water shoogled in her ear, the noise of it crunching about like powdery snow underfoot. Denise tilted her head, trying to get it to run out in case it led to an infection or something. A disease. Her hand moved of its own volition, lifted the plastic tube of an inhaler to her mouth and squeezed it, as if she had been using one all her life. The inhaler gasped twice and tasted of aluminium on her tongue. The old jogging pants the pool attendant had lent her went creeping up at the back, and her ankles were chilly between the white expanse of sock and cuff.

Then she was sitting downstairs on a bus, away from the buzzing on the top deck, her head leaned against the misted glass window; the orange blaze of lamplight outside like a long string of fairy lights strung the length of the road. Her head nodded forward on her chest and she could feel someone sit at the outside of the seat beside her, just on the half-a-bum space left. Then – it must have been later – felt them gone again. She remembered being dozily aware of how stupid it was, how unnatural, to be falling asleep in a dream. But nothing much in a dream was ever very natural. The workings of dreams were something even her sister didn't have a right answer for.

A hard lump of noise came out of her, jerking her body upright in the seat again. She sat up, knowing somehow she had gone by one stop too many. Swaying, she stood and went over to the driver's cabin.

'Let us out at the lights, please, driver?' she said to him.

She stepped out, putting one foot down on the glittery pavement, and hung on to the pole with her carrier bag still strapped to her wrist. She jumped with the other leg, almost the same way she'd got into the swimming pool, just before. Or after, whichever the dream decided it was to be, time not seeming to be much of a concern in this projection.

Down the steps at the side, hung on. The glare of the striplights on the surface of the water; black sprawl of her skirt floating like a man'o'war, just out of reach.

She hadn't any swimsuit with her, she'd said. She'd none. She was sorry. She'd forgot it again. She was sorry.

Maybe she'd like to take a swim in her school uniform then, eh? Maybe the pool attendant would help her into the pool just as she was. How'd she like that, eh?

So she'd gone back to the changing rooms with a bin-liner of spare kit to see what there was. She was still in the shower while the rest of the class went out to the pool; she could hear the noise of the churned water and people yelling.

Something happened then before she had time to do anything about it. She didn't want to be there, she hated it; the numb routine of cold feet on cold tiles and the cold slap in the face of the shower. It took minutes for the water to warm up. She had stood in a place in the corner, holding the blistered silver pipe that ran horizontally along the walls, then vertically to each shower muzzle. She hadn't wanted to slip.

But it just happened all by itself, and her hands went down to try and catch the splashes of red. She felt her eyes wet. She was as much ashamed of the tears as of the blood. Maybe more so, because the tears screamed her weakness more than her bleeding did. They said 'I am ashamed and you have every right to despise me.' She hated the tears most of all.

She put on the too-small swimsuit and walked around in it, back and forth in the empty locker room, feeling like some sort of great big black pudding or something. She pulled at the folds of her lovehandles, pinched at them. She could feel where *she* ended and *they* began; where her ribs began and where they stopped. She clenched her stomach muscles tight and spread out her palm across her belly. All that was loose. All that was not her. None of it was her.

The locker door was open. It wasn't meant to be. Shoes and socks had fallen out onto the floor. The socks, crumpled into each other, lay in a grey puddle beside an overflowing stank. She picked them up and wrung them.

The pool attendant used the big pole to lift her school skirt out of the water, where one of the others had thrown it.

'What's it *want*? It want its *skirt*?' he said.

Denise couldn't make his face out clearly; it didn't seem to be *fixed* in any way.

The pool attendant's mouth stretched into a whitened line, his voice whining round the edges.

She was to get in there with the rest of them, he said. She didn't need her skirt to swim in, did she? She could borrow something to wear after the class. They had plenty of stuff in the bin-liner.

And she remembered thinking it was strange to have to find clothes out of other folks' rubbish. Maybe Alison felt like that when she got the clothes Denise had grown out of.

She lowered herself down the steps at the side and dropped

the last foot, springing up at the same time, not wanting the water to get up to her oxters, it was that cold. The sensation of it was so real that she doubted she was really dreaming it. She gasped and panted a bit, splashing. The shallow end was marked off with red floats. The PE teacher was up at the deep end with the good swimmers, their faces shadowy and distorted so that she knew again that it was a dream after all, that none of it was happening. That was little comfort though; the dream was in control. She stood for a minute at the side watching the phantoms at the other end of the pool. They were practising the crawl.

She took a polystyrene float from the stack at the side and held it in front of her, flapping out, chin held up rigid, and the water going up her nose so she straight away had to make it over to the side again, coughing and spluttering. She let the float drift, hanging on to the lip of the rail, face in towards the tiling. It was good there. Safe.

'Get away from the sides,' the pool attendant said. His body seemed fractured somehow, his voice too. 'Go back out there again,' he said. She had her Bronze Lifesavers' Test coming up, and she'd get nowhere at the rate she was going. She did want to get her Bronze Lifesavers' Badge, did she not?

'Yes,' Denise said, knowing it was the only answer he'd accept.

She'd have to learn how to tread water then, eh? And quick as well. It's not so easy fully clothed, you know.

They were to wear clothes for the test. Get themselves undressed in the water, as if they'd been in a shipwreck. It was all practical stuff.

Next, her feet found her back at the bus stop and walking along a road, knowing where they were going even if she didn't. Perhaps to somewhere familiar, perhaps not. They walked her around a corner, and then another corner before coming to rest at the door of a house. Denise remembered having been there before sometime. In another dream. Her hand reached into her pocket and produced a key. Her dad came to the door before she had a chance to turn the lock: she could hear him whimpering behind it. He must have been lying down behind it, 'cause he was covered in bits of fluff and hair off the carpet. His upper body and arms were wrapped tightly in cling film, so that he couldn't move his hands from his waist. The cling film was manky with the hairs and dirt. He stared out the open door at Denise, his eyes teary. Denise looked away, the sight sickening her. He turned and walked along the hallway, disappearing into another room. She followed him, the newspaper-covered carpet filthy, the smell of decay and a sweet, angry, rottenness. She knew her dad had gone straight through to his place at the kitchen table only because, like hers, his feet had led him there. Denise strained down over her bulging midriff to get the mail off the floor. Except it wasn't her bulge. It wasn't her midriff. Her body was like a rented costume for a fancy-dress party; it could be handed back when the ball was over.

She picked up the sheaf of letters, puffing at the inhaler again, this time because of the strain of bending, and went through to the kitchen.

There were three letters. She opened the brown one that looked like money and threw the other two into the waste-paper basket without opening them. She knew already that one was from her mother, and the other from Alison. The brown envelope contained a postal order, but the writing was so tiny and curly that she couldn't make it out. Perhaps in this dream, she wore reading glasses, but had lost them. Perhaps not. She knew she would have to cash it at lunchtime the next day, before the afternoon's swimming class. That would be the only chance she'd get the whole day. Her dad was sitting on a stool, staring intently at a bowl in front of him. In the bowl was something with the greying look of old tripe, and the bluish tinge of packet noodles that had been left for a day or two.

The sink was stopped up with unwashed dishes, the water

greasy with floating bits of food. The inside of the kitchen window had steamed up. The fish were still in the poke of greaseproof paper in the fridge where they must have been thawing. Golden cutlets. Her dad's favourite. His shirt was caked in dirt at the collar. There was a sort of smell off him as well, not just stale sweat but sharper, like ammonia. But the cling film seemed firm, taut. Most of the cat hairs would come off it when she changed it. She knew now that she did so every night, before putting him to bed. When she looked around the room, she noticed the body of something, over in the corner by the door. A black shape of something. Dead, obviously. Then when she looked again, it wasn't there. The dream couldn't make up its mind. It was the same with the inside of the kitchen; it seemed to warp and bend if she tried to look at it more closely.

'Coconut sponge sandwich for afters,' Denise said, feeling ravenous herself. 'Two for one in Safeway just now. You like coconut sponge sandwich, don't you?'

Her dad was quiet. He scratched the back of his neck by twisting his head vigorously from side to side, pulling it right down into his shoulders, then stared at the bowl again. He was beginning to say something: his lips made shapes.

'I don't know,' he was saying, 'I forget.' He looked up and smiled at Denise. His eyes were sparkly: he seemed about to start singing or something.

She started the tap and began to take the dishes out of the sink, piling pots onto the work top. She got her hand away down under the weight of them, feeling about for the plug, getting it, then losing the thing again. It had no chain: it had broken off long ago. Her dad never got around to fixing it. He never got around to fixing anything. Things just crumbled to bits all around: they stopped working and just never shifted themselves again, taking up more and more space, uselessly. Eventually you would be suffocated, buried alive under the weight of useless stuff.

'Here, let me get you loose,' she said, tearing away the cling film binding that pinned his arms to his sides. He stared down at his two hands as if he'd discovered they were made of gold.

She found the place where the chain had attached and started teasing the plug out with her thumb and forefinger. The water was slimy and cold.

'I'll put the heat on under the fish for you,' she said, thankful now to be free of the filth of the sink. She said it without turning round, a bit louder, her own voice being all the companionship that seemed to exist in this place, this home.

She heard the stool slide away from the table and then a grunting. He was glowering now, she knew. She could just tell. She kept her head bent over the sink and didn't look round, this cloud of ammonia waiting for her to speak, hovering at the edge of her vision. After a while, she turned round.

Her dad was squatting down on the lino, his face straining up, stink rising like a wave, the copper-coloured buckle of his belt clacking against the floor. That lino was filthy. It would have to be scrubbed thoroughly as soon as possible. Soon. Definitely. She took out the matches and lit the gas under the frying pan, moving it to the hob at the front right because of the ones at the back being too slow and also something wrong with the front left: it had been buggered for years. It had never got fixed either. It never would, now. She went to the steamed-up window and opened it full, letting the cold air in.

'Wipe my bum,' her dad said in a monotone. 'Wipe my bum . . . *please?*'

Denise nodded.

They both ate, Denise finding her mouth full of yellowy dyed fish, her hands moving back and forth to her plate, cutting pieces of the fish and pushing them into her mouth, breathing through her open mouth so as not to smell it. It was necessity. The dream controlled it, pushed and pulled her like a marionette. She inhaled deeply through her mouth between the gulps, trying to catch some air, control the desire to vomit. Eventually, it was over, and they both sat still, watching the condensation form into drips on the sagging bulges of the ceiling, stained brown and yellow in places, then fall soundlessly to the floor. Denise wondered about moving a cup under the spot where they fell most frequently, but it didn't seem to be part of the logic, so she sat and stared instead. After a while she said, 'Time to get ready for your bed now.'

'I don't want to go yet,' her dad said. 'I'm not tired yet,' he said.

'No arguments, now,' Denise said. 'Time to away up and get ready.'

'Will the people who write the letters be visiting soon?'

'Maybe tomorrow,' Denise said. 'If we're both good . . .' She paused, then added: 'Just if we're good.' Then, picking up the kitchen knife and starting to hack at the cling film, she began shushing, 'There now, shush . . . There there, everything's fine.'

But her dad struggled and yelped so much that it seemed a long time would pass before the house was quiet again.

Denise sat down at the kitchen table. She was looking at the envelope. She slipped the postal order out of it and read the figure, squinting first at the numerals and then at the type. The numbers and letters refused to corral, wouldn't regiment themselves with any kind of consistency. Just so many hieroglyphics. Just so many lines and crosses, without dice. She set the cheque to one side, flicking through a pile of old opened envelopes gripped by a big bulldog clip that hung from the hook by the dish cupboard. The one that said DAMN'D BILLS! over the upper lip. Everything seemed preordained, predicted in advance. She went through the motions, in control and helpless at the same time. She found a signed one and sat looking at the signature, then turned the brown envelope over and started to write the signature out in blue biro. The flourish was difficult. She mostly had it apart from that flourish at the end, coming off the 'n' of 'Duncan'. The 'Forrester' was easy. His was like hers.

His 'n' hers.

Plural.

It was difficult getting that 'n' right, though. She wrote it out a few times, covering the back of an envelope trying to get it because the woman in the post office would look at her funny and would ask why her father had signed it over to her and Denise would say, 'He's sick is why, he can't come in himself,' and the woman would seem happy with that, and Denise would be in a hurry and would just have to trust the woman to count it all out right. The scenes had shifted now, the backdrop changed, and now Denise was going into the baker's on the way to the bus, a couple of other school pupils passing in their uniforms, so now she would have to wait for them to get on the bus before coming out of the shop, and by the time she did that, she knew the bus would be away anyway and she'd have to wait for another, so she would gulp down the things she'd bought, the food, gagging at the awfulness of it, unable to help herself, the taste and texture of the mince pie and the bridie repulsive to her, making her want to spew it. Now walking fast towards the stop, knowing that it made no difference, it was all happening without her and she'd be late for swimming and that was that. And she'd have the pie grease stuck down the side of her arm and in the water she would feel the numbness of her brow where she was bound to crack it off the bottom of the pool, cramp doubling her, weight of food making her sag, not being able to tread the water any longer, head coming up and then going under again, mouth open and froth sprayed away by her struggles. Tasting the chlorinated water, washing the food down with it in great gulps. Bitten-down nails not able to untie the knot that ran round a belly that didn't belong to her, a drawstring for pyjama pants that didn't belong to her. These were not her clothes; this was not her dream. The weight of this dream-body dragging her under, sting of this dream-water in her eyes and her mouth. Swallowing when she sank under again, retching when she came up. There was panic in control of her and a noose around her that refused to give and then panic coming hard inside her, wanting out. There was shouting and cheering and the big hooped pole slashing out towards her, cutting the surface of the water, stretching out for her, cupping her in its open palm, the metal biting under her oxters. It dragged her backwards and wrongways-up through the water, ducking her so that she sucked in fitfuls of chlorinated water. And she wanted her inhaler and her clothes. She wanted them to let her go home, except she'd no idea where that was. She wanted out of this but she'd no idea how. She went under again and it was the panic itself that tried to drag her up, but there was no

out of this

no exit

her breath coming unstoppable –

let go the knot and stop kicking.

AREYOUDEADDENISE

There'd be no question about it. They'd lug her weight out the shallow end of the pool with the big hooped pole, pyjama pants choked tight round her belly by a drawstring noose, face already turning blue from grey. They'd slap her sunnyside up onto the flatness of the tiling, solid and unmoving. And the tiles would still be dry except where she had spread out; the blood welling first rich and dark from between her legs, then scarlet; leaking over into the pool and clouding pink, finally dissolving into nothing. The sight of her tangled hair would repulse any onlookers, even though they were only dream-onlookers. Just the same as always. Black and shiny. Plastered indecently to her lumpy brow. It would've caused even Denise to look away if she could. The rest of her was just like a lot of sodden pillows looped together. And they'd all have loved it, those people watching – John Burke, Andy McCabe. Her sister. Even Jeedy. Even her mum. How else could you tell a witch if not by ducking?

The pool attendant would bend over, hands on her chest, pumping at it and wheezing in between his words:

Is that swimming? Is it? You'll not get away so easy as that next time. See if you dare. Just see if you dare . . .

The noise of words would lessen slowly in the big hall, surgical in its tubelit brightness. The pool attendant would continue to pump. Finally, a gout of water would come pulsing from her throat, another premonition, another prediction.

'That, I believe, Miss Forrester,' he'd say between her retches, 'is a fail. A very comprehensive fail.'

And Denise would nod, because that fail would be a kind of victory. After all, nobody could seriously expect her to take another swimming lesson again. Not after this. Could they?

This dream had frightened her so much that when she woke up, she'd lain awake trying not to fall asleep again in case she slipped back into it, in case it replayed somehow, or she entered it again at some different scene, some other corner of it that hadn't been fully explored, and the whole thing repeated in some new and terrifying way. When it got lighter outside her curtains, in a real world she couldn't be sure wasn't there just to trick her once more, she braved first the touch of her feet on the carpet; and feeling it solid and ungiving, stood up so that she could brave next the vertical. There was a bit of give to it, but it seemed nothing out the ordinary. She relaxed her shoulders, took a deep breath and walked out towards her bedroom door, half expecting it to dissolve, or burst into flames. When it didn't she opened it and walked to the stairs, climbed down them and went through the hall to the kitchen. The lino lay in comforting rectangles, the cupboard units greeted her with a glad regularity of form. There were no obliquenesses in their design, no bulges or strains where there shouldn't be. She walked over to the fridge and opened it, staring calmly at the contents. Blocks of cheese, opened packet of bacon, box of eggs. And there, on the second bottom shelf, above the drawer where her mum kept the fruit and veg, a fold of greaseproof paper, a yellowy fillet of something dead keeking out from between its leaves. She knew it.

Golden cutlets.

In a way, it was a relief to see them. They were the doorway to the dream, the anchor to it. They, the kitchen, the outside door, were where the two worlds linked up. So there was an element of control to be had. If you could just work out how it could be done, how to control these day-world things, then dreams shouldn't be a problem any more. The workings would give you a correct answer.

Except Denise wasn't any good at sums. When she was sleeping, she would go on being just so much dead weight. So she might as well go back to bed and try to enjoy the ride. To be honest, she was absolutely knackered. She decided to go back up, then changed her mind and put a couple of slices of toast on under the grill. She was famished as well. It was only when she sat down on the couch that she noticed her stomach was still the dream stomach. She felt it growl as the chewed toast descended into it, felt it groan its objection, then there was something else and she was struggling against spasms of pain and then, there it was, something coming out from underneath her nightdress, she was giving birth to something right there and then on the kitchen floor. She looked down at the floor, at the linoleum squares, and saw two doughnuts. Perfect, uneaten sugared doughnuts. One beside the other. And it was this birth that disturbed Denise more than anything else in the dream. Not her dad reduced to idiocy; not the house that was no longer a home; not the drowning in the pool. Not the kid-on reality she'd been tricked into believing. All those things could be explained somehow. All of those had followed some kind of mad rules of their own. But this was too much. These doughnuts were a dream too far.

Denise was the oldest daughter, but was in the middle anyway. In the middle between her dad and her mum, in the middle between her sister and her dad, in the middle between her dead granny and her mum. The only person she wasn't in the middle with was Jeedy. She wasn't sure what he was in the middle of. He was just like some stray cat, wandering the streets, never going to classes, never making friends with anyone. But he'd let Denise get closer than most, close enough that they'd soon stain the old mattress by the railway lines together, the bond between them one of confusion, desire and shared body fluids that would be broken almost as soon as it was formed.

Two years it took her. Two years of hanging around places she knew he'd have to pass sooner or later; two years of loitering with intent. His face was like something carved out of mahogany and his teeth shone like his eyes.

He was beautiful. The way his hands were that pale pinkish-brown colour on the palms, and his skin so black. Really black.

'Nice tan you've got yourself!' her dad said, grinning away like he thought he was funny, the one time she brought Jeedy to the house, *him* with his whisky glass already in his hand and his uniform still on. He looked done in, just after his shift. He had some woman with him. It was three o'clock in the afternoon.

'Yeh, Mr F,' Jeedy said. 'Nice one . . .'

You could see her dad didn't really like Jeedy calling him Mr F. His face had taken on this expression.

'Been using some of that Grecian 2000 suncream of yours in the bog. Brilliant, eh? Doesn't seem to be taking too well on yourself, though,' Jeedy said.

Denise's dad ignored that, but his hand flicked over his remaining hair for a second before he pulled it away again.

'How're yous not in school the day?' he said, surly.

'Free period,' Denise said, dragging Jeedy by the elbow.

'Free period?' her said said. He sounded like he had forgotten what they were talking about already, the woman on the couch reaching over into the open box of fags on the coffee table and taking one out. She was holding it in between her lips, a Bic lighter poised in front of it.

'You on your dabs?' her dad said, him and the woman cracking up with laughter, hers turning to a hoarse wheeze.

Denise flushed beetroot. 'Ha ha,' she said, pushing past the couch with Jeedy trailing behind.

'Hold on a minute there,' her dad said. 'This is my house – and a state it is as well. If you've got a free period for us at home, you can get into that kitchen and get it cleaned up.'

Denise was about ready to scream.

'I cleaned everything this morning,' she said. 'Before you even got back.'

'Never mind that, just do what you're told or I'll—'

He'd what? Throw her out? But the words were just echoing round the inside of her head: *Go on then. You got rid of my mum, you can get rid of me as well. Then there'll just be Alison. You can look after her.* Two down and one to go. *He* could clean her clothes and get her up for school.

'Wait a minute there,' he was saying, beginning to stand up and tower over the coffee table towards her, his glass still in his hand, and the woman pulling her chunky legs out of the road. Jeedy stood between him and Denise.

'Out the road, you,' he said, elbowing past. 'Away climb a tree or something.'

'Right, Mr F,' Jeedy said. 'Calm down.'

'Mr Eff? I'll Mr Effin-Eff you in a minute, my lad! I'll give you Mr F. I mind you when your mother was still around. I mind you and they brothers of yours. Think I don't? I know all about you and your brothers.'

Jeedy was backing away a bit, squaring his shoulders in a way Denise had seen his brothers do, making himself seem bigger in the process. The two of them stared at each other, Denise pulling at Jeedy's arm, trying to tug him round the back of the couch towards the front door.

'Come on,' she said. 'Let's get out of here.'

'Nah, man,' he said, straightening up, eyes and words directed at her dad. 'That's my family, man. You don't know anything about my mum.'

'Just ignore him,' said Denise. 'He's just trying to wind you up. Ignore him.'

'Never mind "ignore him",' her dad snapped. 'I'm the one that'll do the ignoring round here. This is my house.'

'Pretty quiet house now, man.'

Her dad's eyes bored holes through Jeedy. But he wouldn't lower his own. 'What was that he says to me?' he said to Denise, jerking a thumb in Jeedy's direction.

'Nothing – leave it, Jeedy—'

'I was just saying it was quiet.' Jeedy scratched the back of his head and looked about, as if Denise's dad wasn't standing in front of him.

'What does that mean?'

'Nothing, man,' Jeedy said, shrugging. 'Just that it's quiet. It's a quiet house. Not a lot of noise.'

'Jeedy—'

'You think I don't know what you're up to, is that it?'

'I'm not up to anything.'

'You think I don't know what your game is? Think I don't know what you're trying to infer?'

'I ain't got any inference, Mr F. Honest, man. I'm just here with Denise. I wasn't trying to imply nothing.'

'Aye you were. You were implying. And insinuating as well. I know your game, think that I don't? I know it well enough. So I do.'

Jeedy seemed momentarily lost, as if stuck somewhere between innuendo and implication. He wasn't meaning to implicate, he said. Far from it.

'Aye well,' her dad said. 'Should be in school the day.'

'I told you, we've no classes,' Denise added, wanting to get off the subject.

'No classes, that will be right. The state of the place. A midden, in'tit, June?'

The woman on the couch grinned and shrugged her shoulders, half-smoked fag jammed between two fingers, eyes blank like she'd not been paying attention.

'How're your brothers getting on there, anyway? Haven't seen them in a while . . .'

Jeedy shrugged. 'Ain't seen them myself.'

'Keeping out of trouble, are they?'

Jeedy shrugged.

'And you? You keeping out of trouble as well? Haven't had to knock on your door for a while.'

'I've not been in trouble. I ain't ever been in trouble . . .'

'So what was that business with the car, then? Or does that not qualify?'

'I told you already, that wasn't us.'

'Leave him alone, Dad,' Denise said. She didn't know what her dad was on about. He had gone nuts or something. Totally mad. And that woman just sitting there on her mum's couch. Smoking as well.

'What d'you mean, Mr F?'

'Never mind with the Mr F. You know what I mean.'

'That wasn't me.'

'No?'

'No.'

'Who's "us" then?'

'I don't know what you're talking about.'

'If it wasn't you, then who was it?'

'Who was what?'

'The car business.'

'What car business?' Denise wanted to know. It was like her dad was testing Jeedy and Jeedy was seeing what he could get away with.

'I had nothing to do with any car business.'

'Someone did. If it wasn't you, then who was it? Your brothers? Put you up to it, did they?'

'I had nothing to do with any car.'

Jeedy looked up at Denise's dad; something flashed behind his eyes, briefly, and was gone again. Something like fear, guilt.

Jeedy stared at him, his shoulders not so square on.

'You see what it is I'm implying, son? You following my inferences all right?'

Jeedy said nothing.

Denise's dad placed his glass on the coffee table, folding his arms across his chest. It was like he had got bigger, straighter, just by doing that. Denise could see the muscle working in his jaw, a knot of sinew that made him seem so much less a man made out of wooden clothes pegs and more like real flesh and blood. Jeedy's hand went to his head, hovered there, rubbed at his eyes.

'I was just talking about what you were talking about. You asked me.'

'Aye, son, but what I was asking you about was that "car business". And you told me you'd done nothing, that you'd no idea what I was talking about. But here you are signifying to me that you did know something. You follow?'

'I never about meant to signify anything. I didn't implicate anything.'

'Well if you didn't then there's nothing to worry about, is there, son?'

Jeedy's eyes went from his feet to Denise's dad then back again. 'Nah, man . . . I mean, aye . . .'

Denise stepped in: 'Leave him alone! You can't ask him things like that . . .'

Her dad stared at her.

'Ask him things like what, eh? I'm just asking a couple of routine questions here, Denise. About his brothers – just showing a bit of concern. That's all. That not right, June?'

He glanced over his shoulder at the woman on the couch. She seemed to be asleep, mouth open and fag still burning in her hand.

Denise wanted to take the fag out from between her fingers and put it out on the woman's tongue. She'd no right being there in the house. Her mum had only been gone a month or – how long had it been?

'Come on, Jeedy,' she said. 'We'll go to my room.'

'Wait a minute,' her dad said. 'What are yous planning on doing up there, eh? What is it you can do up there that you can't do here?'

Denise flushed beetroot again. Her dad had been making her turn that colour her whole life. But it was worse now her mum was gone. There was one less person to hide behind. She was directly in the firing line.

'*Nothing!*' she said.

'Well you can do *nothing* down here, can you not?'

The woman started awake and looked about like she'd no idea where she was.

Denise felt something inside her, trying to get to the surface, a rage that she wanted to spit in her dad's face, watch his skin wither under it. Instead she made her fists into balls, clenching them tight. She'd no idea why she'd brought Jeedy here. It was stupid. The place wasn't a home any more. It was just the place she lodged at. They were all lodgers here now. Even that woman – June – even she didn't seem all that much out of place. It was as if she had as much right to be there as Denise. She tugged Jeedy round the other side of the couch, towards the door.

'Leaving so suddenly?' her dad said, laughing. The woman laughed too, but you could tell she didn't really know what she was laughing at. Denise ignored them, concentrating on getting the front door open.

'Mind and not do anything I wouldn't!' her dad shouted after them. Denise saw him wink at the woman, pictured him moving closer, her leaning back on the couch, then pushed the picture out of her head, a series of unwanted images slotting in to replace it: Denise and Alison playing in the back lane behind the house – together for once – a game Alison had invented. Throwing a ball at the garage door; early-evening sunlight recoiling from the windows of the back room to blind them as the ball doinked towards the sliding metal door followed by a dull clang; one ball arcing off at an angle; Denise turning her back to it so that it wouldn't hit her in the face; the ball bouncing off her and going over into the garden; Denise going to get it and pausing by the window. There had been funny noises coming from the room; she'd been able to hear them even through the window. Rhythmic, forbidden noises. She stood on tiptoe and cupped her hands against the glass to see inside. A figure on the couch, eyes closed and head thrown back; her hand inside her knickers, skirt pulled up part of the way around her waist, the seam of her tights splitting her pants in the middle as if it had been pencilled there with a magic marker. She flushed and turned away, picking up the tennis ball, and started walking quickly back down the garden path, before Alison followed her up wanting to know what was keeping her so long.

Now she was living these pictures over and over again

in her head; her dad stood over the woman on the couch, unbuckling his belt; her mum's face superimposed on the woman's body; the look on her dad's face; the ball puttering to a stop at the back window; her mum's head thrown back as if asleep, a cigarette burning between the fingers of one hand, the other inside her pants; her dad's face; sunlight deflected into her own eyes from the back windows; the black seam of the tights.

She felt Jeedy take her hand in his.

Again, she felt herself flushing, could feel her ears and forehead begin to burn. The bane of her life.

'What's the matter?' he said. 'It wasn't your fault.'

She looked up at him. How had he known?

'I mean that car business – you weren't to know about that.'

Denise had nothing to say. She would have said sorry but it wasn't her that should be apologising. She should have known, though. She should have known that her dad was never off-duty. He was a full-time pig. Their mum had been right to go. She had put up with it for years and years. Denise hadn't understood until the pictures had come back. Her mum doing that. Them having separate beds and everything. It was like it would have been okay to have seen her doing it if he'd been there as well. Doing it to her. Like he was probably doing it – and worse – to that woman.

She let her hand find Jeedy's again, scared he wouldn't let her take it now, worried he'd be embarrassed. Her palm found his and they fitted, them both walking along for a bit not saying anything. That was one of the best things about being with him. It was like you could exist side by side and not have to know everything. You could wait and it would come out eventually anyway. Denise wanted Jeedy slowly, bit by bit, not all at once. Just this now was enough; he'd never done it before. Taken her hand. He'd never done anything before. But taking her hand was enough for now. She would have him all eventually.

At sixteen, Denise decided she'd have him a bit at a time. Soon enough, on an old mattress by the railway lines, hidden by bushes.

They crossed over onto the other side of the street, not bothering to wait for the lights.

Denise felt a mad something every time she had a class to go to that she knew Jeedy was meant to be in. She would be saying to herself:

Please let him be there. Please God.

It was the first thing she had ever asked Him for. She was ashamed, but she did it anyway. Denise Forrester, that had never needed anybody.

Instead, there were remedial classes with Andy McCabe and Rajan Sood, and old Dode taking the class. The blackboard was scarred with hieroglyphics, but nobody was paying attention. It was always a riot in there.

Andy McCabe was going round the class waving the window pole about, kidding on he was Bruce Lee or somebody. Diane McCarthy and Lorraine Shaw sat, Lorraine plaiting Diane's hair. Some of the boys were arm wrestling at the back and the rest were throwing rubbers and pencils onto the floor then trying to look up Lorraine's skirts when they went to pick them up.

'Get OFF!' she kept shouting, slapping their hands away, but they wouldn't stop.

Nobody bothered trying to look up Diane's skirt. Denise sort of felt sorry for her. She wanted someone to try and look up Diane's skirt just once, just to be fair.

'You boys there! You will NUT behave in this fashion in my class!' Dode was shouting, cheeks flushed and his glasses looking a bit steamy: 'You will NUT!'

Andy McCabe sat down in the next desk from Rajan Sood. He kept flicking his fingers at Rajan's eyes.

'You will NUT,' he was saying to him. 'You WILL. You will NUT. You WILL. You will NUT.'

Flick . . . flick . . . flick . . . flick . . .

Rajan blinked and slapped Andy's fingers away every time he flicked them at him.

'Get OFF!' Lorraine was shouting, a whine coming into her voice.

Flick . . . flick . . . flick . . . flick . . .

Dode paced up and down the front of the classroom, chalk in one hand and a duster in the other, his face a mask of useless rage.

'SILENCE!' he shouted. The mayhem continued.

His real name was Mr Gravesend, but it was as if he wasn't part of the normal school. He took the remedial. It was outside the normal rules of things. You just did what you liked, he couldn't stop you, he was that old and doddery. He was supposed to have been a war hero once upon a time. Denise reckoned that was just a story though. How could old Dode have ever been young? It was impossible. His head sat on top of his shoulders without any neck between, as if it had been rolled up there like a big rock to nestle back in a groove that someone had to hollow out especially. His eyes were greyed, as if he was staring at you through tepid dish-water; he wore tweed jackets with elbow patches on them and brogues polished so's you could have seen your face in them.

'Or lOOk uP lassIEs' skIrTS Wi thUm!' Andy McCabe said, then slapped Rajan over the back of the head. Rajan braced himself under the blow but didn't bother looking up from his jotter. He was used to it. Denise saw the shadow of Dode through the papery membranes attached to the sides of Rajan's head.

Dode kept his white hair clipped short and neat but his

shirts hung out at the front. The buttons were all attached to the wrong holes, buttoned right up to the collars which were always pure manky. There were reddish-brown splotches on them; shaving cuts, or maybe bleeding from the eczema which crept over the backs of his hands the same way the black ink from John's pen did Denise's. Sometimes Dode came in with bits of tissue stuck to his chin or neck, fastened there by a single blot of red at their centre where it would stay until someone told him about it:

'Mister Gravesend! You've got a bit of bum-paper stuck to your face!'

And then the class would erupt all over again.

Dode's face curled up in an ineffectual grimace; he would storm up and down the front of the class looking for a victim.

'Shut UP! Shut UP!'

And he had this mannerism. He would go over to his briefcase, this chalky old leather thing, which he would open and rummage about inside as if he was looking for something: a strap maybe. Or a gun. But they'd taken the strap away from him, there was no more belting allowed. Corporal Punishment dishonourably dismissed. But Mr Gravesend still did this – went over to the briefcase and dug about in there looking, always looking for something that wasn't there any more, that he didn't have any more, the thing that once lost could never be got back again.

What could Dode have done against a whole rammy of sixteen-year-olds about ready to join the dole queue, as soon as it would have them? Andy McCabe was just one. One you could have cowed. One you could have taught a lesson to. Showed the working to. But a whole class? And then another class and then another class? There was no chance. You were doomed. Dode was doomed.

Denise reckoned Mr Gravesend knew that as well as anyone. He was just trying to get through it all, just till the end of the day. Denise had seen him often, walking to the bus stop – carrying a bag of messages. His whole body looked defeated. Shrunken. He seemed not to see anybody.

It was sad.

Denise tried to picture another life for him. Off he would go, get on his bus and then hop off at some cottage somewhere on the outskirts of the city, maybe even further. Folk would nod and smile at him as he got off, the driver would say cheerio. He would stop in at the post office for a blether with old missus whatsername and pick up a packet of chocolate biscuits – he'd forgotten them on the way back. Honestly, he was getting to be so absent-minded these days. Missus whatsername would ask how his wife was and he'd say fine, fine, and he would ask how mister whatsisname was and she would say fine, fine and then they'd both say, fine, well, see you tomorrow and out the shop he'd go, raising his bunnet to her, chimes ringing in the door as he left. He'd take a wander up the road and stop at the hotel – he lived in the country now, maybe out near Campsie Glen or Killearn or somewhere – and in he'd go to have his usual half of Guinness and sit and read the paper while the sun streamed in through the windows in sheets, spotlighting on the cocker spaniel asleep by the brass foot-railing, his paws jerking a bit as he dreamed of chasing rabbits and hares.

It was too much.

No. None of that would happen. None of that had ever happened. It was like Polywka all over again. Dode and the Hammer-man. He would stay here, and be punished, for ever.

Mr Gravesend was a decorated man. Had been dropped behind enemy lines hanging onto the sky with a camouflaged hankie tied up with string. Something had happened to him there. Maybe he had landed on his head.

All the war heroes together.

Denise let John tattoo her hands with black and blue biros,

every day a new drawing. That was when she'd first got the idea for getting her lip done. John was older than Denise. He had been put back a year. Now they were the same age. John said that if he didn't at least try this year, he was going to get booted out.

Him being the same age but older made him seem sort of nice too. He normally wasn't very attractive. On the outside.

One Monday, the tattoo was of a goldfish, eyes bulbous and straining; the next week a crocodile extending down her forearm, each scale drawn in and overlapping the next so that it took the full ninety minutes of remedial French class and some of the break to complete. Denise liked John doing that; he was dead gentle, the ball of the pen dragging slightly on her skin, the look of concentration behind the milk-bottle specs. She wasn't allowed to move. She wasn't allowed to say anything. It was only 'cause of having Dode that they could do it in class. He was totally useless.

A goldfish, a crocodile, a black cat.

Denise only let him do it 'cause John was in the remedial for French as well as arithmetic. That was the only reason. It meant someone to talk to, though Denise never said a lot. It meant, too, that John could afford to extend his repertoire, allow his designs to become more elaborate, let them breathe on their own and take over. Come to life. It was weird watching him do it, weird watching him concentrate. It was hard to sit in total silence, though. The drawing was nice, it felt nice on your skin, but it was uncomfortable too. It was like you were being decorated like a Christmas tree or something. A wall. Curves and angles and straight lines. Graffiti. Denise could have let him draw all day, let him scrawl every inch of her skin, let him write what words onto her that he liked.

The pictures were sort of cartoons.

'How do you not just do art, then?' Denise asked him.

'Why do they call you "witch"?'

Denise went red again.

'I asked you first.'

'I asked you second.'

'They don't call me "witch" any more.'

'They do.'

'They call me "shag",' Denise said, feeling the strangeness of this assertion, defining herself in this way: '*Denise Forrester is a shag* is what they say about me.'

And Denise liked it, could picture the words scratched into the surfaces of desks, carved into tree bark, scraped into still-wet concrete, indelibly. Words stilled and made true by permanence. The thought of it thrilled her.

'You wish. They call you "witch",' John said, taking his pen away from the back of her hand. 'They think you're weird.'

'Don't stop drawing. Do you think I'm weird?'

He looked up at her quickly from behind his thick frames, then back down, his pen resuming its place on the back of her hand.

'Do you?'

'I think you're . . . different.'

'Huh! Big deal. That's just another word for weird. That's what folk always say when they think you're weird. They say: "Oh, she's *different*." They say: "Oh, he's *different*." It just means weird.'

'It's good to be different, though.'

'It isn't good to be weird.'

'Why not? *Vive la différence*,' John said, grinning.

'SILENCE!' Dode was shouting.

Denise lowered her head, letting her hair fall around her brow.

'Is that why you like Jeedy?' John asked after a minute. He kept his eyes on the back of her hand, still holding it.

'Mmm,' Denise said. 'He's . . . *weird*,' she said, giggling.

John smiled.

'He's a nigger!' Andy McCabe said, sliding onto the desk

opposite John. 'How's it going, Denise – still into your witchy ways?'

'Fuck off. If Jeedy heard you say that you'd be in trouble,' Denise said. She dropped her eyes again.

'Aye, right. I'd kick his baldy fanny from here to George's Cross. That not right, eh Burke? Eh?'

'You wish,' Denise said.

'Think Jeedy gives a fuck about you, Denise?' Andy was saying. 'Does he fuck, man. Only this weirdo here gives a fuck about you.'

He skited John over the back of the head, so that his glasses slipped down over his nose. He corrected them again with his forefinger.

John was saying, 'You all right, Denise?'

'She's away with it,' Andy McCabe said. 'Lost the plot, so she has.'

Her period was about to start.

John looked about, scratching his hair and playing with his specs. He was saying nothing.

'What's that you've got on your hand?' Andy asked.

'Nothing. Never you mind.' Denise covered the back of her hand with the other palm.

'Let us see it, eh?'

'Leave her alone, Andy,' John said.

'You can get to fuck, Burke. What is it, Denise?'

'Leave her alone, I said.'

'Some witchy shite is it, eh Denise?'

'I said: leave her alone.' John's cheeks were red now too.

'You going to make me?'

'Maybe.'

'Aye, right. Maybes aye, maybes naw and maybes maybe. Wouldn't waste my time. A fart would blow you away.'

'And you're the fart to do it, are you?' John said, but he didn't look up.

Denise could tell he was scared. She liked him for it, but it was no use kidding on. She'd seen him fight before. He was totally rubbish. Andy was getting up and skiting his hand over the back of John's nut again so that he jerked his head down into his shoulders like a tortoise. Andy went back to his seat behind Rajan Sood, thumped him on the head again, turned and winked at Denise and John: 'Meeting your sister the night, Denise!' he shouted over the noise. 'Maybe give her some hot love action!'

She pictured John turning and sticking his biro into Andy McCabe's heart, and him slumping back, dead. His eyes look clear, at peace, staring into a gentler eternity.

But of course that's not the way it finally does happen, when Andy's throat wheezes out air, it sounds exactly the same as the air that wheezes from the spacehopper that Denise stabbed with a breadknife when she was four years old,

    a distorted

     hissing

       ss . . . ss . . . spl . . spl . . plut.t.t.rr..r.r.r

. . . the real sound of panic and death shaking hands . . . the real sound of a butchered spacehopper.

That was the last time she was getting one of those things from Santa! her Granny *La*mont/La*mont* had said. 'Waste of time, Denise, so you are. What did you want to do that for, Denise?' Granny *La*mont/La*mont* asked her. 'What harm had the spacehopper ever done to you?'

It had wanted to kill her. It came closer in the dark. It was going to eat her.

They had put the spacehopper in the room at night, after Christmas Day was finished.

'Away and not be daft, Denise, how could it want to kill you? It was only a bit of rubber. How could a bit of rubber have hurt you?'

But she had lain there, in her bed, still, and its plastic grin had come sniffing after her, the gap at the door where the hall light came in throwing sudden brightness onto its leering face.

The bed held onto her. Its magic-marker grin moved closer and the lights went off in the hall.

A long while passed before she could move again, seconds that stuck together, lumped, just would not move. Then – all it took was for her just to break the grip fear had on her – she jumped up out of the bed and away and was fumbling in the kitchen drawer. The breadknife in her hand, then in the spacehopper and it was wheezing for breath, the look on its face unchanging.

Denise felt herself calm down again, her heart had stopped thumping like mad.

'Keep drawing,' she said to John. 'Please . . .'

John took up his pen and began to draw again. Denise shut her eyes and imagined the lines being engraved on her. 'Why don't you do proper art?' she said.

'I do do proper art. I'm doing it now.'

'No, I mean *real* art.'

'That's what the teachers say as well.'

'That your drawing's not real?'

'That I have to do other stuff first, before I do my own stuff.'

'Why?'

'Don't know. To make me better at what they want to see.'

'What do they want to see?'

'Don't move.'

'Sorry.'

'It'd be all right if it was more life-drawing or something.'

'To practise drawing people?'

'Yeh.'

'They don't do that stuff?'

'Not much. But that's only part of it. You couldn't draw something like this' – he pointed to the back of her hand with the biro. Something was taking shape.

'That's 'cause that's not real art.'

'How d'you know that?'

'Well . . .'

'It's not even finished yet.'

'But you always draw a cartoon.'

'But why's that not real art as well?'

' 'Cause it's not real life.'

'It's real life inside *here*,' John said, tapping the side of his head with his forefinger, the biro jutting out between that and his thumb like a plastic aerial.

'You pair! Turn round and face the blackboard!' Dode shouted.

John half turned round then turned back. Denise said nothing, but slid her hand back over to where he could start to draw again.

'Can you see it yet?' John was asking.

A black shape had begun to snake itself around her wrist; she couldn't make out what it was yet, tiny slashes of black ink criss-crossed the ridges of her hand, incorporating veins and arteries, growing into something the way Denise was growing into something. Was it Jeedy's face she could see in there, or something else?

It was like John Burke was the only person in the class that was doing any work.

She could see it now; a black cat, the tail coiling round her wrist. Of course, a black cat.

'Good luck, they are,' John said.

'That's if it crosses your path,' Denise went.

John shrugged. 'Black cats, white cats. Does it make any difference? It's all cat luck, isn't it?'

'SILENCE!' Dode was shouting. Denise turned round, then turned back again.

John was intent on the cat, their eyes were locked together, excluding everything else. It would have been a shame to disturb him, bring him back to earth. It was a beautiful kind of exclusion; *his* exclusion. Nobody else's. Just his. Except that

Denise was there with him too, licking the cream from the top of it, saying: *Mine!*

Why not? it was her hand. *She* was the canvas.

Andy McCabe was tormenting Rajan; the boys in the back corner were trying to feel up Lorraine Shaw and ignoring Diane McCarthy, while Lorraine Shaw tried to ignore them and Diane kidded on that she wouldn't like a bit of the attention too; Mr Gravesend was stamping up and down in front of the blackboard looking sad and old.

Denise Forrester and John Burke were better off where they were, excluded together at the back of the class.

She looked at John: the top of his head, bending over her hand, the thick lenses of his glasses. She was feeling something, she didn't know what – an affinity maybe. Or maybe not. His specs were *really* thick. An infinity, then.

'I'd like to get a tattoo,' she said suddenly.

John grunted.

'Want to know where I would get it?' She cocked her head at him; she wanted to tell him this. She wanted him to know.

He looked up: 'Where?' he said.

Denise put her finger to the indent beneath her bottom lip.

'On your chin?'

'Not on my chin! On my lip.'

He looked confused. 'Then everyone would see it all the time,' he said.

'They wouldn't,' Denise said. She tugged her lip back revealing her pointy little incisors: 'On the *inside*,' she said.

She let her lip curl back and sat, looking down at the black cat curling round her wrist.

John stared. 'What would it be?' he said after a bit.

'A word.'

'A word?'

She nodded.

'What word?'

She looked at him, staring past the milkiness of his lenses, trying to make a connection somewhere behind.

'Truth.'

John sat up in his seat. He looked like a big glove puppet, someone's hand working him from the inside, controlling his movements.

'Yeh,' he said. 'Truth . . . I like that.' He was smiling.

Denise smiled too, but then the blushes started to come on again. She couldn't hang on now. She put up her hand.

'What're you doing?' John said.

I have to go to the bathroom,' she said. 'Women's things.'

'Oh.'

Mr Gravesend looked over at her and nodded an unspoken, 'Yes,' and Denise nodded an unspoken 'Thanks, Mr Gravesend.'

As the classroom door creaked behind her, she heard Andy McCabe shout out: 'AyE! iT'S hER bAD wEek!'

And she felt herself wanting to scream, but she couldn't let the words out, not here, not in the school, not while there were teachers about. She pictured blood, spilling out of her onto the floor, and wondered why it was that she had to suffer. She hated this. Even the word for it was horrible. It spelt out her imprisonment, made her a martyr to it: *period*. It equalled unmoving hours in Dode's class. And she hadn't even asked for it. It was a *free* period.

If she could paint or draw as good as John Burke, she would sterilise this bleeding, render it lifeless on white canvas, scar paper for ever with her own blood. There was the hot flush; this sensation of the blood rising inside her, the blood spilling out of her insides, the blood soaking through her knickers and skirt, oozing out of the pores of her skin, soaking her school blouse, the palms of her hands cupping it. Blood spilling out of her onto her jotters, into her schoolbag, or running from her forehead. The dark scores on the back of her hand etching themselves in blood.

All of this she'd put on the canvas, leave it there, ugly words spelt in red and trapped inside white geometry:

Period.

Menstruation.

Puberty.

Denise felt the maddening inevitability of her biology and wanted to scream. It wasn't for her, this growing up. No. Not yet.

She was sitting in the silence of the toilet cubicle, her pants rolled around her knees. They weren't the knees of a woman, she decided. They were dead bony, and she had a scab on one of them. She wondered where she'd got it. There was stuff written on the back of the toilet door, slogans and things. One of them said:

UP YOUR HOLE WITH A BIG JAM ROLL

She sat for a minute, then took a marker pen out of her pocket. On the door, she wrote the words:

Denise F Luvs Jeedy
If Destroyed, True

and drew a heart shape around it, with an arrow stuck through it. A feeling of relief washed over her. She capped the pen and put it back in her blazer pocket. Someone else could take the responsibility. She wasn't old enough. They could decide what happened for her. All it would take would be a wipe with a cloth . . .

Let the canvas be martyred. Let Denise be spared.

Denise minded how the flea-circus man had told her he'd long since parted company with his brains, that the washing machine had stole his right hand off him, and that if you listened up close, you could hear the echo inside his nut when he tapped it with his hook. He always sang the same song, sometimes breaking into a whistle when he forgot the rest of the words.

O, bury me beneath the willow . . .
Underneath the willow tree . . .

He had a funny, cracked voice, like the sound of a car starting in too-cold weather. A sort of revving. He smoked packets of Capstan Shanty, or sometimes Woodbines. She loved the smell of them while they still sat unsmoked in the box. When they were lit, they were horrible. She was scared of the flea-circus man, but wanted to hear the echo.

He bent over, and let her put her ear to his head. She held her breath.

Her dad had snorted aloud when he'd said it, but Denise wanted to listen. She was wondering if it would be like when you listened to a seashell, if you would maybe be able to hear the waves. The flea-circus man tapped his hook against the side of his head, and the sound of it donked through to her.

'Like that, eh? There's no brains in there to get in the way.'

He did it again for her, once, then another time.

It was a good noise. It made you think of caves.

The flea-circus man had all these splashed bits of paint on his clothes, white mostly, but there were other colours too. He told her that he wasn't really a painter, that he had a flea circus. He kept it in his pocket, so's he could keep an eye on the fleas, make sure they weren't slacking. They had a lot of tricks to learn.

Denise looked up at him with a kind of awe. Her own head was so jam-packed with stuff she'd never be able to get any sound out of it. Her dad laughed, sitting on the dustsheet-covered couch, then raised his can of Tennents to the man.

The whole room was covered with sheets, redecoration stripping the skin from the insides of the house. Wallpaper hung in great peeling flaps, layer after layer of it, the covered floor a mosaic of woodchip and broken off bits of plaster. The sun was going down outside the window of the living room, and big swathes of light cast shadows in the corners so that the sheet-covered chairs and tables edged slowly round the walls, as if they were making for the door. Denise's dad and the flea-circus man cracked away to each other, told each other jokes and things she didn't understand. She was sure some of the things were about her.

'Listen,' the flea-circus man said, his big empty head staring down at her like a mouldy loaf from a shelf. 'These are special fleas.'

He held the matchbox up and shook it, but Denise was thinking about the hole in his head where his brains were meant to go, the sound of the donking, and how the washing machine had managed to steal his hand.

He winked at her, made the claws of the hook open and shut like those machines she'd seen at the seaside, the ones that had an arm you were meant to pick up a prize with, except the prizes always fell and you never won anything.

Her dad said, 'Fancy having something like that creeping up on you, eh?' but she ignored him, her mum through in the kitchen clattering the walls, the sound of Alison outside, the whap of her swingball, the hum of passing cars crowding in on her so's she had to try hard to concentrate.

'This old thing?' the flea-circus man said. 'Best thing that ever happened to me, this. A great thing for the ladies, it is. Is that not right, miss?'

His laugh vroomed out at her, her dad joining in.

'Aye, a great thing – they all want to know how this old duffer managed to acquire it, don't they? Want to hear the story. There's not much to it. Off it came, simple as that. Got me old hand stuck in the back of the drum and away it came. Snap!'

He skelped his pincers off his knee and picked up his Capstan out of the paint-tin lid he was using as an ashtray, the smoke curling upwards in blue ribbons through squares of sunlight, disappearing in the shadows, then revealing themselves when they found the light again.

He squinted at her, shaded his eyes with his good hand, took a puff on his fag.

'That was it. Off it came and your man here had to fish it out after the spin-cycle was done. Ho! Imagine that!'

Denise needed no encouragement there. Already she could see the hand birl and dance among the seaweed and foamy clothes.

'No harm came of it, though,' the flea-circus man was saying, her dad slurping loudly on his beer then burping even louder.

'Oof,' he said. 'You could get your lunch out of that.'

He drew the back of his hand across his moustache, and the sun spotlit the top of his bald head.

'Aye. It was a bit of a job getting the painting done after, I can tell you,' the flea-circus man went on. 'Had to retrain, so to speak. Get used to the new recruit and all that.'

Again, he snapped the fingers of the claws together, forgetting he'd been holding his cigarette with them, it falling onto his lap so that he jumped up and did a wee dance, the fag jigging from trouser crease to trouser crease, then onto the floor. The flea-circus man stamped at it, then sat down again.

Her dad was laughing, and Denise giggled too. It was funny to see an old man like him move so quick. He must be nearly as old as her granny, and she moved dead slow, like boats did when they came into a harbour.

Her dad sighed something about getting back to the stripping before it was past dinner time. He was always thinking about his belly, Denise's mum said. That was the only way he knew what time of the day it was, she'd told Denise, using his Foodometer.

'Did it not hurt?' she asked the flea-circus man, surprised at hearing her voice squeak out, the bravery of it.

He grinned at her, his teeth all brown and stained. 'This auld thing?' He shook the pincers at her. 'I'll tell you straight, miss, it did nip a bit at the time. Aye. A hell of a nip. And a hell of a fright it gave me too, popping off like that. Not think it'd bring a tear to *your* eye?'

Denise nodded, shy now, but wasn't sure. Her dad seemed to know, though. He scratched away where the sun was shining on the top of his head.

'Not much of a one for tears, that yin,' he said.

Denise wondered if that was a good or a bad thing.

'Well, it made me greet, I can tell yous,' the flea-circus man went on. 'After, I mean. By the time I got my senses back enough to fish it out the drink, I grat like a wean. I just knew I had to get it back. I had this idea that the machine was going to eat it!'

Again, he winked at Denise.

'I mean, just swally the whole thing up. I was in a terrible state, so I was. Ye see, it had my wedding ring on the finger still. Christ knows what I was thinking. Daft, it was. But that was the idea I had. I says to myself, "Well, Davey, this machine's made a right mess of your business – watch out it doesn't wreck your marriage as well." Ho! There I was, with my good haun in the air to slow down the bleeding, waiting for the bloody spin to finish so's I could get my ring back. I didn't even think about my hand. Just the ring. I was half-dead by the time I fished the thing out, and when the wife gets home she finds me just sitting there on the floor in a pile of washing. Her good linen as well!'

The pair of them were hooting away, Denise's dad and the flea-circus man, but she couldn't see anything funny about what he was saying.

'In she comes, big bag of groceries under her arm, and near deafens me with her screeching when she sees. What a state. "Eh, had a wee accident this afternoon," I says to her. "Bit of a mishap. Caught my hand in the machine." And there I was, still trying to get the ring off my finger before she saw. "Well," says she, "you'll be having another mishap this afternoon if you've buggered my whites, Ahab!" '

Denise's dad was about doubled over laughing. The flea-circus man was too. She pictured him sitting cross-legged on the floor, trying to prise the ring off the finger of the hand in his lap. There was blood everywhere.

The flea-circus man sighed at last, and took another Capstan from his packet on the arm of the chair, tapping it out the box. He tore a nub from the end of it, tapped the rough edge on the back of the packet, and put it between his lips before taking a match from his flea circus and lighting it up.

'What d'ye think of that, miss? Not think that'd make your eyes water? You're darned tooting it would. Not half.'

He looked as if he was thinking about something, and pulled at his ear with his good hand. He had long, silvery hairs growing out of the lobes, and Denise noticed for the first time how droopy they were, great big ears that came right down nearly to his neck. On the crown of his head, where his hair started, was a yellow streak through the white. She liked the streak, and the lines at the corners of his eyes that looked like he'd spent a long time smiling, years maybe. The creases still seemed to have a bit of bounce to them. He sighed again, then said, 'Still, it was a shame to lose it. All the places that auld hand of mine had been! What a life it had. Just the trades it had learned alone. It was worth its weight in memories, if not in gold, that hand. Hammered stone, tiled roofs. Learned to write its name, be Christ! Turned the pages of books, heh. And that auld wife of mine, she missed it as well. Oho! Aye, she might have missed it mair than myself!'

He grinned over at Denise's dad, who was squeezing the empty Tennents tin, and standing up. He stood there a minute, and by the way his body hung together Denise knew he was wanting to get back to the stripping. He kept nodding, but you could tell he wasn't listening any more.

'Aye. She wasn't wrong when she called us Ahab, eh? He smiled again over at her dad, then said, 'Still getting the prickings of the old dismembered spar.' He raised his tin to Denise. 'What think ye, Starbuck?' He leaned over and snatched her hand, too quickly for Denise to move out of reach.

'Here, now!' her dad said.

But the flea-circus man just looked over at him sharply, then back to her. He held her hand in his live one, and it felt so warm and friendly that Denise wasn't frightened.

'Feel how warm that is,' he said. 'And rough, too? Now, close your eyes. Go on.'

Denise looked up at her dad. He nodded, once.

She closed her eyes. Cold hardness of metal touched her palm, and she felt the man close her fingers around it.

'Cold, in'tit?'

She nodded, her eyes still closed.

'Nothing hurts that yin. It cannae feel a thing. But it misses the old hand, wishes it *was* the old hand. Feel it?'

Denise said, quietly, 'Yes.' And it was true. She knew then that the claw wanted to be flesh and blood. It wanted to be a real hand.

'Ye can open your eyes now,' the flea-circus man said.

Denise opened her eyes, and looked at his old laughing face.

'Now, it's back to work for us old seadogs, miss.'

Denise wanted him to tell her more. She wanted to hear about how he'd lost his brains. She wanted to see his flea circus, watch them perform their tricks and stunts.

Her dad said, 'Right enough. We'll have to get cracking if we want to get this all off the day.' He slapped his hands together and rubbed them. 'Right!' he said.

The flea-circus man stood up, draining his Tennents and dropping his fag end into the empty. Shaking his overalls, he straightened their creases and smoothed any spilt ash off them, then went and picked a scraper off the mantelpiece.

Denise drew strength from inside her, and said: 'What about the fleas?'

He grinned down at her. 'Heh. Just matches. That's all.'

Denise tried again. 'What about your brains?'

The flea-circus man shook his head, grrring like a bear. 'Brains? I've mair than most men my age can claim!'

Denise looked down at the paint tin, the stubbed-out Capstan lying on its lid. If they weren't true, why had he told her these things? Why did he want to make fun of her?

A funny look came into the flea-circus man's eyes. They seemed to soften. He came over and got down on his hunkers. He smiled.

'The hook, Starbuck. Remember the hook!' Then he clapped her on the top of the head and walked off.

But even the hook wanted to be a real hand.

So she may know that I am sleeping . . .
And perhaps she will weep for me.

The flea-circus man was singing again.

There was a hurry to get things done, get the room stripped at least, that night. Denise's mum said her mother was coming over, so they better have something to show for the after-noon's work other than empty lager tins. That ought to be like a red rag to a bull for her dad, she said, 'cause of him and Granny *La*mont/La*mont* having this mutually antagonistic relationship.

Denise didn't know what she meant, but wandered back and forth from the kitchen or the good room to the front room, wanting to see how things were going, it being a sort of magic room now, a place where anything might happen, so long as the flea-circus man was still in it.

'Tell the truth,' her mum said, hands still wet from the sink and talking more to the dishes than to Denise. 'Be good if we could get that old buffer out before she arrives. The rate they're going they'll be half-drunk by the time she gets here.'

Denise listened to the whap-whap of Alison still playing her swingball in the back garden, though it was now dark out. She went back through and stood at the door and watched the two men working, never quiet for long, just pausing now and again while one or the other of them pointed to something unforeseen, or chiselled at a tough section of paper. They had the radio on now, a station that played bumpity-bump music, the same kind she knew the flea-circus man would like, though he kept interrupting with his own contrary tune. His long body in its overalls jerked at the wallpaper, and the layers gradually came off, revealing more layers underneath. On top, when they'd started, the paper had been just cream woodchip. Underneath that, there was another layer the same. Next was a pattern with maroon flowers. At the start, a lot of layers came off at once, but now they seemed to be all together. Some bits had been too tough, and her dad and the flea-circus man had moved on to an easier bit, leaving it till later.

'Lazy get,' her Granny *La*mont/La*mont* would have said if she could have seen.

'Thinking of his belly,' her mum would have said, if she'd thought it would make any difference.

Denise said nothing.

Now, the room was left all scabby and half-done, as if it had got some kind of disease. Denise wondered if the house could get ill too, like people. But there was something good about it like this, the dustsheets everywhere, all the furniture looking like ghosts. It looked like a place Granda could come to and stay.

Alison came in late, tired out with her game, the swingball left plugged into the garden lawn. She said she wasn't hungry and went up to her room to play her notebook games, make plans, invent strategies.

A problem had arisen. Her dad came through to the kitchen and said, 'You better come and look at this.'

He looked as if he might laugh. Her mum said: 'What?' but he just shook his head and tugged at her arm for her to come through, Denise following behind. They went in and stared.

The flea-circus man winked at her and cocked his head.

'What is it?' her mum asked.

'Up there,' her dad said. He pointed a long finger up at one of the corners, above the mantelpiece. 'See it?'

Denise's mum looked angry. 'See what?'

She squinted up, one hand on her hip. The flea-circus man looked as if he was about to say something, then thought the better of it. He stared instead at the wall as if he was seeing it for the first time.

'Oh for crying out loud,' Denise's mum said. 'This is all we need.'

Up on the wall, there was a big drawing somebody'd done. Denise couldn't quite make out what it was. It looked like arms and legs.

'You see it?' her dad asked.

'Yes I see it. The question is, what are yous two going to do about it?'

'Us?' her dad said. He looked over at the flea-circus man, who shrugged.

'Been there a long time, I reckon,' he said.

'We've just uncovered the one wee bit,' Denise's dad said. 'Just the now. There might be more underneath. We could paper over it. Or paint it.'

Denise's mum looked like she would scream. 'My mother'll be here in an hour!'

Denise stared at the legs and arms. It looked like a naked person. A man. There was a big willy sticking up from between his legs. She giggled and her mum snapped round to her and glared.

Her dad stroked his head.

'If we leave it as it is, she might not even notice. I mean, you only noticed 'cause we pointed it out.'

'Not a bad talent, the fella that did it,' the flea-circus man chipped in, then took a sip from a can of beer.

Denise's mum shot him a look, and he stared down at his shoes.

'To hell with leaving it. Pull the lot off as fast as you can. And get some paper over it. You've an hour.'

Then she turned round and stamped through to the back room. When Denise followed her through, she found her lying on her back on the floor, a cushion under her head. She had her eyes closed and had switched the light off. Denise hovered in the doorway.

'Leave me alone,' she said, very quietly. 'Just give me peace for a while, can you not.'

Denise turned and left.

Denise saw the flea-circus man move faster than he had all day, her dad too. All the talking had stopped. The radio had been switched off. There was no more bumpity-bump music.

Once, her dad saw her in the doorway and said, 'Get out of

here, you,' but then seemed to forget she was there at all, his face taking on this determined look.

The two of them seemed to move in time, the one stepping in to compensate for the other, no words needed. She sort of wished that's how she could be too, not having to say anything, just act. The bits of paper came off in jaggy tears, showing a bit more here, a bit more there. There were more arms and legs underneath, more men with big pointy willies. There were women as well. You could see their fannies and everything. The whole of the wall above the mantelpiece was covered with them.

Denise's dad stood back and stared. He looked over at the flea-circus man and wiped his head. The flea-circus man looked like he needed the toilet. He seemed like he would burst.

'Aye,' he said. 'And you wondered what we used to do before they invented television.' And he burst out laughing.

Denise's dad wasn't laughing, though. There was a nastiness there, waiting to get out.

'Listen, Ahab,' he said. 'You think losing a hand's bad? Her mother gets in here and sees this, ye'll lose your balls as well. Is that paste nearly ready?'

The flea-circus man stirred at the plastic bucket by the ironing-board they'd set up for the paper. He nodded.

'Right. Well you get that first strip pasted and I'll scrape this bird's arse clear.'

The flea-circus man started to laugh again, then got it under control. 'Aye, aye, captain,' he said. He saluted over at Denise, and she saluted back.

'Mind if young Starbuck here gives us a hand? Many hands make light work and all that . . .'

Her dad looked round and saw her, then just said, 'Aye, but get on with it the pair of yous!'

Denise shuffled over and looked up at the flea-circus man, and he clapped her head again. Denise liked it when he called her Starbuck.

'Here,' he said. 'You keep stirring this stuff while I get on with the pasting.'

She took the piece of wood in the bucket and began to stir. It was dead thick and looked like the porridge her granny made that Denise always refused to eat.

'It's not going to be the best job in the world,' her dad said, yanking and pulling the strips off, 'but it'll do till the old biddy's away back home again. We can take it down the morra. It'll come off easy.'

'You'll stay for something to eat, Davey?' Denise's mum asked, not taking his 'No No, I'll be fine, Mrs Forrester' for an answer, and they all sat down at the table except Denise, who stared at the blank television screen and wondered if it was too late for cartoons to be on. She could hear Alison creak about in her room, but wanted to stay where the flea-circus man was for a while. He'd taken off his overalls and sat, looking like he was having a rare time as they slustered through the soup and put a dent in the ham. He wore a white shirt, and had all these pens in the top pocket. When Denise's granny arrived, he'd been upstairs getting washed and she wasn't sure she liked him so much with combed hair and smelling of turpentine and soap. His one hand looked big and clunking at the table, as if it wasn't used to company. He kept his pincers out of sight under the table and her mum sliced up his food for him so's he wouldn't have to bother with a knife.

Elsa *La*mont/*Lamont* looked him up and down and must have decided he was all right. Denise reckoned they must have lots to talk about seeing as she was missing bits of her as well. She cut up her ham into tiny pieces so's her falsers could manage, but really only touched the potatoes and the vegetables. She kept on mentioning when she could get a look at the next-door room, she wanted to see how it was coming on. When she said this, she'd glance quickly at Denise's dad, who kept his eyes on his plate.

'Oh, we were in a bit of a rush there to get it finished for you, Mrs Douglas,' the flea circus man said. 'Knew you'd have a good eye for that sort of thing. Details, heh? That's what it's all about. Attention to details.'

Denise's granny smiled at him. 'You've been in the trade a long time, Mr Bell?' she asked him, discreetly chewing her food like a horse. Denise could see she must have got a bit round the back of her teeth. She always did that when she got a bit round the back of her teeth.

'Davey's been a painter and decorator for – what is it Davey? – thirty years now?' her dad said. The flea-circus man nodded and took a gulp of beer before answering. He was drinking out of a glass now.

'Thirty year, right enough. Aye. Never even thought of retiring, neither I have. Just get in the way of the wife. She'd have me throttled in a fortnight!'

Denise's granny laughed, covering her mouth and going a bit red. Her mum smiled. Her dad made a funny noise.

'Ye're a married man, then?' her granny went on. 'Children, have ye?'

He shook his head and sighed, looking up at Denise's granny. He shook his head again. 'No, Mrs Douglas—'

'Call me Elsa.'

'Elsa. No weans now. Had a boy once, but he died.'

Denise's mum said, 'Mum . . .'

'Don't you worry yourself about it. A long time ago, so it was. Though it doesn't seem it sometimes. You're lucky to have that girl there, Mrs Forrester. My boy was younger'n her when he died. Pleurisy it was. A serious business in they days. Aye.'

Everyone round the table went quiet for a minute. Then the flea-circus man jerked his head round to Denise saying, 'Everything shipshape over there, Starbuck?'

Denise nodded.

Her mum got up and said, 'Anyone for a refill? Davey? Mum?'

Her dad harrumphed a yes, and her mum nodded. The flea-circus man's eyes lit up. With new drinks everyone seemed to cheer up, Denise's granny cackling out loud. Now and again the flea-circus man would lean over and say something under his breath to her, and she would tut, then burst out laughing all over again.

Finally, when they'd all eaten – except for Denise, of course – the flea-circus man sat back in his chair and lit a Capstan. Denise's mum brought him an ashtray and he looked sheepish.

'Bad habit of mine, awful sorry, Mrs Forrester—'

'You can call me Anna, Davey, for God's sake!'

'I can never mind the rules in other folks' houses,' he went on, oblivious. 'Aye putting my size fourteens in it, so I am. D'ye mind if I smoke at the table?'

'Lead on, Macduff,' her dad butted in.

'Great bit of ham that,' the flea-circus man said. 'The wean not having anything?'

'Acht, she'll not touch anything. A very faddy eater is what she is,' Denise's granny said.

Her ears burned when her granny said that. She didn't want the flea-circus man to know that. She didn't know why. She just didn't.

The flea-circus man looked round at her and winked.

'Careful about what she eats, is she?' he said, talking to the room but grinning at Denise.

'Careful's not the word,' her granny added. 'Hardly touch anything other than chips.'

'Nothing wrong with chips. Chips are a great thing. Thank God for the Italians, eh? Or the war would have been terrible!'

'Right ye are, Davey,' her granny was cackling. 'It was a rare treat to bring chips home then. Ye mind eating pieces in margarine with sugar sprinkled on, Anna? We used to give ye that when you were wee.'

Denise's mum sighed: 'Yes, Mum. And with a digestive biscuit in the middle. And with dripping.'

'Did you fight in the war yourself, Davey?' Elsa *La*mont/La*mont* asked.

'Me? Fight? I was *in* it. I don't know that I did any fighting. A waste of bloody time, was what it was. Tramping about the place, all these youngsters raring to pot a Jerry. Me being a bit older, I wasn't so keen. Anyway, all I ever did was sit about and get hungry. Sat about getting hungry, getting dirty and getting cold. And bloody wet with it. No, I'm not much of a one for fighting.'

The flea-circus man's mood seemed to have soured for the first time. His mouth straightened out and he breathed heavily through his nose, then picked up his glass and drained it in one go.

Denise's granny was quiet, too.

After a minute, the flea-circus man spoke again.

'Tell the truth, Elsa, it was during the war I lost my boy. He was called David too.'

He looked up and smiled. 'After myself. It was while I was over there, in France, that he caught the pleurisy. He was dead six months before I knew. All the time I was sitting in that bloody trench not firing a shot, he was here dying. Hell of a cheek that, I've always thought. There's the war for you!'

Everyone was quiet, and the flea-circus man placed his palm slowly on the tablecloth. Denise saw him open and close his tweezer hand under the table. It was coming to life.

'Ehm, how's about a look at yon living room?' Elsa *La*mont/La*mont* said, draining her own glass and then keeking in the bottom as if to make sure it was really empty.

A look blinked between Denise's mum and her dad. He shrugged. He looked at the flea-circus man. The flea-circus man made no commitment, either way.

'Yes, let's all have a look,' said Elsa *La*mont/La*mont*. 'See how this pair of reprobates are getting on.'

They all slid up out of their seats, and edged round the table, so that the good room began to go back to normal. It was a shame, Denise reckoned. She liked it with the lights on and people in it. Even if it was just her family. She got up and trailed through to the other room at the back of everyone else, squeezing between them to get in.

Her granny was staring all around and not saying anything, just going, 'Mmmm,' occasionally. They had put a wee lamp on in there, instead of the big light. Someone had taken the bulb out. It was dim as anything, but you could see what her dad and the flea-circus man had done together. All the walls had been stripped down to the plaster, the room all turpentiney-smelling. The torn-down paper had been piled in rubbish bags so that even the floor was clear. The chairs sat silently under their sheets, the wee table and the cabinet under theirs. One single wall had been prepared. The one above the fireplace.

' 'Course, we were a bit rushed the day,' her dad said. 'Had a bit of trouble getting some of the layers off. But once they started to come, everything was fine.'

'Aye, so I can see,' Denise's granny said. She went squinting and shuffling up to the wall and put her hand on the wallpaper.

'Careful, mum! It's still wet!'

Granny *La*mont/La*mont* rubbed the glue between her thumb and forefinger, then sniffed.

'Is that the colour yous're using?' she asked after a bit.

'Aye, well. It's to be painted over. That's just to cover the plaster with. You know, so's we can paint on it,' Denise's dad said. He looked at Denise's mum, who shrugged back.

'Oh, right enough,' Denise's granny said. 'Well! It all looks very swish, I must say. It'll be great when yous have the rest done. what d'you think, Davey? D'ye like it yourself?'

The flea-circus man squinted at her in the light from the table lamp, then shrugged.

'Everything looks grand to me,' he said. 'The wife despairs of me. Any time she asks me something like that I just say, "Aye, not bad."'

'Well, I think it's smashing,' Elsa *La*mont/La*mont* said. 'It's going to be rare, so it is. Well done you two.'

Denise's mum looked relieved. She ushered Denise out of her way and said, 'Shall we all sit back through and have a refill, then?'

'A wee whisky and ginger might be nice,' Elsa *La*mont/La*mont* said. 'What d'ye think, Davey? Do ye take a whisky yourself?'

The flea-circus man cheered up a bit, following the rest of them back through to the other room. 'Indeed I do, Mrs Douglas—'

'Elsa.'

'Indeed I do, Elsa. Man like myself can only afford to drink spirits. In lieu of fresh water, obviously. Another thing I learned in the war. Now, of course, there's even more reason for it.'

'Why's that?'

'The Soviets, Elsa. Don't drink the water, and don't breathe the air.'

Denise could hear her granny cackle, as the two of them walked through, then she heard the flea-circus man sing a few bars.

O, bury me beneath the willow . . .
Neath that weeping willow tree . . .

Then it stopped.

Denise sat for a while, staring up at the dark corners, listening out for the groan and clank of the old pipes, their friendly noises. She heard the floorboards creak above. Slowly, she got up and went to the wall above the mantelpiece. She put her hand out and touched it. It was wet and sticky. There was a bit of a bubble on one of the wallpaper rolls. She pressed her finger against it, smoothing it. Then she stepped back to look at it. Slowly from the top, the entire length slapped down and hung like an old bandage above the fireplace. A man's big pointed willy poked out at her from underneath. She turned and ran out the room.

Denise remembered the tenement flat of her granny, all ticking clocks and porcelain dogs on the mantelpiece. She pictured the old wireless that worked with a glass valve, shaped like a brown Hovis loaf. She pictured the recess for the bed, and the view across the back court, the dyke and the middens, but couldn't be sure how much of it her memory had filled in for her, how many absences had been altered, changed, tricked into coherence. The pictures she saw were like her granny's stories, the people that inhabited them, their towns and villages, their shadow lives flickering, vividly living only for as long as she gave them life. The stories contained something like truth, something like life. But they all ended in tragedy, every one. Now, when Denise thought about them, they seemed only calculations themselves. But even so, her granny used to laugh at a lot of them. Maybe that was because she'd invented them and could do what she liked. They were her own calculations, working themselves out. They were free in a way that the world wasn't. Even death was only temporary inside one of them.

Once, she and Alison had been waiting for their dad to come and pick them up and take them home. Granny told them a story to stop them from getting bored.

There had been a woman who'd lived not far from here, Granny *La*mont/*La*mont had told her, long before your granny was even born herself . . . And this woman drank quarter-gills like a fish, so she did . . .

'Why?'

'Why? Why would she not? It was a hard, hard life she'd had. Nothing was easy in those days, so it wasn't. Up every morning before it got light, up in the freezing cold and get into her working clothes, the only clothes she had, so thread-bare and worn that ye could practically see through them. The wool was thin on her skirt. Her stockings were held together by the wool she used to re-darn them every night. Nails came up through the soles of her shoes and stuck into her feet . . .'

That had sounded horrible. A nail straight through your sole. Denise wondered what kind of boots vampires had worn. She remembered they hadn't liked the texture of food either. They were mainly drinkers.

'She'd come to the town for work,' Granny said. 'She was a country girl, but there was folk out where she came from that didn't care for her; says she had the Evil Eye, they says she could turn any man's head, so the other women took a dislike to her. They were aye just jealous, 'cause she was more beautiful than the lot of them!'

'What did she look like?' Alison had asked.

'Well, she was tall for one thing! That lot out there? They were just a lot of wee smouts. Make a midget look tall, so they would.'

Denise and Alison stared at each other.

'But we're wee too,' Alison said.

'Aye . . . but yous are wee 'cause of not being grown-up. This lot were wee 'cause they were above average-size for being shites . . .'

Granny turned a winking eye at the pair of them, leaning forward in her armchair and looking about as if to check if anyone else was listening to her say the bad word. Their dad wouldn't have cared if she did say it; their mum would just sigh. Denise was turning the word over in her head; getting the feel of it. Shite.

'. . . And she had black, black, hair that hung down her

back almost to her waist, black, black, eyes that glittered like a cat's when it gets caught in the headlights of a motor . . .'

'Cat's eyes?'

'That's what I said, isn't it? Cat's eyes.'

'That's those things in the middle of the road. They're yellow, not black.'

Granny *La*mont/La*mont* huffed her folded arms under her giant chest. 'Cat's eyes. Rabbit's eyes, doesn't matter does it? It's all eyes, in'tit? Eyes are eyes are eyes, eh? Am I right or a meringue?'

They nodded: A meringue.

'Right, well . . . she had these black eyes, ye see; black hair, black eyes and the clearest, palest, whitest skin ye've ever seen. Like whipped cream it was, except for the rosy-red in her cheeks. And the rest of her?'

Granny *La*mont/La*mont* sat back and carved an hourglass shape into the air in front of her. Denise stared at it, transfixed for a second, before it evaporated into nothingness in front of her. You couldn't have said that with words.

'. . . The women in the place she came from, they wouldn't let her be. She was an orphan and had worked the landlord's farm since she was old enough to carry a pail. But all she ever felt from him was the sharp end of his tongue and the sharper end of his birch.'

'Why did she not run away?'

'Where to? She was only a girl, but she swore to herself she would as soon as she was big enough. But between now and then many hard years would have to pass . . . So she scrubbed floors, shone the brass in the big house, washed and pressed the laundry, aired the rooms, stoked the fires in the kitchens; whatever she was told. And when she'd done with her polishing and her shining and her washing and sweeping and sewing, then she would maybe get a few minutes to herself to think. A dog's life, so it was . . .'

Denise watched her granny tap the old tobacco out the end

of her pipe, then tamp a new lot into it, take a match and strike it on her sole and take two or three puffs till it caught.

But the master of the big house could see she was growing; she wasn't the waif he'd let stay on after her ma and da had shot the crow . . . She was growing, right enough. She was growing into something else entirely – and he couldn't take his eyes off her. Bewitched, so he was. Here was this *new creature* living in his house, in the cupboard room below the stairs, eating in his kitchens and scrubbing his floors . . . but . . . but . . .'

'But what!'

'But she was something *else* now. And he might be her master and her provider – he might be God for all she knew – but she didn't belong to him. And he couldn't stand it. Made her life a misery, so he did. He knew fine well she would never be interested in the likes of him. For one thing, he was old and past his best. For another, he was married already – his wife was nearly as old as he was. And last but most important of all, he knew fine she could never have fallen for someone that treated her the way he had treated her. He looked at her and what he saw was purity and goodness and beauty – everything he wanted but couldn't have 'cause of not being good and pure and beautiful himself. Every day he'd take any excuse he could to pass by the kitchens, or inspect the cleaning going on in the hall. He'd hover over her, watching and longing and thinking about how he could have her, how he could make her his. 'Course the wife was to know none of this – it was all to be kept a secret. So he plotted and he schemed and he racked his brains; and he watched and he longed and made himself sick in the process . . .'

'Why did he do all that?' Denise wanted to know.

'Why? I'm just after telling you why.'

'No, but *why?*'

' 'Cause he was in *love*, stupit. Why'd ye think?'

Love. It sounded like some sort of illness. It sounded like

something that would grow and grow inside you, something that would make you sicker and sicker until finally it killed you. What could be worse than to die from *love*? There was nothing worse. The slowest, most painful death of all. She shuddered.

'Well,' Granny *La*mont/La*mont* went on, 'he harangued her and harassed her and tormented her, but never in the sight of anybody else. He would ring the bell in her room in the middle of the night and get her to make him a toddy or punch and bring it to him in the big room, where he always sat when the rest of the house was asleep, staring at his face getting older and uglier by the minute in the big golden-framed mirror above the fire. And he blamed her for it . . . It was all her fault; she was to blame; she had put the evil eye on him, it was plain as the big purple-nose on his face, ruddy with all the toddy and punch he was putting away.

'One night he just couldn't stand it any longer. When she brought the toddy in, he gets down on his knees and begs her just to let him kiss her, just once; he greets and he wails and he stamps his feet and gnashes his teeth – but she refuses. No matter what it was he says to her, no matter how he threatens her, she refuses. She stood her ground and told him to stop, leave her alone, just leave her alone, it was no use, no use what he says, she would have nothing to do with it . . .'

Granny puffed her pipe and sat, looking like she was thinking. She was nodding slowly to herself. Then she went on:

'Finally, he just sits there, this grim look settling on his face, looking even older and uglier than when she'd first come in the room. "Very well," says he, "but I know now what it is you've done to me. You've put the Evil Eye on me and I can see now that you mean to destroy me. But you won't succeed. You won't be the end of me. I'll be the end of you! Now get out of my sight!" he says, hammering his fist down on the table at his elbow so's the toddy glass jumps up in the air and goes rolling along the carpet. And she goes rushing away, just glad to get out the room . . .'

'What happened next?' Denise asked, crossing and recrossing her legs on the floor in front of her.

'Next? Nothing. She went to her scratcher. But she never saw the master the next day, or the day after that, or the day after that. But rumours had started. So the girl decides to sneak out for a while, while she's on a message into town. But it's not just a message . . .'

'What else is it?'

'It's a meeting. She's away off out into the woods to a secret meeting place that nobody knows about. Nobody except one person . . .'

'Who?'

'Ach, nobody special.'

'Who!'

'Just the curly-headed farmboy from the next place along. See, she's known him since the pair of them used to go about together, before her ma and da died and she went up to the big house. Well, they'd been meeting in secret all these years, whenever they got the chance. And now they've decided to run away together, as soon as they'd got enough money to get them started on the road. They just had to pick their moment. But the farmboy tells her that someone's been spreading rumours and lies about her, that folk are saying she's an adulteress, that she'll do anything for money, that she'd designs on folk that were her betters . . . and once ye'd got a name for yourself in this place, that was you done for – your life wouldn't be worth living anyway. Of course curly-head doesn't believe any of that, but they're a right ignorant lot around there, and once ye had a name for yourself that was it. It stuck. That was your name.'

'What name was it that they gave her?' Denise asked, a feeling of dread spreading cold fingers over her back.

'They called her *a hoor*.'

'A hoor?'

Granny *La*mont/La*mont* nodded, her face tight. 'That's right,' she said. 'A hoor is a special kind of person. Sometimes it's a man but most of the time it's a woman. A woman that gets all the worst, all the dirtiest jobs and none of the thanks for it. And folk just needed an excuse. So she and curly-head decided they'd better get going on the road soon. And they decided on that night . . .'

'Where were they going to go?' Denise asked.

'As far away as they could get,' Granny *La*mont/La*mont* said. 'As far away as the nearest big town or city, somewhere they could get board and bread, somewhere they could disappear, somewhere they could get lost in; somewhere there were thousands of folk just like themselves walking up an' down the streets, breathing in the ash and soot that passed for air; a place that had been stained black by a thousand chimneys belching out dirt into the sky; somewhere the weans sailed peerie boats down the gutters that ran with all kinds of filth, and folk worked themselves into an early grave, went to jail or the poorhouse; somewhere they could get a single-end in a soot-stained tenement building that squatted like some fat black beetle on the brow of a hill so that it just had to shake itself once in a while and the dirt and the filth would come rolling out and down the slope; somewhere the pair of them – *him* and *her* – could get themselves swallowed up along with the rest of the tide of people going from frying pan to fire. Somebody had told them the streets of the place they were headed for were paved not with gold, but with lead. The gutters were lined with lead and the lofts were stuffed with fibres that would choke your lungs . . .'

Denise and Alison looked at their granny. 'What was the name of the place?' Alison asked.

'The name of the place? It would have been any place. But the place they were heading for was called Glasgow, a city with a glass eye and no teeth; a city that had let itself go . . .'

Denise felt the pipes grunt at her through the walls of Granny's tenement; it was like they were laughing at her. It was like her granny had tricked her, as if she had left a trail of breadcrumbs for her to follow . . . a trail that had led her here . . . right into the middle of the story. She was inside it now. She was trapped. They were all trapped in it together.

'They never got there, though. Leastways, not together. The girl went back up to the big house to get her few things ready. She was to meet curly-head at the crossroads where one road went east, and the other went west. The master of the house had an idea she might try to run away, and spent the night pacing up and down in the big room in front of the mirror, and ordering bowls of punch, till pretty soon he was rolling drunk. The poor girl couldn't slip away till after she heard him begin to snore, well after midnight. Curly-head would have waited, surely? She was desperate to get away and begged the Lord that the master would sleep soon and she could go . . . Well, the good Lord above answered they prayers of hers, and bye and bye she hears the snoring coming from the big room. This is her chance. She gives it a minute to make sure he's absolutely sound asleep. Aye. Definitely out the game. Quick as a flash she grabs her things and sneaks her way out the door and down the road, fast as her legs'll carry her – on and on she runs, determined not to stop till she sees the sign up ahead . . . *Please God let him be there*, she wishes. *Please*. And there's the signpost up ahead, finally. But no curly-head. He must have set off without her. He couldn't wait any longer.'

'What does she do next?' Alison asked. Her eyes were big and round, like puddles on a pavement. Denise wanted the story to go backwards, she wanted to change it so's that curly-head would still be waiting at the signpost. She wanted a happy ending. Why could it not have a happy-ever-after?

'So the poor girl decides she'll try an' catch up with him somehow, in the city maybe – she'll hunt high and low for him till she finds him, do anything in her power to track him down. Everything. But the trouble is, she's never been to a city before, never even imagined the size of the place, the number of streets, the number of houses, the number of people. As soon as she's got herself a hovel of her own, and a job scrubbing the floor of the nearest hospital, she sets about searching for curly-head. She searches every place she can think of, up an' down the streets, the parks, every pub an' park bench she comes across. But it's no use. Nothing. Finally, she even checks the morgue . . .'

'What's a morgue?' Denise was wanting to know.

'It's a place where dead folk go for a sleep, before they get fitted out for a coffin. Somewhere for dead folk to put their feet for a bit, get themselves ready for the afterlife and that.'

'Oh.'

'She looked at the poor dead faces lying on the slabs around her and she wondered about how it was they'd come to be here, now, instead of somewhere else enjoying themselves. They could be walking down the road, just the same as she had been earlier. They could be working behind the counter in a shop. They could be a coal-miner or a policeman or a bank robber or anything. And some of them so young as well! Nice-looking boys, a lot of them – the ones that still had faces. 'Cause they were in all sorts of states when they came in. Some of them were mashed up pretty bad, they'd been in accidents or they'd got their throats slit down some dark alley, or got their skulls stove in with a hammer . . . That was just the ones that went quick – the ones that had died of diseases were even worse, would give you nightmares to think about it, so it would . . .'

Denise could feel the cold marble slab against her back just the same as if she was lying there; she could feel the chill air on her flesh, hear the cold tap of shoes tap-tapping along the marble floor, smell the smell of cold, dead flesh, formaldehyde and surgical spirit. She felt herself floating, naked inside a giant glass pickle jar, insides laid open for everyone to see, flesh blue-grey and her hair afloat about her like the tendrils of a jellyfish, her dead arms trying to cover her dead nakedness while people filed past, staring, mouthing things to each other that she couldn't hear . . .

'At last,' her granny was saying, 'the poor girl comes to the end slab, and the attendant slips back the sheet. She can't believe it. It's curly-head. He looks so pure an' white that he might still be alive, only his eyes are shut for a minute. His hair is as red and ringleted as it ever was. She imagines that if she was to kiss him, there, on the lips, that his chest will start to rise and fall; that he'll sit up and open them, like they'll fill up with tears when he finally sees her. But he doesn't. He just keeps on lying there, still and cold and with a label tied about his toe. Then the mortuary attendant quietly slides the white sheet back over him and they walk to the door. And the funny thing is, that she can't feel anything. Oh, she was shocked right enough; but she'd been expecting it somehow. It was as if it was all part of the plan. That it was inevitable somehow. It was the strangest feeling. And when she asks the mortuary attendant what happened to him, how had he died, it was as if she had known it all along.

' "Of a broken heart," the mortuary attendant told her. Then she left. Walking along the road she had the feeling he was there with her; walking along beside, just on the corner of her vision. And sure enough, there was a wound there, somehow marked on her skin . . . She could feel his love. It was still there when she got home to her room. It rubbed up against her, kept her warm. But in the morning when she got up for her scrubbing job, it was still there, following her about. It was beginning to irritate her. It stayed with her all that day. And at night, it followed her home, climbed into the bed with her and shifted about so's she couldn't get peace. It was the same the next day, and the day after that. It followed her everywhere, snuggled up against her in the outside lavvy, suffocating her, never letting her alone. It was as if it was joined to her by an invisible thread. She began to scream at it *Leave me alone!* in the middle of the street. The only way she was immune to it was if she took to the gin. So she did. She tried to remain as drunk as she could for as much of the time as she could. Just so's she could rest in peace. Well, in time, she lost her job. She tried to sober up but the presence of so much love was unbearable to her, and she never managed to keep it up for long. She had to stay numb. As soon as she was sober, there it was: love in her life again. She went back to the gin. She lost as many jobs as the empty gin bottles she piled around her. Eventually, she couldn't make the rent and was chucked out by the landlady. She slept on park benches and in alleyways, and the only job she could get was the hooring. All that just to stay drunk. By the time she was thirty, she was like an old woman – toothless, grey-haired, blind from drinking unripe spirits. And that was the end of the hooring. She had a gaggle of weans, mostly dead, and the others having to fend for themselves on the streets: she was no use to them, so she wasn't. She spent her days sat in the dirt and the muck and she begged; she spent all day begging on the street. As soon as she could she'd get herself some kind of cheap spirit; she'd fill herself with it till her cup ran over. She would live only as long as she had the spirit inside herself. When it left, she would die. One bitter winter's morning it did – the police found her lying on a doorstep in the street: she was frozen solid. *Who is it?* the one policeman says to the other. *Ach, just some auld hoor, says the other.'*

Granny *La*mont/La*mont* winked and stared at the two of them. Denise felt breathless. Alison just stared.

'Mother's Ruin,' Granny said, tapping the tobacco from her pipe once more. Then she burst out laughing.

What was funny? Denise wanted to know.

'The faces on you two,' Granny said. 'You should see yourselves!'

But Denise could see herself too well. All she ever did was see herself.

At nights, Denise often went down the Dummy. It was called that 'cause of it running parallel to the railway lines. The dummy-run; where they used to go when they still went about on their bikes. Denise didn't bother to take her bike out now 'cause of it being so old; you had to get off it every ten minutes and straighten the wheel. Plus the mudguard wrestled with the rubber, made this rasping noise. It was a terrible old thing, all rusty and that.

Alison still rode hers. She didn't get it. She didn't get why Denise would rather walk somewhere, get there last and miss everything, all the excitement. Denise would rather walk. If she did, someone would trail back with her. Never any of the girls, though. They still treated her like an outcast. They even called her things sometimes: *smelly*. Right to her face!

She just ignored them. She was used to ignoring them. She only bothered if they tried to hit her. But they never did, not any more. They were probably worried she'd put a curse on them or something. A hex.

And they were right to worry. They were right to be careful. Denise would stick pins in drawings she made of them and scatter them about Eulalia, stamp on them and set them on fire with the matches she took out the kitchen drawer – the matches her mum and her dad and her granny and everybody else were always telling her she wasn't meant to be playing with, because they were dangerous. But it wasn't matches that were dangerous: it was Denise. Now that she was grown-up. Her mum wasn't here any longer so she was the lady of the house. She was boss and could do what she liked. So she snapped the matches alight and the pyres would go up all over her country, orange flame that lapped at its papier-mâché central belt, spreading north and east and south and west till the room stank of burnt paper and cardboard. The hills and valleys blackened and scorched, the lochs hissing and curling back. And when, finally, the fires went out, the blackened words of which the universe was made began to creep through and became visible.

But, when Denise would go to school the next day, the inspiration for her effigy would be standing there none the worse for having been burnt alive.

Still, it made you feel better to do it.

Nights were always spent the same way: hanging about on streetcorners, getting someone older to go into the offy for you, trying to take up smoking 'cause it made you look older, more grown-up. Big groups of alliances would spring up and dissolve; there were betrayals and defections, loyalties shifted and power swapped hands; gangs of boys decorated the ground around them with flicked gobbets of spit shot from between the teeth, marking their territory, the same way that dogs marked theirs by pishing on lampposts; girls giggled at private jokes you knew they were never going to let you in on. Sometimes there were fights. Sometimes one big group of guys would start a rumour that another big group of guys who went to the Fenian school up the road were around the corner right now, swear to fuck, man, right now, round the corner, man, tooled up and everything, swear to fuck.

Then the first big group would go haring after the rumour, try to catch it, white and stunned, try to make it real, but by then it would have turned on them, and a hasty retreat became the politic option. On and on it went. Night after night.

Sometimes they would get hold of somebody and five or eight or ten of them would gather about the body on the ground and kick and punch him – it was always a *him* – until he managed to scrabble up somehow and get away, or until he stopped moving, or until the pigs arrived and one tall thin one in particular, a man like a lot of loosely arranged clothes pegs, would eye over the crowd on the lookout for a girl who used to be skinny but was filling out now in all the right places, and their eyes would connect for a second before he would look away, all the connection between them that there ever would be.

Sometimes they passed around pills marked with pictures that stood for things, states of mind they could induce. Denise didn't know if she believed in them or not. Maybe she would try one someday. Maybe not.

Down the Dummy nobody could see you. In the bushes, drinking bottles of peach-flavoured soft drinks that were really full of alcohol. Peach was Denise's favourite. Sometimes they had fires: her and John Burke mostly. Sometimes Alison came as well, and they'd sit and glower at each other. Every night Denise wished Jeedy would come. Sometimes he did, sometimes he didn't. Sometimes she let John put his arm round her. Sometimes not. Not if there were any people there. Not if Alison was there.

They didn't talk all that much, just sat on the old mattress and poked about in the fire with sticks and drank their bottles of stuff.

This time, they were sitting there, quiet, huddled up against the embers to keep warm, watching the glow. Denise Forrester and John Burke.

'Red man say paleface build big fire, stand far away. Cold bum,' John said in a kid-on Red-Indian-Pakistani voice. 'Red man build small fire, stand close up. Warm bum.'

Denise smiled.

There was something crashing about through the bushes; it was roaring and snorting. Denise nearly shat herself. So did John. He jumped up and started shouting, 'Who's there?'

Jeedy strode out of the bushes. He stood there staring at the pair of them, the whites of his eyes brilliant in the darkness.

'Give you a fright, did I?' he said, grinning.

'Don't do that, man! I nearly pished myself,' John said, his shoulders relaxing, letting out a deep breath.

'All right, Denise?' Jeedy said.

Denise couldn't help smiling. 'Yeh,' she said. 'You?'

He shrugged.

'Mind if I come in out the jungle?' he said.

John laughed and looked about to make some remark, but then must have thought the better of it and shut up instead. He was going to sit down but Jeedy had already sat down where he had been sitting, next to Denise. John stood, toeing bits of the embers back into the fire. He didn't look at them.

Denise had already forgotten he was there.

She could feel Jeedy's leg touching hers and was keeping as still as possible so's she didn't frighten him off. She was wishing he'd hold her hand again. Maybe if she waited long enough. If you waited long enough and wanted it bad enough, anything could happen. She could feel his body through his clothes, the heat of it, she could taste the taste of his skin on her tongue. She squeezed her legs together, then realised what she'd done. Now he'd notice when she put her leg back. She'd just have to sit there the way she was. It was excruciating.

'Anything left in that bottle for me?' he said.

She handed him the bottle, watching him tip it back, the glug of the liquid going down, travelling down his throat, past his heart, his lungs and kidneys, pooling into his stomach. Glopping around inside. That was daft, though, being jealous of a liquid. Mental, so it was. Pure mad.

John kicked at the fire. 'Think I'll head now,' he said. He was looking at Denise but she wasn't paying any attention.

'Yeh?' Jeedy said.

Denise looked up. 'Oh, you away?'

'Yeh,' he said. 'I'm off.' He waited a bit, then added: 'Well, see you two tomorrow.'

'Yeh,' Denise said.

'Maybe,' Jeedy said. 'Maybes aye and maybes naw.'

'And maybes maybe,' Denise finished for him, then flushed hot red. She was glad of it being dark out, so no one could see her.

John made his way out through the bushes. As soon as he was gone Jeedy took her hand, then he was kissing her and she was flushing again this time, but different. His hands moved inside her top. Her hands copied his, went under his top, feeling his nipples get hard. His skin was soft. Softer than she'd expected. His tongue licked at the edges of her lips. Then he broke away.

'I ain't going home tonight,' he said.

'Why?' Denise went, feeling the dampness of the mattress sticking her knickers to her.

'My brother wants me to meet him in the house. I don't want to.'

'Your brother wants you to meet him?'

'He wants me to help him steal a car from the garage round the corner.'

'Can you drive?'

'Nah. He wants us to shove it up the road. Roll it, know what I mean? The guy in the showroom's left the driver's door unlocked. My brother's mate has an empty garage round the corner from the flat.'

'What'll you do with it?'

'Spray it, get different plates. I don't know.'

'Then what?'

'I don't know. Sell it I suppose.'

He spat into the fire. 'So I ain't going home tonight. I'll go back tomorrow, when my brother's not in.'

'What'll he do?'

'My brother? Waste me, probably. Kick me about the place a bit. But I won't have to steal the car.'

'What if your brother puts it off till tomorrow night?'

'Then I'll have to stay out tomorrow night as well. He's fucking nuts, my brother. He locked me in a cupboard once. For a whole day. My other brother just laughed when he found me. He had to lift me out 'cause I couldn't stand up any more, my legs had been cramped so long.'

'How come your other brother can't help him instead?'

'He doesn't get involved in stuff like that. He doesn't know anything about it. He'd just say our mum would kill us if she was alive.'

'What was it she died of?'

Jeedy shrugged.

'She got sick,' he said. 'She had cancer and she had to have these operations and then treatments. Her hair fell out. She looked like she was a hundred when she went.'

'How old was she?'

'Forty-one.'

Denise stared into the fire again, the embers cracking and splitting. Jeedy put his hand up to the back of her neck, rubbing it. It was as if her mum was the one who had died, and she was the one getting comforted.

'How're you going to keep warm tonight?' Denise asked.

'I'll be okay. I'll sit here and get the fire going again.'

'It won't last all night.'

'It'll last.'

'What if somebody comes.'

'Who's going to come?'

Denise shrugged.

'Your dad? On duty, is he?'

Denise didn't answer that.

'Off to *crack a few nuts* eh?'

'That isn't fair . . .'

'Yeah. Fair. Fair's fair, eh?'

Denise said nothing.

'Pigs would love to lock my brother up. Any excuse, they'd fucking love it.'

'Don't say that.'

'Say what?'

'That word . . .'

'*Pig*? That's what your dad is, isn't he? A pig.'

'He's a police officer, not a—'

'Not a what? Say it. Go on. Say "pig". Pig. Pig. Pig. Pig.'

But the word Denise was saying over and over was a different word. The word that Denise was saying was:

'Stop. Stop. Stop. Stop. Stop.'

And then she was going to hit him on the shoulder but he caught her hand mid-air; then they were wrestling together on the mattress and they were hugging. Her eyes were wet. It was water. There were real tears there. Real water. Wetness was coming down her cheeks. It felt like losing something of yourself, an exposé, a scandalous loss. She wiped at her eyes with the backs of her hands, letting her hair fall down over her face. Her last resort was always to hide.

Jeedy stared at her, his own eyes registering nothing, telling nothing about what he was seeing.

'What's the matter?' he said, as she managed to turn the crying into embarrassment, a single, lonely snort escaping through a runny nose.

'I think I realised something,' she said, smiling quickly up at him, then letting her hair fall over her face once more.

'Yeh? What?' He scratched at the back of his head.

'I think I might be missing my mum,' she said. 'Yes. I think I miss my mum. That's all.'

The words escaped, only to fall spent onto the mattress where she was sitting. Denise felt lightened. But then she couldn't be bothered to think about it any more.

She was drinking first from a bottle of brown-coloured stuff that had a foreign name on the label. It looked like it was Spanish, but you never knew. The word on the label said:

RON

Lukewarmish in the mouth; she held it for a second or two, afraid to swallow. Sweet, fiery. She made a grooing face.

The liquid in the next bottle was clear:

VODKA

'Vodka,' she repeated, handling the word on her tongue the same way she'd handled the brown stuff. It tasted terrible, even worse than Ron had. It was like petrol or something.

'John,' she said. 'Let me have a fag.'

'You shouldn't smoke,' he said. 'It's bad for you. Specially after drinking petrol.'

Denise giggled. 'So's this minging stuff. How can folk take it?'

'It's good with Coke in it. Or lemonade. Or orange.'

She wasn't convinced. Coke or lemonade or orange. All soft drinks. That was like the yin-yang thing. Soft/Hard. Masculine/feminine.

John took another bottle out the cabinet. They were sitting on the carpet in his mum's living room.

Brown liquid, like the first one. There was something a bit different about the smell though. Sweet.

'Sherry,' John said.

It was terrible stuff. Another bottle had some kind of

creamy-yellow stuff in it that smelt like bananas. It was a long time since she'd eaten a banana. They had a horrible texture, but the texture of drink was much better than the texture of food. It was . . . *wetter*.

'Let's have a disco!' Denise said, starting to giggle again. Her lips were dead sticky from the creamy stuff.

'My mum and dad'll be back soon,' John told her. He lifted another bottle from the cabinet and looked at it: again, it was clear, but with a milky sediment at the bottom.

'What's all that stuff floating about in it?'

'Floaters,' he said.

'They've sunk.'

Her eyes had gone funny. She was having to squint to get a good look at him. His face was sort of out of its usual shape or something. Or he was a different colour from usual, less pale. He had taken on a tinge, especially around the nose. She decided he must have a light bulb inside him that only got switched on after dark. They were both just robots, their organs and entrails really just battery packs and electrical cabling. Drinking this stuff was a kind of short-circuit that made things seem hazy and colour-saturated. It was like a colour matinée after an afternoon watching black-and-white films, a last defence against sterility. All the stupid thoughts Denise kept to herself seemed like good ones now. All the pictures and plans and maps.

'Let's dance,' she said, rolling back and lying flat out on the carpet. She liked this room. It was full of things you could pick up, things you could hold and handle then put back. Denise's house didn't have any stuff like that in it. Her Granny *La*mont/*La*mont's house had, but not their own. She smiled up at the ceiling, where God was, on the other side, looking down at her.

'He's a jealous god, up there,' she said.

'What?'

'He's an angry god,' she said. 'Jealous of me. You're all jealous of me. Everyone just wants to be me.'

226

'Whatever.'

'Let's dance,' she said again.

'I can't dance.'

'Neither can I. But there's only the two of us. We can both be spazzys together.'

'I can't dance.'

Denise sat up; she was feeling a bit funny now. 'I should be getting back,' she said suddenly. She felt a bit sick.

'Aw. They'll not be back for a while yet.'

'Give us some more fire-water then, Injun Joe.'

'Who's Engine Joe?'

'Don't know, Injun Joe. Don't know. S'just a name. Let's phone Jeedy up.'

'He won't be in,' John said, giving her this funny, quick look.

'Let's phone him anyway.'

'Here. More fire-water,' John said, ignoring her and slouching the bottle over toward her, his arm wobbling about. Denise took it and had a gulp, the liquid burning all the way down, the feeling beginning to flower inside her the way words sometimes did. But this was freer, spreading into her arms and fingers, the top of her nose. It was like she could say what she wanted, do what she wanted. Nobody could stop her. Not her mum. Not her dad. Not Alison. She giggled, remembering how her granny used to warn her and Alison about the dangers of Mother's Ruin: Denise wondered why she had listened. It was like the veil had been lifted. She decided she never wanted to be normal again. She sat staring at the carpet, her vision getting blurry.

Mother's Ruin, the Curse – who cared.

She was lifting the bottle up, tilting it into her mouth; some of the liquid trickled out the side. Nice. Banana-ey. Like creamed bananas. It didn't even taste like it had any alcohol in it. That was good.

'Phone Jeedy,' she said.

'He won't come,' John said. 'He'll be away out.'

'He was sitting cross-legged beside her, leafing through his mum and dad's albums. There was a lot of Michael Jackson and stuff like that. The Commodores.

'Let's have a disco,' she said again, giggling.

'A concert . . .'

'Sing something, then !'

There'll be no holy water in the Cup – thank fuck!'

'No, something proper . . .'

'Like what?'

'Like a *song*. Or . . . something.'

Denise lay back on the floor again, her cheeks feeling dead warm, the thoughts slow and trickling, like treacle dripping from a spoon. She was wanting to say something. What had it been? There had been something. Something about something. She couldn't mind. She slapped the flat of her hand against her forehead. Her brain was in there somewhere rattling about . . . she felt numb. Maybe this was as good as it was ever going to get. Maybe it'd be best to die now, if it was.

'If you were going to kill yourself, how would you do it?' she asked John.

'By eating two hundred Mars Bars in a row,' he said.

'That would just make you sick.'

'By eating three hundred Mars Bars in a row.'

'Eeech . . . What about two hundred Milky Ways?'

'Not potent enough.'

'I'd drink a bucket of banana-ey. I'd inject myself with it.'

'I'd sit outside a fire-station and wait for a fire to start somewhere . . .'

'How would that work?'

'Sooner or later a fire-engine would have to come out and roll over me. Squish,' he said, flattening the palm of his hand against the floor.

'Splat,' Denise said.

'Flattened . . .'

'Pancaked . . . Give me some more banana-ey.'

'None left,' said John, shoogling the empty bottle then lying down on his back next to her.

'Awww . . .' Denise said. 'Will your mum and dad not be angry?'

'They'll take months to notice. They've had it for years. Nobody drinks it here.'

'If it was my house I'd drink it every day. I'd have it on my cornflakes for breakfast.'

'I thought you hated cornflakes?'

'I do. But I like banana-ey. Tell me something.'

'Tell you what?'

'Just tell me something. Anything.'

'Like what?'

'Something about yourself. Or something about me.'

Denise turned her head to see him, eyes half-shut, squinting against the brightness of the lights though it was only table lamps that were on in the room.

'Something about you and me?'

'Yes.'

'I don't want to.'

'Why not?'

'I'm embarrassed.'

'Don't be.'

'Okay then. But you might be embarrassed.'

Denise giggled. 'I won't be, I promise.'

'You can't promise that. You don't know what I'm going to say yet.'

'Yes I do. I know everything you're thinking right now. I can read your mind.'

'Uh-huh.'

'I can read your mind and I can see your thoughts swimming about in your head . . .'

'What am I thinking right now then?'

Denise smiled at him: the way his hair was ruffled up like that made him sort of cute. He was like some sort of owl thing with his specs on. She held up her arm and stared at it, letting it hang in the air right above her. She let out a sigh, then took a deep breath and did it again.

'What're you doing?'

Denise closed her eyes and exhaled deeply, from away down inside, emptying herself out. 'Helping myself go to sleep . . .'

'You can't fall asleep here, Denise. My mum and dad'll be back in a bit.'

'I know. Just for a minute,' she sighed again, letting her hand sit up there like a weather vane.

'C'mon, Denise. You were about to tell us what I was thinking . . .'

'Mmmm,' she said, drifting away, the floor feeling good there underneath her. The carpet. Her arm came back down to her side.

'Denise!'

John was tugging at her shoulder. She snapped awake again and sat up, blinking dumbly at the light.

'I should get home,' she said. It was getting on. She was drunk. She was supposed to have been in ages ago. Not that anyone would worry about her. As if.

John Burke looked at her. 'I was going to tell you something about us,' he said, looking at the carpet. '*You* were going to read my mind . . .'

'Too tired now,' Denise told him, covering her mouth to yawn. 'Too tired. Have to sleep soon.'

She got up and started to get her things together, swaying a bit as she did.

John looked a bit hurt. Maybe what he was going to say had been important. Oh well.

He stood up, too. 'D'you want me to walk you part of the way?'

'No,' Denise went. 'It's all right. It's not worth it.'

She wondered if she should have said that last bit. Maybe he would think she was blanking him. Well, she was. Sort of.

'I mean come if you like . . . but it's all right. I can take care of myself.'

John snorted.

'What was that meant to mean?' she said.

'Just the idea of you taking care of *yourself*.'

'What?'

'Nothing. Just—'

'Just what?'

'You always take care of yourself. You're an expert at taking care of yourself. Drives me nuts sometimes . . .'

Denise felt herself getting flushed again. 'What d'you mean?' she said. 'What's wrong with that?'

'Nothing. It's good. I mean . . . *sometimes* . . .'

'Sometimes?'

'I mean, it's like you don't even notice the other people about you sometimes. It's like if they all dropped dead – if *we* all dropped dead – you just wouldn't care at all. Would you?'

Denise was trying to reply, but the words weren't there; a stutter was all she could manage.

'All this' – John opened a hand – '*talk*. About dying and that. Killing yourself. Sometimes I think you would too . . . I mean, just to *spite* people.'

Denise just stared at him, fists clenched.

'You want folk to *see* it, that's the trouble. You want them to *see* it and *feel* it and keep *on* feeling it. Appreciate the sacrifice *you're* making, being here with us. Other than that, it's like we're just here to populate *your* fantasy, *your* world.'

Denise felt caught in the act, she wanted him to stop, didn't want to hear, wanted to stick her fingers in her ears, because it was true.

'And it'd be dead glamorous being drunk all the time,

too. You could just disappear right up your own arse then, couldn't you? You'd have your excuse then, wouldn't you?'

John was jabbing a finger at her, his face a crease of frowns.

Denise said nothing.

'You've no idea about what I'm thinking. You haven't the first clue what I might be thinking. You haven't the faintest idea what I might be thinking or what anybody else might be thinking either.'

'Stop it,' Denise was mumbling.

'Can you tell what I'm thinking now? Can you? Getting any clearer, is it?'

'Stop it. Please.' She couldn't understand what it was that she'd done to make him so angry.

'You'd like to tell me what I'm thinking, wouldn't you? That'd be it – *tell* me.'

'Stop it, John.'

'That's the way you deal with people isn't it? You'd like them to bow down and worship you.'

'John . . .'

He stopped, took a breath, and began to put the bottles and the decanter back into the cupboard, brushing at the thighs of his trousers. He avoided her gaze.

'You better go,' he said. 'It's getting late.'

He emptied the ashtray into the bin and put it down again on the carpet. 'Go on,' he said. 'Go. I'll speak to you tomorrow or something.' He began to footer with the glasses.

Denise was staring at him, waiting for him to say something else. An apology. But he was right. Why should *he* say sorry? *She* never would have, and all this was making her feel really drunk now, her head fuzzy with it. She swayed a bit putting her jacket on. Then she turned and went to the front door. John came out too, unsnibbing the door for her, holding it open. She went out into the porch.

'Denise, I—'

'It's all right,' Denise said, opening the porch door.

232

'Wait.'

'I can't,' she said. She thought she might start to cry. It had happened once. She couldn't let it happen again.

'Okay,' he said, closing the door behind her, waiting in the porch, watching while she walked away.

As she stepped from the path onto the road, she turned and jerked her lower lip down at him, knowing he could see the word that wasn't yet written there, her first tattoo, waiting to be inscribed.

TRUTH

The word was freshly inked, black, truth waiting to be told.

He stared at her, then shook his head.

Denise didn't like these streets she was walking down; didn't like these houses. These main roads that led onto other roads and side-streets like the veins in a dead body. It was just all one great big body. She could hear shouting and yelling somewhere nearby. She turned past a bus stop with the glass lying all about. A brick lay inside. There was graffiti on the inside of the metal frame.

UDA ALL THE WAY

The Red Hand of Ulster beneath, except it was just a black outline. Someone else had scrawled I LOVE RUSTY, and somebody else had written TUBES next to it, using a different tone of spray. In the light of the street lamps, everything was the colour grey, or the colour orange. Colour blind, tone was all she had to go on.

She had never intended it to be like this. Greyness was what she'd wanted to avoid. Now, she was drenched in it.

She kept walking. Maybe it was true. Maybe she really was like that, like the way John had said. She didn't know. She knew she had been singled out somehow, if only by herself. She knew she had been marked in a way she didn't understand. There were things about herself she was only half aware of. There were things about herself she didn't like all that much. But at least they were *her* things. At least they were a part of *her*. At least she could say: These things are *mine*.

There were all these pictures of her, a jigsaw in stained glass. She'd nothing else to go on.

If anyone dares to risk my fisk . . .
Its buff and its wham, understand?
I'm strong to the finish 'cause I eat my spinach . . .
I'm Popeye the sailor man!

She was what she was. Like Popeye. I yam what I yam.

Sounds of feet and running. Someone ran across the street up from her, full pelt. Other figures ran after. Some of them were carrying sticks or something. She couldn't make out who was who. They passed her and she pulled herself into the side of the pavement next to the privet hedges and railings and palings so's not to get knocked over. Now she recognised some of them. Andy McCabe was there, running past, nearly elbowing her out the way.

'FUCKING DIE!' he was shouting, then paused, looked at her winking, as if whatever he was doing was just a bit of fun: 'All right, Denise? Still up to your witchy ways?'

And he was away again, tearing after the rest of them.

'FENIAN CUNT!'

She was alone again, almost wishing Andy would come back so's she wouldn't be. She felt like she might start to cry again.

When she got back to her street, she made her way up the steps to the house. There was noise coming from inside, but her brain was too fogged up to register it straight off. She fumbled the key into the lock. Music was playing. Loud music. Ceilidh-band type stuff. Bumpity-bump country and western music. All the lights were on.

Her mum came stamping out the living room. *I'm leaving* she was saying, *I'm leaving right now.*

Alison was sitting on the stairs. She looked frightened. Her mum saw Denise and came over to her, grabbing her by both arms. 'I'm sorry, she was saying. 'I'm sorry, Denise.' She turned and looked at Alison. 'I'm sorry, Alison,' she said. Their dad was striding through the hallway, a drink in his hand.

'Wait,' he said, 'Please.' He grabbed Denise's mum by the arm. 'You're not going anywhere.'

'Don't you ever try and manhandle me,' her mum said, raking at his face with her nails. Denise's dad cupped his hand to the side of his cheek. She'd cut him. He was bleeding.

'I'm going, Denise, Alison. I have to leave. I can't explain it just now . . . Just, I have to leave.'

Denise's dad stood, one hand dabbing at his cheek, the other still nursing its drink, the glass moving from chest height to mouth in a reflex action. His eyes were red. Even now he wouldn't put it down, she could see. If her mum had knocked him down he would have found a way to protect it.

She pictured him tumbling backwards through the air, taking the impact of the ground with the full spread of his back, the glass held up out of harm's way, not even a drop spilt. It was disgusting. She stared at the two people who equalled her parents and didn't know what she was meant to say or do. They had never fought. They hardly ever even had discussions. Only silent, unspoken ones. Ones they conducted with their eyes.

'Let me get my bag, Duncan.'

Denise's mum stared at him. He said nothing, his mouth set as if he was afraid of opening it. They stood in silence while she dialled a taxi number. Nobody was saying anything, Alison huddled on the stairs, eyes all watery. Their dad went through to the living room, then came back out again. He was carrying a suitcase; he walked over to the door and set it down without saying anything. Then he went back through to the living room and didn't come back out again. A country and western singer plonked out a tune.

Denise's mum ordered the taxi, then nodded for her and Alison to follow her into the front room. She sat down on the good couch, Alison and Denise on either side of her. Denise stared at the floor not knowing what to say. She tried to make herself feel something about what was happening. But she just felt drunk and stupid and disconnected.

Alison had started to greet.

'Come on, don't cry,' her mum was saying, wrapping her arms about her and pulling her in. 'You'll make me cry too . . .'

'Why?' Alison was saying. 'Why d'you have to leave?'

'I can't explain it right now. You'll understand when you're older.'

But for Denise that was no explanation at all. Neither she nor Alison would understand when they were older. They would never understand. It would mean a lifetime of explanations from her to explain a lifetime of reasons. Or at least a marriage's worth. If she explained well enough – if they gave her the chance to explain – perhaps they might understand some of the reasons. Still, there were things they would never understand. Things she could never explain. She could try and try and never even get halfway there. And Denise knew, too, that they would both resent her for it. She knew that. A lifetime of questions ahead, for all three of them. A lifetime of penance for their mum.

'But *why?*' Alison was saying.

'Listen,' Anna said. 'Your daddy isn't a bad man, don't think that. It's just that . . . I can't explain just now. Just promise me you'll not blame him for this. He just . . . I can't explain.'

Denise felt her mum reach out behind her and take her hand; she nearly jumped at the touch. She stared down at them, those two hands, the one clasping the other, squeezing it hard, communicating something to her, some kind of signal.

'I'll be in touch, I promise. Just let me get myself settled somewhere. And when I do, I'll be in touch. You'll be able to come and see me . . .'

'*When?*' Alison asked.

'I don't know that yet. Soon. But you'll come and see me, won't you?'

Alison nodded.

'Denise?'

Denise didn't know what to say. If she told her the truth, that she didn't know, that she'd no idea what she might feel about that *if* and *when* the time came, that maybe she'd hate her, despise her for walking out on them, then it might destroy her. What use was the truth if it hurt people? She couldn't tell the truth now; she wanted to but couldn't. She had no idea what the truth was. Perhaps there would be another time for truth; perhaps there would be a chance to get it all out. But not now. Denise drew her hand away.

'Yes,' she said, because it was what was needed, what the situation called for.

Her mum smiled weakly at her. It was something. No matter what happened now, Denise had given her this much. This chance. She stood up and went to the curtain and looked out.

There was the sound of an engine outside, then the phone rang once, twice, and died.

'That's him now,' she said. 'I better go.'

Denise went up to her room, locked herself in and sat with the whisky tumbler and the half-bottle she'd picked up off the breakfast bar in the kitchen. Nobody would notice. Nobody would care. Her dad had plenty; he was sitting in the living room, the stereo belting out 'My tears have washed I love you from the blackboard of my heart.' Her sister chapped on her door.

Denise, she was saying. *Let me come in, Denise.*

But Denise wanted to speak to no one. Not to have to listen to anyone. Not to see anyone. The room was still hers. The things in it were still hers. They couldn't leave. Her walls and her bed and her ceiling. Her papier-mâché and her paintings and her sculptures. Pyramids and sphinx and rivers and lochs and towns and hamlets, roads and arteries and fly-overs and underpasses, all populated with her gangs of boys and girls, her laybys and roundabouts where folk could leave flowers by the side of the road, wreaths and red roses, white roses and cards that other folk might stop and read. White roses, wreaths to be put there, 'cause somebody would have died there, hit by a car, stabbed for a pound, beaten to death for no reason at all other than boredom . . .

The rot had set in long ago.

But there was no rest to be had in this house. There was numbness, but no rest. It was not the same.

Let me in, Denise?

She could hear her sister through the door.

Please . . .

Denise was staring at the painted outlines on her window-pane, the ones she'd watercoloured in, the ones she'd traced the contours of the outside world onto, all miracle blues and greens, distant low hills, skyscrapers that jutted like teeth from diseased gums against the horizon, wondering what was beyond the next hill, and then the next hill, and then the hill after that.

She could hear her sister crying out there. John Burke's words were still jangling in her ears:

We're just here to populate your fantasy, your world. That's the part I hate about you.

Well, the population of this fantasy was dwindling.

$4 - 1 = 3$.

Her sister was still outside the door. She was crying. She was crying 'cause their mother had left them. 'Cause their dad was drunk downstairs. She was crying and Denise wasn't. There were no tears this side of the door. There might never be. Denise went over to the door and stood. She put her ear up to it. She cupped her hand around. She could feel her sister on the other side. She could feel her sister's breathing, the rise and fall of her chest. Denise waited.

The numbers were just numbers. They didn't equal anything unless you said: One green bottle plus another green bottle. That gave you two green bottles. Two people plus two people gave you four *people*.

Denise listened again at the door, but her sister had gone away now, too.

Not long after her mum left, Denise began to notice the change in the house. It was different now. It seemed to be in a kind of grief, a kind of mourning. When she put her key in the lock and went to turn it, the whole place altered just before she opened the door. Denise would go in and listen to the emptiness. Nobody. Nothing. Through in the back room, the wallpaper still hung from the same walls, but everything had changed just the same. Did the house know it too?

Her dad had changed seats. Now, he sat in the one her mum had always used, the times when she wasn't just lying on the floor. He had a collection of empty beer cans round the chair, *Daily Records* that were gradually piling up. Denise had tried to clear them once, while he sat there asleep, mouth open and his police shirt unbuttoned at the collar, his tie loosened and skew-whiff. There'd been white spittle at the corner of his mouth. Snoring came in jolts, his forehead with a dirty mark on it that he must have rubbed there with fingers inky from the newspaper that was open on his lap. A topless girl stared up from it. When Denise'd gone to pick up the cans he'd shook awake and stared at her like he'd no idea who she was. Denise had jumped. She noticed his undone fly.

'Leave them,' he said, wiping his forehead. He closed his eyes again, and she began to straighten the toppled cans that lay on the floor, then he took the newspaper and whipped it against the back of her head.

'I said leave them!'

She turned and walked out of the room slowly, closing the door very quietly behind her. Then, she ran up the stairs to her room.

Here she was now, standing in this room, listening once more to the sound of emptiness. She clicked on the TV: there was a cartoon showing. One of the ones with the coyote in it, and a sheepdog, and some sheep. The coyote made different plans, used different devices to try and catch the sheep. Every time he seemed about to succeed, his ACME-made contraption would backfire, or the sheepdog would appear and beat him up. It was terrible and sad. The coyote never got the sheep, his eyes always filling with the same recognition of utter futility and the inevitable knowledge of his imminent demise. If he wasn't a cartoon coyote, he'd have been killed long ago. But there he was again, ready to start over every time. He never gave up. And at the end of this cartoon, he walked up to a punch-machine and clocked off. So did the sheepdog. And then they both said goodnight to each other, called each other by name. In the morning they'd begin all over again. It was the most depressing thing she'd ever seen in her life. But then again, it was funny too.

She clicked the set off and stood, looking at the lager tins collected in their usual positions. There were ashtrays and cushions and wet patches on the floor. She started rearranging things, clearing some of the mess away. She plumped up the cushions and opened the curtains and windows, getting some air back into the room. Then she stood at the wall, pressing her hand against it. Those pictures were still under there, waiting to come out and scare her all over again. Likely they'd be under there until the house fell down.

Denise went into the kitchen and put the radio on: it was tuned to one of those bumpity-bump stations her dad liked. She thought how nice it'd be if nobody else came in for a while, just left the silence and emptiness to her. Let Denise enjoy the peace. Let her enjoy the quietness. Of course, the place was almost always empty now. But still.

There were things her mum had left, reminders everywhere. Denise sort of wished her mum could have taken a big box and thrown everything into it, everything she'd ever owned, everything she'd ever touched, everything that had ever known her presence, no matter how big or small, and then carted it all away so's Denise wouldn't have to keep coming across them. They kept surprising her. They jumped unexpectedly out of drawers or from behind settees. They fell from the tops of wardrobes or rolled from underneath the sinks. They were coughed up by the Hoover or appeared from the pockets of old clothes, clothes Denise could never recall if her mum had worn or not, clothes she couldn't remember ever having seen. There was a box of jewellery, rings, a necklace made of tiny white seashells, ones she'd told Denise were too small to hear the sound of the sea in. A pendant she'd got on holiday in Wales, a picture of a red dragon painted on white enamel. Framed photographs of Denise and Alison as toddlers. Their Granny *La*mont/La*mont*. Their mum wearing a fur coat she said she'd smuggled out of Poland away back in the sixties, meaning to sell it in France except it turned out to be a fake.

'All fur coat and nae knickers,' Denise's dad had said, and they'd all laughed.

'A wild lot, they Poles,' said her granny, maybe having old Polywka in mind at the time, though he'd never seemed all that out of control to Denise. The opposite, if anything. His whole demeanour had spoken only of quiet tolerance and a kind of inevitableness.

There was a drawing of the moon that Denise must have done in nursery or primary school, a big round flat nothingness with black all around. It'd been folded between the pages of a Barbara Cartland novel, one where all the women spoke in a kind of breathless, expectant away. Denise had no idea why. She'd folded up the picture and put it back between the pages, slid the volume once more into its place on the shelf. It made you feel like you were looking at something you were never meant to see, finding it there. Like you'd caught somebody in the act of something private. She decided it would be best to leave it there for someone else to discover or not at all. It would be fine to her if it just stayed where it was, in its own inky universe.

Once, she'd asked her mum which the stars were, and which the planets. Her mum hadn't known, but her Granny *La*mont/La*mont* told her that you could tell the difference if you looked hard enough.

'See that one?' she said, pointing up at the darkened sky.

'Uh-huh.'

'See how it doesn't twinkle?'

Denise had stared hard at where she thought her granny was pointing. After a while, she found one that didn't seem to twinkle.

'That's a planet, not a star. Stars twinkle. Planets shine.'

Up there, between the blacknesses, there were stars and there were planets and the stars were twinkling and the planets were shining.

She wanted to throw all these things, all these reminders into a big box and leave it out on the street, or build a bonfire and set it ablaze. But there wasn't any point. There were too many reminders, and even if you did manage to get rid of them all there would still be the big, empty house. Because the emptiness of the house was her mum's too. It was an emptiness you could touch, permanent and unyielding.

Someone was at the door letting themselves in. Her dad. He nodded his greeting, a nod with nothing behind it. It didn't question and didn't expect a reply. That was fine with Denise. She'd nothing to say to it anyway. He came in, loosening his tie, hat already off. He'd been to the shops. He was carrying a paper grocery bag, the sounds of bottles clinking from inside.

'Don't expect you'll be cooking, will you?' he said.

She moved to one side to let him pass, but when she did, he brushed against her, his body momentarily pressing hers so that she shrunk in to herself. He seemed to be smirking at her. She couldn't be sure.

He went into the kitchen, Denise watching, unsure what to do with herself now. She'd wanted the quiet for herself, but now she'd have to share. Her dad put the carrier-bag on the worktop and stood for a minute looking out of the window, one arm leaning against the frame, milky sunlight turning him into an outline. A silhouette.

'Lawn needs cutting,' he said, not turning. 'And that hedge.'

Denise said nothing.

'Something smells in here,' he said. 'Something's gone off.'

He turned and opened the fridge door, bending to get a look inside, picking out an old lettuce head then putting it back in again. He peeled the lid back off a milk bottle, sniffed it, then took a gulp. He cocked his head over at Denise.

'Cat got your tongue?'

Denise dropped her head, shifting from one foot to another.

'I'm having guests later,' he said. 'You might want to be out.'

'Why?'

''Cause I says so.'

He turned to the worktop, lifting a whisky bottle from the paper bag and putting it heavily down on the counter so Denise knew he'd already had a drink before getting home. These days, doors always got slammed. There was a weight to everything he did. Everything he went near seemed to cower, as if afraid of what he might do next.

'June's coming over,' he said, then took a dirty glass from the sink and filled it two-thirds full with whisky. As he raised it to drink, he winked an eye at Denise and grimaced.

'Purely for medicinal purposes,' he said, and took a drink, making a face as he did. 'Jesus Christ,' he said. 'That's what I get for buying cooking whisky.'

He put the glass down on the counter hard enough for some of the liquid to jump out. The bang made Denise start.

'This bin,' he said. 'Been emptied lately, has it?'

Denise shrugged, her housekeeping skills still not perfect.

Her dad was looking at the bin, hands on hips, suspicious of it. He was looking like he was scared to open it, frightened of whatever rottenness might be hiding inside.

Finally, he stepped on the pedal and the lid sprang back, releasing a cloud of black flies, furry and huge, their massed wings filling the kitchen with buzzing.

'Ah!' he said, and Denise shuddered, covering her mouth, the flies veering off in erratic trajectories about her dad's head, him flapping his hands at them so that his body danced and jerked stupidly. He stepped back from the bin and covered his own mouth and nose with his sleeve, the stink rising from the bin along with the flies.

'Do something!' Denise said, a buzz of flies surrounding

her. Her dad was crouched over the bin, lifting a lump of dead thing out with thumb and forefinger. He held it at arm's length and fumbled in his trouser pocket for something with his other hand, not able now to cover his mouth and he kept it open, breathing through it to avoid inhaling the smell. Flies landed on the meat and took off again. Flies crowded to the window. Flies clogged up the edges of it or began to bash themselves uselessly at the glass. Her dad had fished his keys out and was trying to flick through the bunch with one hand while still holding the thing – pork chop, steak, fillet, whatever it had been – as far away from himself as possible. It was itself a crawling mass of flies again.

'Open the door,' he said, throwing the keys to Denise. She caught them and shivered through the kitchen to the back door, putting first one wrong key in the lock, then another. At last she got the right one in and turned it, flinging the door open wide, her dad already behind her, then he was out into the garden and tossing the chop so that it landed, trailed by flies, in the middle of the lawn. Denise stared at it lying there. It was true. The lawn did need cutting.

She decided to stay in, even if that June woman came round or not. It was her house too. Alison went out as usual. Denise sat in her room, hearing the noise of laughing and music coming from downstairs, the thump of footsteps as they climbed up to the bathroom. The sound of urine splashing. The sound of the cistern's ball-cock. Every time someone came up, she was sure they were going to come to her door and say some stupid fucking drunken thing to her, ask her some stupid fucking drunken question, embarrass her in some stupid fucking drunken way. The woman, June. Her dad. She felt like she was under siege. It was like being in prison. Here, in this big, empty house, full of people.

She got up and went to the window. Her watercolour was still painted there, matched to the view beyond. Except it was too dark to see either properly. The pork chop, steak, bit of meat, still lay outside on the lawn, hidden by the grass. Maybe a cat would come along and drag it away. Maybe a fox or dog would come and fight over it. If they were dead hungry.

All she could make out was the outline, a shape squashed into the grass like one of those crop circle things.

She went and opened the door a crack, listening to her dad and the woman, June, talk and laugh downstairs. She was loud, but you still couldn't make out what she said through the slur of drink. The hallway smelt of cigarettes. Denise went through to the main bedroom and stood. She was sure she was standing exactly above them. She could feel the floorboards creak under her weight. They were old. Loose. She walked over to the bookcase and picked out the book. She opened it at the place where the drawing was, took it out, unfolded it. There it was, the moon. Alone in the night. She decided that was okay, though. That was fine. It'd be best of all if Denise could be really alone too. Even here, in this room with the two single beds in it, one with a duvet and one with wool blankets and linen sheets, the room her mum had slept in, Denise wasn't alone. There were the books lined up in queues of unread and read, all with their thousands of breathy words; there was the chest of drawers she'd kept her underwear in, lined with newspapers dating back to when they'd first moved to this house. There was the big mirrored wardrobe with the bevelled art nouveau designs on the front, and inside the few things she'd still to come back and pick up. A fur coat, lustreless and shabby. A crimson velvet beret still in its sealed bag, the kind of bag you'd get if you went to the baker's for a Paris bun or a Danish pastry, one side ordinary paper, the other cellophane. There was a row of shoes, the cracks along the bit where her toes bent them showing the wear that had been got out of each pair, dating them as efficiently as the yellowed newspapers in the drawers.

She stared at the bed her mum had slept in. The one with the wool blankets, because she'd never got used to the duvet, said it got too hot in the summer and wasn't warm enough in the winter.

'It's unhygienic,' her dad had said. 'Encourage infestations, so they do.'

'Mmm,' her mum had said, not paying any attention.

And here was the moon she'd given her, that her mum had left behind, forgotten about. Denise thought it was weird that somebody could forget the moon. She remembered some lines from a Japanese poem she'd heard at school. She didn't know who'd written it, but it had gone something like:

Though you are thousands
Of miles apart
You are united
By the moon.

Maybe it hadn't been Japanese, though. Maybe it had been Chinese, or some other place. Egyptian, a poem in hieroglyphs. Anyway, the moon was still here, in this book on a shelf. They weren't united by it. But the emptiness was still here. Her mum had left that behind. She felt its chill hug against her and shivered.

Outside, across the street, were other lives behind their net curtains, framed by their own yellow streetlights. They were laughing, and watching television, playing Monopoly. If you were dead quiet, you might even hear them. They might speak their lives to you, spread Chinese whispers.

Shssh. Pass it on. Shssh. Listen. I have to tell you something. Yes. Listen. Pass it on.

She folded the picture again and put it back inside the book. She stopped, thinking she could hear foxes screech outside, somewhere nearby, maybe attracted by the chop on the lawn. Maybe not. Denise switched the light off, stepping over the creaky place in the floor and going out into the hall. She saw the frame of a man silhouetted against the light, as he'd been downstairs earlier, in the open doorway of the toilet, the sound of heavy splashing in the bowl. He hadn't bothered to shut the door. She heard him cough loudly, a cough that pretended it was casual, spontaneous, but was anything but. Denise tried to step by quietly, but she must have done something, alerted him somehow, caused some ripple in the atmosphere that told him she was there because he turned, glancing over his shoulder at her, sensing her presence. And then he turned to face her full-frontal, trapping her there. His fly was open, his penis hanging down. It was a different colour from the rest of him. Olive dark, where his face was pale and prone to rosiness. He put his hands on his hips and grinned.

'That is . . . not appropriate!' she said.

She took two steps towards her room and slammed the door shut behind her. Inside, she could feel him still standing there on the other side. Then, the lumpen sound of his boots heading down the stairs again.

It was a long while before Denise could push that picture to the back of her head, and when she did, she wanted it to stay there, the dustsheet drawn over it. But she knew that a wind might blow through her head at any minute, threatening to uncover the picture, leave it exposed and blatant. At any moment.

Denise got out of her jeans and put on her black mini, then put her trainers back on. She ran down the stairs and into the back room for some change. Her dad was sleeping on the couch; she slipped her hand into his jacket pocket and took out his wallet. She folded away a five-pound note and slid the wallet back in, then went out, clicking the front door behind her, walking fast to get to the back lanes. It was cold, too cold, but she took off her sweater and tied it around her waist anyway, then opened a button extra on her blouse. It was all she could do to stop herself running down the road.

She pushed the door of the café open. It was warm inside, a living warmth. She went over to the booth they usually sat at and slid in.

'All right, Denise? Jeedy said.

'All right.'

The guy that nobody spoke to nodded at her.

'Yeh, but I have to get some ice-cream for after tea.'

It was just Jeedy and the guy that nobody spoke to. Denise wished he would bugger off.

'I'm only here for a minute,' Denise said. 'Just to get the ice-cream and some flakes.' She got up and went over to the counter, not looking behind. She caught Jeedy staring at her in the mirror. Caught his eye. He smiled at her and she smiled back. It made her clench her bum in a kind of funny spasm. She even did it again, on purpose this time, tighter. He was talking to that guy now – the one that never said anything –

leaning forward like they were conspiring, sharing things that she'd never get to be privy to. Maybe they were talking about the car or something.

Old Turtle-face came up to the counter. 'What d'you want?' he said.

'Two one-pound-twenty tubs and four flakes, please.'

'Is that it?'

'Uh huh.'

He smacked his lips and waggled over to the freezer on his bandy legs, creases on the front of his trousers like he'd ironed them in. Surely nobody ironed creases into jeans? Denise started to smile a bit: just the thought of it.

She took the bag and turned round. Jeedy smiled a big, gleaming smile at her. She went over.

'So what happened about the car?'

The guy that never said anything looked at the table.

'What about it?' Jeedy said. He was angry again. She'd made him angry. Everything she did seemed to make him angry. Everything *anybody* did. She didn't understand him at all. Did he even like her? It was impossible to tell.

'The car business . . .' he said. 'Nothing. Yet.'

She nodded, wishing she'd never sat down. It was as if nothing had happened the other night. She'd felt like they'd overcome something, like there was a connection between them, something that bound them together, a shared something, a mutual something. She'd felt it. She thought he had too. But now she didn't know.

Jeedy leaned over to whisper in the guy that never said anything's ear, and he smirked. Denise couldn't hear what he said, but it felt like it was about her. She flushed.

She got up. 'Well, maybe see you later,' she said, wishing she had the bottle not to say it, wishing she was totally not bothered, totally did-not-give-a-fuck. It was too late though. The words had just jumped out and there was nothing she could do.

Jeedy looked up at her. 'Maybe,' he said. Then he looked away again.

Walking down the road, she was still hoping Jeedy would come out after her. She was about round onto the main road when he finally did. 'Wait up, Denise,' he said. She stopped and turned round, squinting at him in the cold sun. 'Thought you weren't going to wait,' he said. She tried to look offhand, but he put his arm around her hip and said, 'Had to talk over some business with my man . . .'

Denise kept walking and not saying anything.

'Not want to know what it was about?'

Denise shook her head, arms crossed across her chest, her nipples stiff in the cold.

He was unfankling the wires and putting the tape into the player of a personal stereo. Grinning, he handed her one of the earphones and took one himself. 'All right?' he asked.

'Okay,' Denise said, but didn't know if she'd shouted loud enough, because of the headphones. It was some mad stuff, something she'd never heard before. But Denise didn't know anything about music; she couldn't tell you the names of groups, or who was number one; she'd no idea if what she liked was cool or not, what year it was recorded or what label it was on. She just liked tunes. If someone like Jeedy was to ask her what she liked to listen to, she'd only have been able to shrug. She might have hummed a few bars, picked a few notes from something she had heard recently on the radio, or television, because she'd no records of her own, except ones she'd been given as presents. And she never does pick up the habit of categorising her tastes; she leaves that to others. What particular instrument, the variables of flat tunings, the sharps, the heave and yawl of pitch, these seem to Denise to be constellations that hum and bring their weight to bear. It was a conclusion she was sure of; the working was irrelevant. Music was in the fabric of everything.

But, like everything, the music could sometimes get too loud.

'Turn it down a bit,' she asked Jeedy, 'so's I can hear if I'm shouting.'

Had she got home all right the other night? he was asking. He'd not been able to leave the Dummy till he was sure his brother would have gone out. Then he'd slept all day.

'You better not come any nearer the house – my dad might see you,' she said, ignoring the question, nervous as they got closer.

'Don't care if he sees me or not,' Jeedy said. 'I got as much right as him to be out here.'

'Yeh, but you know what he's like . . .'

It was even dead romantic, like the Montagues and the Capulets. Doomed, star-crossed lovers. The thought saddened Denise, but in an enjoyable kind of way.

Then Jeedy was going to snog her, with his mouth open, and she hadn't even been going to let him, but then she opened up her lips a bit and it was all right, really. Better than before, and his breath was cleaner and he tasted of Wrigley's spearmint. It was nice. They leaned up against a garage door round one of the back lanes and she felt him pressing up against her, and she reached down there and rubbed the flat palm of her hand against the lump. It was funny but it didn't even disgust her to do that, it was all right really. She had thought it would disgust her. If she tried to picture it, in her room, alone, she stepped lightly over the specifics, did not picture genitals or fluids; even nakedness. A veil covered the rude mechanicals, a smokescreen that made the violence of sex palatable. Because it was a violence, a violence made of ugly words and uglier actions:

Fuck.

Penetrate.

Orgasm.

Yes, there were always other pictures, other images. But

they were best avoided. Best kept secret. Even if it was from yourself. Denise snapped out of her thoughts, letting Jeedy put his hand up around the back of her skirt, squeezing her, a bit too gentle but okay. That was all she wanted just now, she didn't need any more. She could only take a bit at a time. She felt dizzy in her belly.

The night before his seventeenth birthday, Andy McCabe walked down the road with Alison Forrester, teasing her about what she was going to get him for a present, listing ever more extravagant and expensive things. They'd be laid out at his funeral. Alison, unlike her big sister, feels some kind of regret for him dying, throat slashed on a suburban streetcorner. But it's a regret tinged with guilt; guilt for telling him that it was over; guilt 'cause it was the night before his birthday; guilt 'cause she's going off to meet somebody else, though she says there's nobody. Of course there's nobody.

And, of course, the police had arrived, and the ambulance and a crowd of folk all trying to get a look, get a photo. One of the police was a tall thin guy with a baldy head and a moustache, who kept looking over at a girl with long dark hair and pale skin stood over in the corner by an ambulance, a girl who wouldn't say anything. And the girl looked at him too, and something passed between them that didn't seem to require the effort of words, though of course the girl was a witness. She would have to say something eventually. The law required it.

She could get him a new watch, Andy said, or a set of gold clubs . . .

'As if.'

Or just the cash equivalent would be fine.

'That'll be right.'

Andy and Alison walked down the road, him insisting on

putting his arm over her shoulder. Alison kept herself contained, made her body small and compact, tried to give away nothing of herself to him. She concentrated on how she was going to tell him. Maybe he'd take it really badly. It would be terrible if he cried or something.

Did Alison want to go in for an ice? Andy was asking.

She didn't. She'd already been to Burger King with her sister. Denise had been there with John Burke. She had even *smoked*. Nobody'd been saying anything to each other. Alison and Denise stared at each other as though enemies, neither of them sure how it was that they'd arrived at their positions of mutual contempt.

Alison and Andy McCabe kept on going past the café, Old Turtle inside mopping the floor. He looked at them and kidded on he didn't recognise them. The café was closing down, but she didn't really believe that. It didn't seem possible. Where would they all go? They'd just have to wander about the streets all night getting hassled by the folk from the school round the corner.

'Here,' Andy said, 'I know what you can give me for my birthday . . .'

'What?' Alison asked, trying to sound as if she was interested.

'Follow me.' Andy cocked his head and grinned. His skin was clearing up; he looked quite manly. Alison wondered if she looked womanly, suddenly aware of her body.

She let him take her hand; it felt cold and clammy. He stopped a second and went to snog her but she pulled herself away so that he could only get her cheek. She had a kind of shiver then. It was odd. She'd decided to chuck him, and now he disgusted her.

A few hours after being at Burger King, Denise drank too much vodka, too much Ron, felt them swilling about all inside her, curdling, pictured the contents of her stomach burble like a lava lamp, then realised she'd pished all over the couch in John's mum and dad's house. She started shivering, John Burke trying to get her to take her wet skirt and knickers off. Denise's hand went to the buckle of his combats and got them open while he sat back staring stupidly at her, not understanding. She tried to will him into being Jeedy, just for a second, but he was missing something, would never have the necessary ingredients, never be the right mix for Denise. Perhaps for Alison, but never Denise.

For one thing, he wants her to say *sorry*. For ruining his mum's couch. It's just a word. That's all it would have taken for them to be fine again, but instead here he was lifting up his arse to help her slide the combats down.

Denise got them off and then rolled a wad of hankies around her hand from the box sitting on the glass tabletop and began to mop herself up with them. There was stickiness all over her jacket where she'd spilled her drink while unconscious. She got up and got her things about her. John Burke even began to notice.

'Denise,' he said, as if she was still there in front of where he was sitting, knelt up in against the side of the couch, his feet curling under him on the carpet, one elbow in the dark spreading stain in the middle of the couch. He flapped his hand about in front of him, like he had something important to say but couldn't remember what. He has white sports socks on that are pulled halfway off, just the boxers on.

'Denise . . . 'msorry. 'Msorry, Denise. Why am *I* saying sorry?'

'I'm away now,' Denise told him. She had nothing to be sorry for. It wasn't her fault if it was Jeedy she liked. She told herself that, but there was something that didn't feel right about it. It sat in her belly uncomfortably, like food.

''Mon Denise, an' not be—'

His trousers were far too big. She had to fasten the belt away up to the last notch. Denise put her wet things into a carrier bag and managed to get it into her jacket pocket. John Burke sat there, eyes glazed over and stupid-looking, his glasses off so that he looked even more lost than usual.

'Denise . . .'

John Burke's socks were somehow too explicit, the dirt showing on the soles. They hung down like a pair of used johnnies. They were an obscenity.

Boys. Only after one thing. Denise tucked herself in at the waistband and put John Burke's packet of cigarettes in her pocket, picked up the bottle of alcohol-flavoured soft drink that was lying on the glass coffee table, *SlaZinger*, it was called. She put the bottle to her lips and swallowed, her teeth and lips sugary from the stuff. Her favourite.

She didn't know why she picked the fags up. She didn't even smoke. Not much, anyway. Then she went out the door, clicking it shut behind her.

Of course, John Burke *was* only after one thing. He'd wanted Denise Forrester to say sorry, but it would never happen. Denise went out into the hallway, trying to think what to do now, where to go. Maybe she'd go down the Dummy. Jeedy might go there. Or somebody might be there that knew where he was, 'cause he might want to see her, it was possible, anything was possible, it was still dead early. She might walk out and round the corner and he'd be standing there under a streetlight, waiting for her. She might just take a few steps out and he'd jump up from behind the privet hedge, go *Boo!* and surprise her. And she'd go *Jeedy!* and put her hand up to her chest, it palpitating away like mad, the engine that kept her alive, slick red and marbled with yellowy fat, pulsating like a kettle-drum about to burst. Or he might be down the Dummy already, sitting on their mattress – which is how Denise always thinks of it, this mouldy, damp, stained object – the campfire going, his eyes gleaming in the darkness. Which is the way Denise actually does discover him, after an hour wandering about in the dark, searching everywhere she can think of, going back and forward to the same places over and over again in the hope that he'll turn up.

'Stop, Andy,' Alison was saying. 'Stop it!'

He was holding her too tight, wouldn't let go. She broke free and fixed herself.

'I'm sorry all right? I didn't mean it.'

He was staring at her, his eyes wet. He'd started crying as soon as she'd told him. Alison straightened her blouse and jacket. She hated it, this crying. It wasn't as if they'd been dead serious or anything. He'd always acted like he didn't care about fuck all. He looked sort of limp now, standing there. Not like a man really. Alison had her back to a garage door.

She looked at him: just a boy, that was what he was. Just to look at him. She'd no idea what it was she'd seen in him, now.

'But it's my birthday,' Andy was saying, sort of pleading.

Alison shot him a look. 'Grow up. It isn't your birthday till tomorrow.'

Andy came over and started to put his arms round her, pinning her so she couldn't get away. She began to struggle a bit, but he had too tight a grip on her, so she just sort of hung there like she was a kid in one of those carrier things folk strapped to themselves. After a bit, he began kissing her cheek, his hand slipping under her blouse, over her tits.

'Andy,' she said, quietly. 'Andy?'

He just kept kissing her.

'Andy, just face it,' she said. 'It's *over* . . .'

His face moved round to meet hers, his eyes wet again.

'I'm sorry,' he said again.

He was kissing her, and she was kissing him as well, surprised at herself, this feeling of pity and guilt coming over her, his hand on her tits, the other working down the back of her jeans, feeling hot against her cold bum. 'No, stop,' she started to say, trying to draw away from his mouth when he went to kiss her again. 'Stop, there's no point . . .'

But he wouldn't stop. He kept on trying to kiss her, his hand continued to work its way inside her jeans. *Stop, Andy*, she was saying. *Please*, he was saying, *Just this once. No*, she said. *Stop. Please*, he said again. He was trying to work her bra off, trying to push it up over her tits. She squirmed and wriggled away from his touch. *Stop, Andy*, she was saying. It was like this mad sort of stalemate, this weird wrestling match. He would try another avenue; she would counter by drawing away, somehow neutralise the movement. All the time she kept saying *Stop*, and he kept saying *Please*. It was like body chess. For every attack there was a counter, an evasion. She was even sort of getting used to it.

But she was getting tired. And angry.

Then he had his hand down between her legs at the back of her jeans, was trying to get his fingers inside the material. She began to twist and kick at him, pulling her arse away from his hand by arching her back, but he was pinning her too well, it was just wasted energy. *Stop, Andy*, she was saying. *Just this once*, he was saying, and she felt him pull her hand down to the level of his groin and push it in there, his own hand on top, so's she couldn't pull away, rubbing the big stiff lump in his pants, just rubbing at it, his other hand pulling out from the back of her jeans, pinning her opposite hand to her side; her loosening the buckle of his jeans and saying, *All right, all right,* kissing him on the mouth, feeling the heat of his breath, and then holding it in her hand, hard and smooth, stroking it a couple of time so that he relaxed a bit, loosening his grip and she was kissing him again.

His eyes were shut. She looked at him, stared at his face, this weird feeling of power and control coming over her. She gave his dick one almighty yank and he yelped and jerked back, pain and fright in his eyes.

'FUUUUUU-CKKK!'

He was fumbling with the buttons of his fly.

'BITCH!' he shouted, his panic turning into rage. But Alison was already walking away.

'As I was saying,' she called over her shoulder, a smile turning the corners of her mouth: 'You're *chucked.*'

And it was odd, because in less than an hour's time, Andy McCabe would not only be chucked, he'd be dead as well, no time to make sense of his short life, no time to put it in perspective and say: *Yes, if I had the time over again, I'd do this differently,* or, *If I had my time again, I'd do that differently . . .*

No extra time.

No rewind.

No chance to put those penultimate moments on pause, duck out of the way of that glinting object swinging through the air towards him; the face of the stranger before him, a stranger, yes, but familiar somehow, a face he can't quite place. And then incomprehension. A sudden cold pulsing in his throat. The sight of the blood pooling its unbelievable, shocking redness onto the pavement, the blank stunned look of the girl in front of him, hand up to mouth as if to stop herself from screaming, and him *trying* to scream, trying to shout for help, but no sound coming out. Then being suddenly, pointlessly, taken by the thought of that as he slumps down against the wall behind him, the only sound coming out an airless guffaw. Not even having time to feel pain through the shock. Not even having time for that.

The bottle of peach *SlaZinger* was nearly done. Denise shoogled it, swirling it around, then threw it over a hedge into someone's front garden. She reached down into the pocket of John Burke's trousers. There was maybe some money in there, hiding away like a mollusc, in a corner. A folded-up fiver or a pound note tucked away inside the right-hand hip pocket. She reached her fingers into the corner and dug about, hopeful. Nothing. She kicked at a stone on the pathway, clear moonlight making it gleam silver in the darkness. The railway lines sat silent on the other side of the fence, but if you put your ear to them, they would sing. It was better than listening for the sea in a shell. Places that weren't here. She kept on walking. The mattress wouldn't be too far – she could lie down there for a while until it was early enough to go home. It would have been nice to have had something to eat, though.

There was a shape sitting on the mattress, a dark shadow. It was hunched over. Denise stopped dead. Something cracked underfoot. The shape looked up at her, startled Jeedy. Denise could see he was crying. She walked over to him and sat down on the edge of the mattress.

He sat with his head bowed forward; she could feel his insides heave right through his back.

'It wasn't meant to happen,' Jeedy said, the tears slowing down.

'It's all right,' Denise said. 'Take your time.' That was

terrible. She sounded like an adult. 'What's happened? What's the matter?' she said. Jeedy wiped his nose with the sleeve of his jacket.

Denise was too steaming for this. She didn't know if she wanted to find out what this was all about.

'It was an accident,' Jeedy said. 'Totally, man. It was an accident . . .'

He started to cry again. Denise said: 'Shhshh, it's all right, everything will be all right.'

But clearly everything wasn't going to be all right.

'Just start from the beginning,' Denise said, letting her voice go quiet and trustworthy, the way people did when they wanted you to tell them your secrets.

They both sat silent for a minute.

'What happened?' Denise said.

She looked at him, his beautiful face carved out of mahogany, white gleam of moonlight on the profile of his forehead and cheeks.

'Have you any cigarettes?' he asked.

'I think so.' Denise reached into the pocket of her jacket, taking two out the box.

'Smoking now as well, are you?' Jeedy asked.

'I don't . . . usually,' Denise said, lighting the cigarettes with John Burke's lighter.

'They new trousers?' he asked, looking at John Burke's trousers.

'Em, yeh,' Denise went, wanting to change the subject, aware of the wet knickers in her pocket: 'What happened?'

Jeedy's hand shook as he put the fag to his mouth and inhaled. Denise lit one and copied what he did, inhaling and letting the smoke funnel out her nose.

'I had to go steal the car with my brother.'

Denise waited.

'We got chased by the pigs. Probably your fucking old boy as well.'

He looked at Denise. 'My brother wrapped the car round a set of traffic lights, trying to get away.'

Denise sooked on the fag, looking over at the corrugated fencing with the empty cans and bottles all around it. Someone had sprayed on it, covered up a bit more of the past graffiti. Soon the past would be covered by the present. That was what happened.

'Are you hurt?' she asked him.

Jeedy shook his head. 'No, not me, man.'

'The car?'

'A write-off. Totally wrecked.'

'But you're all right?' She had her hand on his back, was rubbing his shoulders. 'You got away?'

He shrugged her hand away.

'I don't think so . . . I don't think I got away.' Jeedy flicked the cigarette over at the corrugated sheeting, sending orange sparks into the air. He began to cry again. Through the tears and snot he was saying how he had never wanted to go in the first place, his brother made him, it was just an accident, what was he meant to do now? He couldn't go home, it wasn't possible to go home, but there was nowhere else he could go, nowhere at all, he would have to run away, maybe he could get a hitch somewhere, but all he had were these clothes he was wearing and that was it, no money, nothing, he would get lifted straight away and flung in jail. No doubt about it, man. No doubt—

Denise stopped him. 'But you're okay? That's the main thing, isn't it? You never got hurt . . . ?'

He was shaking his head, his head hanging over his knees. 'No, Denise, not me. My brother . . . he was driving,' he said. 'It was really fast, man. We were going really fast. I told him to slow down, but he was loving it. I told you he was nuts . . .'

'Is he all right?' Denise was shaking, just wanting him to say it now, get it over with.

'. . . he was going really fast.'

'Jeedy . . .'

'What d'you want me to say? I don't know how he is, all right? I panicked. I got scared and fucking bolted before the cops could get me as well. I shook him, but he wouldn't wake up. There was blood coming out his nose. There was blood coming out his head. I got scared, man. I don't want to go to some detention centre.'

'Calm down,' Denise was saying. 'Just calm down . . . It might not be serious. We can find out . . .'

'You don't get it, do you?' Jeedy said, lifting his head up to look at her. 'He'll go to hospital, they'll find out I was there. Either way I'm fucked . . . That's how they'll catch up with me. That's how your *dad'll* catch up with me . . .'

It was true. That was how her dad would catch up with him.

They'd find his brother in the hospital. They just wanted to go round the wards. It was inevitable. But his brother could be dead for all he knew. If her sister was hurt or something, would it bother her? She was looking at Jeedy and not understanding him: it seemed obvious enough to her that she would be worried if it was her brother. It'd be his brother who would get most of the blame for making him go along with it. But maybe Jeedy had done loads of stuff. She didn't know anything about him, not really.

'You'll be all right,' she said, unsure, rubbing his shoulders. 'Nothing's going to happen to you . . . I'll see if I can find out what's happening. Where was the crash?'

Jeedy looked at her. 'At the roundabout.'

He couldn't have picked a worse spot. Half the country must have seen it.

'Okay,' she said, standing up. 'Stay here. I'll see what I can find out.'

Jeedy was staring up at her. 'We could just leave,' he said. 'You and me. We could just get lost.'

She looked at him, hunched there on the mattress, staring at his fingernails, and knew she couldn't get lost with him. Not now. Something had changed, something essential. Something had changed or was lost, or maybe had never existed in the first place. She put a hand on his shoulder and said quietly: 'Let's just see what we can find out. Wait here. I'll be back soon.'

Denise never does get the chance to find out what happened to Jeedy's brother, at least not that night, because on the way back, after stopping and waiting at the green man, after passing the café and John Burke's house once more, where lights were still on, curtains drawn over, after quickstepping along pavements, earthbound, Denise wanders into the middle of another witch hunt, faceless shapes carrying bits of wood and homemade knuckledusters, going after anyone they can find, anyone within reach, someone they can smash with iron bars, driving the rest back to their side of the Dummy, bludgeoning everyone within reach, trapping those that tried to escape in the corners of lanes and alleys, forcing them into huddled balls on the ground, and Denise tries to put herself between them and this particular figure on the ground, break it up, pulling and scratching, biting and kicking till the three or four guys kicking and punching begin to realise that this isn't quite what they had in mind, that this isn't in the script, who is this fucking witch with the nails and the teeth, and they begin to back off a bit, just enough so that the boy on the ground has enough time to uncurl, except he doesn't, he's too scared, he stays right there even after someone grabs a clump of his hair and rips it out, leaving a bloodied bald patch beneath.

One of them dangles a pair of nunchaku from his hand. They look homemade too.

'You're claimed as well,' he says, pointing his finger at her.

Another holds a weighted cheese-wire, a makeshift garrotte.

For a minute, Denise pictures them engulfing her, dragging her off, stripping her, shaving her head, baseball bats raised. She sees herself yanked round the neck with a cheese-wire garrotte, feels the bite of it, knowing they would kill her over and over again if they could, but that once for her would be enough.

$1 - 1 = ?$

But instead, they turn and begin to look about nervously, listening for sirens, leaving only one behind.

Andy McCabe.

Denise feels the blood jump through her veins, she could have sworn she'd been possessed, she's never ever felt anything like it in her life, this delicious feeling of being totally alive; it's like all these years she'd just been dozing, and now here she was actually alive, and they couldn't hurt her because she was too powerful, she could take them all. And now she sees what it is that they see in it, in this violence, and as the other guys wander off, hearing a siren coming closer, Denise stares into Andy McCabe's eyes and he smiles at her, it's like he can see, it's like he's saying, *You and me, we're not so different after all, are we?*

And it's like she's saying back to him: *No.*

The words flash silently between them.

Neither of them is really aware of the boy uncurling on the ground, getting up, standing, walking towards them. He can't be more than seventeen, a year older than Andy McCabe will ever be, tall with square shoulders, not a pick of fat on him. Bad skin, cheekbones jutting like they want to escape from his face. His face. Bloodied, a gash over his eye that looks worse than it is; his shirt stained with it. Neither Andy McCabe nor Denise Forrester really registers this boy coming towards them. He looks like he's reaching out to shake hands, but then flicks his hand suddenly across Andy's throat. And it's a surprise, this sudden hot gout of blood leaping into his hands, hands that understood instinctively, hands that went up to hold it in, the blood, hands that press uselessly at the wound.

Denise's own hand leaps up to cover her mouth. Andy's eyes are pleading with her. Andy McCabe sits wheezing against a hedge, hand to this throat. Blood bursts out onto the pavement in front of him. Denise has her hand over her mouth. He makes a noise like laughter, as if there is something funny about it, the way the blood comes out. His eyes continue to beg something from Denise.

But he is running out of things to beg for.

Denise's muscles were tight, contracted, as if she was bracing herself: the more he relaxed, the more taut she became, even as the light went out of his eyes and she knew there was nothing she could do. She could see that he would be dead before anyone got here. She ran up the pathway of the first house she came to, banged on the door, tried to shout. A man came to the door. She flapped her arms. He asked her what was wrong. She pointed at the wall. 'Up there,' she said, finally. 'Call an ambulance.' What was wrong? he asked. An accident, she said. The man went part of the way down the path, not understanding. 'An ambulance,' she said again, 'an ambulance.' He looked out onto the street, looked left. Then he must have seen it. His whole body jerked. 'Jesus Christ,' he said. He ran up the path, shoved her into the house. 'Call an ambulance,' he said. 'Go!' She walked into the hall. The phone was right in front of her, on a glass table with wrought-iron legs. The wallpaper was nice. Kind of a marbling effect, very pale green. She picked up the receiver of the phone. It was an old-fashioned one with a dial. Nine . . . nine . . . nine. Ask for Emergency Services. A voice came on. It was a woman. Which service did she require? the voice asked. 'Emergency services,' she said. Then felt stupid. 'Ambulance,' she said. The woman asked where she was. In the hallway, Denise said. There was a mirror in front of her on the wall with a bronze frame. She couldn't mind the name of the street, she said . . . But the voice seemed to know anyway, without Denise telling her. Is this the street? she said. Yeh, that was the one, Denise told her. The voice said someone was already on their way. Denise put the receiver down, looked at herself in the mirror. She looked old. She stared at her reflection. Her hands were covered in blood. She'd no idea how it had got there. She couldn't remember. It was a mystery.

The man came back in. Had she phoned? he asked. She nodded.

'He's dead, isn't he?' she said. She knew already. The man said nothing. There didn't seem to be anyone else in the house.

AREYOUDEADANDY

No question.

Nothing to work out.

Dead singular.

Could she use the phone again? she asked. The man nodded. His hands were shaking. He went into one of the rooms. She took the business card out of her jacket pocket, where it had been sitting for weeks. She stared at the name on it. It was of a Bed and Breakfast.

The man came out. He was carrying a blanket.

She dialled the number on the business card. The tone rang out several times. She waited. A woman answered. 'Mum?' Denise asked. 'Who?' the voice answered. She was looking for Anna Forrester, she said. Oh, okay, hold on. She waited.

'Alison?' the voice seemed strange, anxious. She could hear sirens. There was a car drawing up outside, a police car, and an ambulance.

'Denise,' she said. 'It's Denise.'

Two policemen got out the car. One of them walked in the direction of Andy McCabe. The other came up the path, taking his hat off. His hand went to what was left of his hair. He saw her. He was looking at her hands. It was her dad. He looked angry. He came towards her.

Her dad stood in front of her. He was saying something, but she didn't catch it. He put a hand on her shoulder. Denise shrugged him away. His touch stung her back to life.

'Denise?' her mum was saying. 'Are you there, Denise?'

In the back of the police car was Jeedy.

She went out and stood in front of the car. Jeedy didn't look at her. He was looking through the front window. He was looking at the body on the pavement. There was a blanket over it. But its boots were uncovered. They were sticking out.

A big crowd of folk turned out for the cremation. They held each other's hands, and stood with bowed heads. They wore dark, sober-looking suits and had darker bags under their eyes. Andy's older brother Grant had to support his mother; his dad stood stiffnecked and stared straight ahead, an arm round her waist. A fat woman Denise didn't recognise, her sparrow's-nest of grey hair imprisoned under a brimmed hat, offered her condolences between nervy drags on a Regal King Size, and when she'd smoked that right down to the beef, lit another one off the end of it.

'A terrible shame,' she said, 'when someone so young as that goes. A terrible pity for his poor mother and father, out-living their own son.'

Another lady asked Denise if she'd known him well, and Denise hadn't known what to say. Well enough, she wanted to say, but even she knew that there were times it was better to keep your mouth shut. Alison, standing beside her in a navy blue skirt that was too big for her – neither of them had any clothes that were suitable for such an occasion – nodded politely in Denise's place, let the woman clasp her by the shoulder, transmit her sympathies by touch.

'It was a lovely service,' the woman said, before moving away. 'Andy would have liked it. He'd have liked it a lot.'

She stared over at the urn they were going to put his ashes in, the ones his dad was going to scatter on the eighteenth hole at Gleneagles.

They'd played two songs Andy had liked; his brother had picked them out, so Denise supposed he probably knew best. The first one was 'Is There Life On Mars?' by David Bowie, who, as far as Denise could recall, Andy had always said was a past-it poof in a clown's outfit. As the people filed out past Andy's family, each person said a couple of words to his mum and dad, and the track spooled on to the next selection Grant McCabe had made on behalf of his dead brother. It was 'The Girl From Ipanema'. Apparently he'd loved it as a wean, used to samba about the coffee table and everything. Denise liked that song as well, and for the first time that day felt something like sadness when it came on. She felt something like loss. She wasn't sure who or what for. For everyone, maybe.

Between the end of that service, and waiting for the next party, she and Alison wandered about the cemetery, reading the names on the tombstones. Denise was sure that Granda had been buried up here, but there were so many stones it'd take all day to find him. There was no stone for her granny. Like Andy, she'd been cremated, the ashes scattered. She pictured the graveyard overrun with coffins, one piled on top of another, queuing to get in the ground, some of them fallen open to reveal the corpses inside. Cats prowled everywhere. She saw her granda sat resting on one of the low walls that kept the lawns in check, rubbing at his hands, taking his bunnet off and rubbing his forehead. He looked too hot in his long herringbone coat and that bunnet. Denise smiled, and Alison started to ask her what she thought was so funny, but gave up when she got the answer. She decided it was just Denise being Denise.

A taxi had drawn up at the edge of the cemetery lawns, on the red blaze of the driveway. When the door opened, Denise saw that it was her mum. She got out and stood, looking over at them.

'Coming?' Denise asked her sister, but she shook her head.

'I don't want to talk to her,' Alison said. 'Not just now.'

Denise shrugged and walked over.

'How did it go?' her mum asked, playing with Denise's hair, pushing it out from her eyes and behind her ears. Her mum seemed tired, but there was nothing new about that.

'It was all right,' Denise said, shrugging again.

'I can't stay long,' her mum said. 'I've an interview for a job after lunch.'

Denise nodded. Neither of them said anything for a bit, then her mum said, 'Look, there's something I have to tell you.'

Denise waited.

'It's about your dad. I'm as well telling you now, while your sister's over there. Maybe it's best if you hear it first.'

'What?'

Denise wasn't sure if she wanted to hear anything about that man. She recalled what her mum had said when she'd left that night. How he wasn't a *bad* man.

Her mum took a breath and said: 'He's not your dad, you know. We should have told you before, but . . . Well, the timing's never right with these things.'

She looked at Denise. 'We met when I was pregnant with you. And got married. Seemed like the right thing to do at the time. I don't know why, really.'

Denise nodded. 'Who was my real dad?' she asked.

'Just a man. I only knew him for a day or two. He just disappeared. He never knew about you.' Her mum gazed at her. 'Denise?'

'I'm all right,' she said.

'Your dad's Alison's dad, though. I expect she'll be fine knowing about you. Once she's come round.'

Her mum stared over at Alison, who was sitting arms folded across her chest, her back to one of the headstones.

'You know, once I'm settled, you could come and stay with me if you like,' Denise's mum said. 'I mean, once I get a better place and everything. You could come over and visit.'

Denise nodded.

'Denise? You sure you're all right?'

'I better go now,' she said. 'The next service'll be starting soon. I better get Alison.'

'Oh. Of course,' her mum said. 'What'll happen to Jeedy?'

'I don't know,' Denise said. 'He's still under sixteen. Maybe he'll get taken into care or something. He should be here soon.'

Denise's mum nodded. She cupped her hands around Denise's cheeks, looked ready to cry. 'Well, I better get off. Give your sister a hug from me. Tell her to ring or something.'

'Okay.'

Her mum climbed again into the back seat of the taxi and closed the door. Then, she wound the window down and said: 'Wish me luck!'

Denise looked puzzled. 'What for?'

'For the interview!'

'Oh. Good luck, then.'

'You're sure you're all right?'

'I'm all right,' Denise said. 'You better go.'

'Okay.'

Her mum wound the window back up and pressed her palm to the glass, the taxi reversing, then turning, a crunch of blaze under the tyres.

Denise stood for a minute, watching the first cars draw up for Jeedy's brother's service. It would be a while yet before Jeedy arrived. She went over and sat with her sister. Alison scratched shapes in the dirt with a stick.

'Well,' she said. 'What did she want?'

And Denise was wondering what to tell her but then couldn't think how to begin, so she just said: 'Who, mum? You know, the usual.'

But for the life of her Denise had no idea what the usual was.